It was not a good day for mail. Two of my stories that had been picked up for anthologies were suddenly without a home. The projects they had been picked up for had gone under. To make matters worse, I received notice that a magazine, which was considering yet another tale went belly up and yet another story was returned to me with the deadly but efficient quote, "We loved it—but it was not right for our requirements." So it was that these stories were replaced in a growing pile of tales that were orphaned, stories that just fit a particular market, or were 'too unique'.

I talked with other writers and it seemed that all of us have these little files. Stories with nothing wrong except that they failed to meet the capricious demands of what ever editors or publisher they were submitted to. Into this picture stepped my wife, Mary Ann. Lacking the sage wisdom that controls today's literary marketplace, she poised the question, "Why not lump all those stories into an anthology?" Of such earthly observations a project was born.

ORPHANED EPICS is a collection that is unique in that it adheres to no particular genre. Its tales cover a variety of scenarios from the clashing of two cultures in THE BORDERS OF VALHALLA, to the night prowling of a murderous streetwalker in JASMINE IS THE SCENT I LOVE. There is south sea adventure in THE STORY OF A HEAD. The issue of capitol punishment and vigilantes is addressed in CANDLES ARE BUT WHISPERS OF GOD. There is dark futuristic Horror in PARTS IS PARTS and madness rules in THE GORGON. A Bushman runs afoul of escaped slaves from early Egypt in THE COPPER PEOPLE. In APOTHEOSIS, an off Broadway production garners praise for its unusual cast. A Wakamba guide encounters a ghost— and a mystery in SUNLIGHT. In all there are fifteen tales and four poems that I hope will entertain your late night—or weather the daily commute.

1

It is my hope that this will be the first child of a series of such volumes. In the course of time I will seek out the lost children of other writers to be placed in future editions. For now though, it will be just you, dear reader—and me to settle down in a comfortable chair and see if magic is to be made.

Enjoy.

~Frank Menser 2007

ORPHANED EPICS

(Tales of the Unusual)

By Frank Menser

ISBN 978 0 6151 6777 0

For Mrs. Gene Maupin, who taught me and so many others the love of the printed word. And Mr. Ogden who read them to us so well.

We would like to thank the following persons and organizations who through their efforts, assistance and support have made this volume possible;

Laura Stamps, Tracy Carbone, Nick Cook, Bobby Willes, The members of the SHOCKLINES WRITERS GROUP.

Table of Contents

ON THE WIRE

By the fence that split the hill
In the grass untrimmed and tangled.
It watched the wires threading through
In hopes that something tasty dangled.

Slept the owner of that spot
(A natural beast...or from the pit?).
No explanation can suffice,
Just that death's blood satiates it.

Should it take notice of the road?
There cars and children pass each day.
It sleeps—yet filled with gnawing hunger,
It waits for those who walk its way.

There was a time one walked alone.
She sat upon the fence to rest.
A scratch of cloth, a bit of hair
Who knows what happened to the rest?

A cry was heard one evening past.
No one answered the pitiful screams
They ran from claw marks on the ground.
Rescuers found odd shapes it seems.

It was those tracks (?) burned in the grass,
That made the men all tell their wives
That this spot be cursed...condemned.
To be shunned for their very lives.

It's now been weeks since it has fed.
It waits within the highest grass
The spot stays clear, but on the road
It smells the living things that pass.

Its hunger draws it from its den.
Its starving jaws all flecked with foam.
It waits for something on the road.
Something it can follow home.

BABBA YAGGA

"Five and a fig,
Is a merry, merry fig.
Five and a fig,
Goes merry, merry down.
Five enter in,
And go for the fig.
Five go on in,
The sixth one will drown."

Old Babba Yagga
Called to the children,
"Come little darlings,
Quick like a mouse!"
Six came in,
To play by her fire.
Six came in,
But none left her house.

Old Babba Yagga
Sang as she cooked them
Sang as she nibbled
On their tiny little feet.
One is a fig,
That is lost to his father.
Another is a flower
That tastes really sweet.

Old Babba Yagga
Squinted as she cooked
And rocked her old house,
With it's strange chicken legs.
"Five little figs
I rolled in the flower.
One little fig,
I boiled with the eggs."

CANDLES ARE BUT WHISPERS OF GOD

"Burkland," Porterfield said, "Like I have been saying, this new thing about electricity is obscene I tell you, just obscene." Burkland watched as a drop of gravy dripped onto the round man's vest. Porterfield's consternation had little effect on his appetite-even at this somber dinner table.

"So what about you doctor? Do you feel the same?"

"Yes, I agree with Porterfield on this," Dr. Bainbrook said. "What with all that is to be done with electricity these days, why continue to pursue it in this unfortunate matter?"

"Gentlemen," Burkland said in his calm melodic voice. "You both didn't think it was a bad idea, when you invested in this project."

"I dare say, what do you mean?" Porterfield set down his cigar and nervously sipped from his brandy. The glass shook with the trembling of the disease that palsied his hand. Burkland watched as he steadied his grip with his other hand and placed the glass back onto the table.

"I mean you were interested enough to throw your money into this thing, when a rich profit seemed up for grabs. You spoke of Bell, and the possibilities of his contraption. You all were pretty keen on getting into the ground floor of this. Now that Edison seems to have the inside track on this device. We are given, alas by calamity, a means to pull ahead. Now you balk in the name of morality.

"Why look at this headline." Burkland held up a copy of the Herald. "See Edison and Westinghouse know opportunity. They are at each other's throats for it. Are we so wrong to seek every advantage for our selves to cash in?"

Porterfield the banker read the story and then setting the paper down on the table, leaned back in his chair. Burkland could tell he was busily calculating.

"My friends," Burkland continued, "science has taught us that all of life...in fact, well, everything about us, is comprised of particles of pure electricity. Why even that slice of mutton you are cutting doctor, is comprised of billions of particles of atoms and molecules all carrying a charge. There is no escaping the fact that electricity comprises everything in our lives. With so much to explore, there is boundless opportunity."

Burkland stood and removed the bib from his neck, placing it on top of the newspaper. "This project you invested in gentlemen has a known value. So instead of grousing about it, we may as well continue our look into how the thing goes about its business of death."

"I think your speculations go well beyond business."

"True enough, Porterfield. As a mystic, it is my belief that electricity is both positive and negative not just in polarity, but also by its very nature. We all know for example, that an electric charge may be used as Dr. Bainbrook has mentioned before, in the treatment of mental illness. I find it fascinating that the same charge when increased in intensity becomes lethal."

"Quite so, Burkland," the doctor said, "Hence our project. Your point is, sir?"

"Simply, it is not necessarily the obvious physical properties that control whether electricity is beneficial, or detrimental. Perhaps there is something more subtle in control. I mean to use this opportunity that has fallen upon us to find it."

"Good Lord man," the banker said, "you talk like the blasted thing has a bearing on our soul or something!"

"Perhaps Porterfield, it might," Burkland said. He stepped back from the table, pulling a cigar from his vest.

"Are we not ourselves, comprised of the same electricity as that, which we send through wires, see in the sky as lightning, and recognize in the atoms and molecules life is built from. Yet, the theologians claim, we are unique in having a soul—unlike those other things. Pray, what if their wrong? What if this match I now light, carries with it that divine essence?"

"Bloody Pagan sounding, if you ask me," Porterfield said. "Next you'll be saying rocks and trees have souls too."

"Perhaps, old boy, but what if good and evil were as simply defined, as the product of a singular frequency, or charge of electricity we were born with?"

"Rubbish! God gave man free will; you sound ready to excuse it as bad tuning on a dial, tis silly nonsense!"

"And yet, here we sit gentlemen, toasting tonight the memory of a friend and the proposed passing of his killer; both events involving the same essential essence."

"And you're a cool one for that, Burkland," Porterfield said. "Dr. Baker was a good man, and our associate. I can't say I wish him dead, even if his use of electricity was to kill poor Wilson. Are we so very sure we are right?"

"I care not for his purpose, Porterfield, "McMartin said, "Burkland and I both saw his hand on the switch. Kill he did. His end must be found in that chair he built as well. Wilson's death must be answered, as the court would demand."

"But why can't we just turn him over to the authorities?" Dr Bainbrook said. Why do we take this on our shoulders, when the law would serve?"

"Because Doctor, It was our friend who died, whose body lies in the parlor. It is right in our measure, to take this unfortunate opportunity and use it to have a test subject. That's something even Edison has not had. We have it here gentlemen, to safely test our electric chair before presenting it to the state. We all agreed on that...didn't we?"

13

Burkland looked around the room. Porterfield grunted and lowered his head, Doctor Bainbrook looked away. Only McMartin looked directly at Burkland. His eyes were pinpoints.

"Aye, we did," he spat. "Wilson deserved better than to be that bloody bastard's victim. Damn, but he must have been hot to try it on a human!

"And yes, we do deserve the contract that New York offers for the chair, not Edison and Brown."

"Lord forgive us for the task we have chosen," Porterfield said, taking a sip of sherry. "But you Burkland...You just want to watch the man die, so you can explore your blasted ecclesial theories! Good lord man, with all this mumbo-jumbo you're almost as crazy as the poor soul we have downstairs."

"Perhaps that's so, Porterfield, but my cousin deserves to be avenged," McMartin said. "If Burkland gets some notes to speculate on and we make a profit, it's a fine return for what Baker did."

"Perhaps gentlemen," Dr. Bainbrook said, "we should attend to the drawing room for cigars and brandy to fortify ourselves. I fear we have the devil's work to do tonight."

*

Dr. Baker sat buckled into the lethal chair he helped to build. He sat alone, but fortunately not in the dark. A candle on a small table provided him with light so his musings were at least not compounded by the uncertainty of the dark. He looked around the room at the cabinets and the control panel. Baker could still smell the cheap wine that was on Wilson's breath when he came in.

The voices of his former colleges were clearly audible to him. He knew they were aware of his dislike for Wilson. The man had been a bully and a lout. Yet, Wilson had on occasion, been disposed to exhibit a certain charm, despite his raucous nature. It made him well liked-which added to the discomfort of the quiet man strapped into the chair. The chair that had been the source of all the events that led to this.

*

They had read of the battles in court between Edison and Westinghouse. The state of New York offered rich contracts to whoever came up with a humane electric chair. Burkland said that there was an opportunity to slip their own design in, while the others battled. Porterfield and the rest had jumped at the chance to invest.

While Buckland had been the visionary, it was the hard scientific reasoning of Baker that had propelled this project beyond the mere speculation of friends who talked over wine and cigars. Yes, Burkland had been the visionary, but he, Baker, had the knowledge of alternating and direct currents that pointed the right way for them.

Burkland had wanted originally opted to use Direct current for the chair and Baker had quickly pointed out that Alternating current was much more humane as DC left the test animals tortured—but alive.

It was a grim business to be sure, but Dr. Baker had seen hangings. It was the cruelty of that form of execution that drove him to push for a painless device.

*

Now Baker reflected on this as he sat strapped into the device waiting for hours, while the men upstairs discussed putting it all to the test-on him. The irony was not lost on the doctor. Then as the stress of waiting became almost intolerable, the cellar door opened a crack.

"Dr. Baker!"

"Yes?" Baker recognized the voice. It was Bainbrook.

"Would you care for a sherry, or something?"

"A drop of Port would be fine, if you can spare it. I am a bit dry sitting here."

"Well, I will see if we can provide. Give me a moment."

"Take your time," Baker said. *By all means, take as much time as you can, gentlemen. This chair will wait with me.*

Baker looked closely at the switch on the wall that powered the chair. What could have happened?

Bainbrook came downstairs with a glass and a decanter. Setting it down on the small table that he had earlier moved next to the chair, Bainbrook unstrapped one of Baker's hands.

"How much?" Baker held up two fingers. Bainbrook poured the liquor and placed it on the table.

The doctor drained the spirits in a single gulp.

"More?"

"Thank you," Baker said, as he watched Bainbrook pour again.

"I don't think you will have too long to wait, Baker." Bainbrook said.

"Don't you see Doctor? This is murder you discuss up there!"

Baker went to reach for his pipe but found his action blocked by his bound right hand. Frustrated, he glared at Bainbrook. "This is not justice, you know."

"A fine subject you bring up, Baker. We all know you hated Wilson."

"Damn man, you know he was a bully!"

"I didn't say, you had no cause to do it, but you were caught in the act!" Bainbrook sat on his haunches and looked into the doctor's eyes. "Look, it's not me who is pressing this. Burkland and McMartin seem most disposed to carrying this out. Porterfield is wavering."

"Then perhaps you could call the authorities and let them sort it out."

"I think not, Baker." McMartin stood at the top of the stairs with a glass of sherry in his hand. Behind him were Porterfield and Burkland. "I think it's high time we finished this."

"In a hurry to be the grave digger, McMartin," Bainbrook said.

"For the last time, Dr. Bainbrook," McMartin replied, thumping his fist on the stair rail. "You aren't going to believe that tale he contrived that Wilson fell into that chair while a test was being run? Paugh, His lies make me sick!"

"That is how it happened," Baker said, "Your cousin came into the room while I was working on the switch. He must have been standing close to it. He was staggering drunk, from the sound of him. Wilson must have bumped into the chair. I heard a thunk, and when I turned, he had fallen into it! I never saw him before he fell."

"Why would he do something that foolish?" Burkland said as he pushed past McMartin and came down the stairs. "Look man...He was drunk, maybe, but he was not daft. Wilson knew never to touch the thing. Even if he did, he was grounded by his shoes."

Porterfield walked down the stairs easing his massive body down slowly. "Tell the truth, how much is this really about Baker? It's about money, Gentlemen.

"Peterson said Edison's device would be selected by New York. We all know he became the committee head, while he was still employed by Edison. Our only hope was to guarantee our device worked better.

"So here we sell our souls to use this man as a guinea pig, so we can get that contract and be wealthy men. So how much really is this about Wilson? Like Bainbrook, I feel we were hasty to judge this man. Let the authorities deal with this."

"You know this will be dragged through the courts, if we let the police handle this," McMartin said, slamming his fist again on the rail.

17

Baker jumped at the sound. He could swear he heard the wood crack. The small Scotsman was florid. *If his face gets any redder he'll have a heart attack,* Baker noted. The others seem to hesitate for a moment which propelled McMartin to an even greater fury.

"Damn you all then, I will see my cousin avenged!" McMartin shouted and raced down the stairs. Bainbrook moved to stop him, but was too slow. Porterfield was in the way, so McMartin pushed him with his shoulder. The fat man fell down knocking the table over...and with it the candle. From the floor, a flash of fire blossomed and as quickly died. Burkland dove down the stairs and grabbed the candle, cursing as the hot wax from it seared his hand. He replaced it on the table Bainbrook set back up. McMartin seemed pinned to the wall, his anger temporarily forgotten.

"What was that flash?" Bainbrook bent to sniff, "Smells sour."

"Smells like burnt wine," said Porterfield as he raised himself onto his elbows. "If you look under the cabinet, you can see a half spilled bottle of it. I happen to have a good view, from my position here on the floor."

Burkland walked over and retrieved the bottle from its hiding place. His face was pale. "How did we miss it?"

"Because we had no reason to look for it," Bainbrook said. "Did you see where the flash came from...right before the chair? We all ignored the alcohol smell, as Wilson was quite inebriated. I wonder if we check his shoes, might there be a burnt remnant of the wine he must have spilled?"

"Which would have negated his being grounded," McMartin said. His voice sounded hollow. "It was a bloody accident."

*

"The four men were silent, as Burkland unstrapped Baker from the chair. The little scientist stood up and pushed his way past his ex-captors. He walked with his face expressionless, as he went up the stairs and left.

McMartin shook as the tears of his loss finally welled and over came his anger. For all the rest, there was nothing to dwell upon...Nothing but shame.

"You know Burkland," Porterfield said as he got up from the floor, "You maybe, had the best grasp on this of us all."

"How…so?"

"With all your mysticism about the marvels of electricity and souls, did you notice the truth emerged from the light of a simple candle's flame?"

Porterfield walked past the others and also left. Bainbrook turned to McMartin who was sobbing uncontrollably and held him, as Burkland stared at the small candle's flickering light.

"A whisper from God," Burkland said. "A whisper from God."

THE GAME

Desmond Nidbit sat at the circular table staring across at his opponent. She looked tired. Her face was damp, covered with tiny sores, some of which were leaking an amber colored fluid. He knew far worse things were happening further down her body.

Nidbit hesitated. It was his move and he knew at this level what he played, would result in someone getting hurt or even killed. Someone, maybe the one he loved above all else; like the woman sitting across from him.

*

The ad had been simple and straight forward. It asked for couples to meet at a specified location to test a new game. The amount of money mentioned was sizable, all too tempting to Desmond's wife.

"Des, this trial is close to here. It takes a weekend away from us, but five thousand dollars would really help catch up on some bills."

"I don't know, Anna, the amount sounds awful high for just a product test. It might pan out to be one of those promotional scams."

"Well, I think we should find out," Anna said reaching for the phone. "Worst that can happen is that we get bored with a timeshare deal, or something. Besides, we can always leave."

Anna punched the digits. A feminine voice, which was obviously a recording, read off a list of instructions. The voice coaxed her through a long questionnaire about their personal habits and preferences.

Anna hung up the phone and said to Des, "Ok, we are entered."

"Remind me to cheer later," he groused.

"You are such a grump," Anna said and threw a cushion at him.

Two days later, a slick looking manila envelope arrived in their mailbox. The label read:

IT'S YOUR CHOICE Inc.

Inside, there was a black glossy flyer and two plastic tickets. The flyer explained in smart looking white print that the test would be a two day live-in event and that all personal needs would be supplied free to the players that qualified. The two days on location would be spent testing the game, which was planned for release to the general public early next year.

Anna studied the flyer reading it out loud. Des knew from her comments and eager look, there would be no talking her out of going. Secretly he groaned, as the date for the test conflicted with a football game that he really wanted to see. But Anna was set on it and making bedroom eyes. If he turned that look down, Des knew he would be racking up couch time for the next month.

*

Desmond drove his car into the parking garage at the address specified. When the heavy door closed, Des heard a distinct click. Somehow, he knew it had been locked behind him. He drove up the ramp trying to ignore the vertigo he always felt when snaking his way around a coiling parking ramp. It felt to him, like he was driving up the edge of a giant concrete spring, ready to collapse and crush their car any second. Anna, sensing his discomfort, grasped his hand and smiled.

"At least we know the car will be safe, till we get back to it."

When they reached the top of the parking garage, Des pulled into an empty space. The garage was empty except for a few parked vehicles. On the other side was a line of doors. On each door hung a sign marked with a name; Bill, Sandra, Marty, Deanna, Desmond, Anna, Paul and Natasha. Anna took the two tickets out of her purse.

"I suppose they are key cards," she said tapping them on the palm of her hand.

"Must be," Des said. "Look's like we split up here. Sure you want to do this?"

"Come on party pooper, you can stand a little time away from me."

Anna giggled as she tossed Des his card. She got out of the car and ran across the lot to her door.

"Last one in gets the consolation prize!"

Anna unlocked her door, and after sticking her tongue out at Des, she ducked inside. Desmond looked at the key card in his hand.

"What the hell," he said.

Once inside his door, Nidbit saw a long corridor. He followed it ignoring the bare concrete that felt close, too close. The hallway led to a flight of stairs that led first down, and then back up before going sharply left. When Des reached the end of it, there was a door with a card attached that said:

Wait for the buzzer.

As it turned out, his wait wasn't long. In fact, just as he finished reading the card, a low sound, not unlike the buzz of a sweat bee, indicated that it was time to enter. With a soft click, the door opened, revealing a ramp with high grey metal walls on either side that met at the ceiling. The ramp narrowed so the effect was like being in a giant triangle. It sloped downward for about twenty feet, terminating in a space just wide enough, to allow someone to sit at the chair and desk at its end. The desk it self faced into what looked like a clear plexi-bubble that blossomed out into a darkened room. On the desk was a computer which was already turned on. On the screen was written:

Hi Desmond Nidbit, push ENTER when seated.

This was printed across the black screen in bold white letters.

Des seated himself and punched the key. When he did, the lights went on illuminating the room before him. Des linked shielding his eyes against the glare. When his vision cleared he examined the room. The chamber was perfectly round, its floor level with the top of Desmond's desk. Its yellow surface was spattered in places with what looked like red paint. Black lines split it to eight sections like a giant pizza.

Seated directly across from him—encased in another bubble window, was Anna, who blew him a kiss. *She is still giggling. Damn, she'd be comfortable anywhere.*

Des looked around and counted seven more compartments like his, including Anna's. Each compartment held a man or woman. *The other players...I guess.*

There was a brief crackle of static, and then a disembodied voice spoke.

"Welcome, players."

Des listened close, as it did not seem to come from the computer. Then he saw a microphone nestled in a niche in the ceiling along side a camera, its cherry light winking like the eye of a demon.

"Welcome to, IT'S YOUR CHOICE, Spyrex Corporation's newest reality game."

The voice continued its monotone, which reverberated through the chamber with an annoying loudness.

"The rules are simple, Wish for pleasure for yourself, and post that on the computer before you. That wish will be granted.

But then, your choice will result in something painful happening to another player. Pick pain for yourself, and another player chosen at random will benefit in pleasure.

I advise you there is no picking what will happen—or to whom. Nor is there any choice of picking alliances, or partners. You are now each one of you on your own. The game is won by the one who prospers most.

But remember, your own good fortune may result in…ah, pain and suffering for the person whom you love most."

"What do you mean," Desmond asked, "by pain and suffering?"

The voice was silent. Des asked again but only silence answered his words. *I don't get it, pleasure or pain? Anna, what did you get us into?*

Desmond signaled to Anna that is was time to go. He rose from his chair and walked back up the ramp. When he tried the handle he found the door was locked.

"Ok, I don't like this," Des said.

"Please return to your seat, Mr. and Mrs. Nidbit, so the game can begin," the voice said.

"Why is the door locked?" Des said as he tried the handle again.

"For security reasons," the voice answered, "The doors will stay locked till the product test is over. Now please return to your seats."

Desmond sat down and looked across the table at his wife. Anna looked back with a mixture of amusement and annoyance.

"Just play the game," she mouthed.

On the console before Des, a green light flashed. Then a table appeared on the screen like the one in the room before him, with numbered seats. Next to it on the display was a list of the players. Des scrolled down the list and found he was player three. Below was a row of buttons listing the five senses. A red and a green button blinked below.

"Pick one of the above symbols and then tap green or red for pleasure, or pain. You have ten seconds," the voice said.

Des tapped the button marked Sight and then Pleasure. Anna smiled at him.

"What a lovely bird, how sweet," she cooed.

The symbol on player one's seat flashed green.

"Player one," the voice advised, "You now have one minute to make a choice."

A choice of what(?) Des wondered. It made no sense to him. He studied the images on the console looking for a clue to what was happening.

"The symbol for pleasure flashed green on the screen. From the computer came the sound of a man's voice.

"Wow, it smells like my wife's perfume." Seat four lit up. A second later, a voice said, "Mine smells like...well you wouldn't want to sit here."

Des looked at the screen, that voice belonged to Natasha. Des laughed in spite of himself. This was silly. But still, he wondered *how do you win or lose at this?"*

Meanwhile, player two, Deanna, got the scent of roses. Player six, Marty, got rotten eggs.

It was his turn to receive again. Des sighed, as a brief excerpt from Rimsky-Korsakov's SHEHERAZADE filled his room with a moment of pure joyful sound. It was an excellent recording.

"Delightful," he said.

"Better than what I'm getting," Anna scowled. "I hate Jazz."

Round the game went, till all players had contributed. Des got a second of blinding light from his console as Natasha's screen filled up with the image of a beautiful crystal. Sandra got a pill that tasted like peaches, Paul got a glass filled with old prune juice.

Desmond relaxed after receiving a tiny electric shock which was his gift from Deanna. Not too bad this game, even if the point of it eluded him. He paused in his thoughts as the voice spoke.

"That was the warm-up round. From here," it said, "It will become more intense. You may pick a small pleasure or large, it will have no bearing on what your opponent gets in return."

Des hesitated, *how intense do they mean?* He looked on his screen and saw the Pleasure and Pain buttons now had a scale with increments from mild to extreme.

"Round two," the voice said. "Player one begins."

The green light on pleasure flashed and seconds later Bill said, "Damn, who needs a woman after this? Oops! Sorry honey."

A scream issued from Sandra. Bill called out, "What happened?"

Des looked across at her. The woman was shaking. Before he could signal to her, the voice announced player two. There was a long pause. Des looked at Deanna. She had pushed back her chair and was staring at the console with a worried expression.

"Number two, make your move, or the penalty will be severe."

"Des watched as she gingerly reached out and touched her computer. The light indicated that she chose pain. Des watched her body jerk repeatedly. *Electric shock. What will the pleasure be?"*

Sandra moaned in ecstasy. For a moment she was lost to her pleasure, and then she sat panting, her long fingers touching her mouth. Her lips wet, her eyes glazed.

"Oh...God," she sighed.

"Player three...It's your move.

Des turned from Sandra to stare at Deanna who was crying, and then at Anna who looked confused. There was no way he was going to allow this to go on. Des rose in his eat and said, "Game over. Open that door, NOW!"

Suddenly, Des felt himself slammed back into his chair Restraints shot out of its frame wrapping him like in a giant cocoon from shoulders to knees, locking him into a position where he could only move his hands. Des tried to squirm but the bonds held fast.

"Do not struggle against the restraints. Players must play, or the penalty will be severe."

What the Hell? Des couldn't move an inch. He could see Anne across the way was now bound up like him—as were all the rest. *She looks scared.* Des could not hear her, but her eyes pleaded for help.

A needle emerged from the side wall. Anna could not see it, but Desmond watched as it approached her from behind and finally pierced her neck just below the right ear. Anna's eyes went wide and she choked as the needle went in deep. An amber fluid was injected. Then the needle retracted.

On Desmond's console, a message appeared:

Player three, Your wife has been injected with a lethal dose of an advanced form of Smallpox. If you wish her to live, keep playing.

Des stared at the console and then quickly punched in pain for himself. Nothing happened. Then Anna began to scream in earnest. Des fought with his restraints, helpless to stop the new torment inflicted on his wife. Somehow he noticed that the straps were staining with red where they pinning his wrists.

Then it was over. Anna slumped in her chair. Across the way, Marty started thrashing. From the expression on his face Des could tell he was getting the pleasure.

On the screen, the words formed:

You chose pain.

Then it was Natasha's turn. The lovely redhead pulled at her blouse as pleasure excited her beyond any control. She squealed and went limp. Her eyes looked like those of a predator, wild with lust satiated. Across from her, Paul went rigid. Then the glass of his window went red speckled with blood and bits of brain matter. Des suddenly realized what the red speckling on the floor was.

"Player eight is out of the game," the voice said. Player five, it is your move."

*

The game continued for another hour. Bill, Paul, Deanna and Sandra were all dead. Of the couples, only Des and Anna were left. Anna's face was covered in small sores, some of which leaked an amber fluid. Marty looked desperate, Natasha had the look of insanity in her eyes. It was Anna's move. The console displayed her choice. It was Pain.

"We now enter the sudden death round," the voice said. "Any choice will kill."

Marty gagged and struggled as if something was strangling him. Des strained to see and caught a glimpse of a steel wire that apparently emerged from the back of the chair to throttle him. His eyes bugged out of his head and then he stopped twitching and just hung with his purplish tongue hanging from his mouth. Natasha started slamming her head back into her chair, fear totally commanding her body.

"Player three, it is your turn."

Des looked across at Anna. He knew that what ever button he pushed was likely to kill her, or Natasha. He was afraid. There was no choice, but there was only his choice now. *Damn you Anna for getting us into this.* Desmond's finger hovered above the console. Could he deliberately kill either of them?

Des relaxed his hands. Anna saw the look on his face and cried out what must have been, "No!"

"F—You!" Desmond yelled at the camera, "I forfeit!"

From out of the sides of the compartment, gas issued. Des held his breath for as long as he could, but the sour smell burned his eyes and nose. The strain on his chest and throat became unbearable. He finally reached the edge of his endurance and despaired as his body forced him to take a small breath. Des felt himself thrash, as the toxic effects overwhelmed him. His body convulsed like he was gripped by a metal claw that crushed his throat and shook him. Before he passed out, Des saw through his bleeding eyes that Anna's room was also turning cloudy. *What kind of monster made this...*

*

Des awoke and found he was no longer bound to the chair. Somehow he managed to stumbled up to his feet. The smell of gas was gone. *How?* Des looked back at his window, but the room with the table was dark. In front of him the door to the outside was open. Tucked into the handle, was an envelope.

Inside, there was a check for five grand. For a moment, Des toyed with the idea of shredding it to pieces. The cost of the game was far...far too severe. It made the money seem like an insult—no an abomination.

Des grasped the check and started to tear...and then stopped. No, he'd earned the money. Besides, if she were still alive, whatever they did to Anna might require the funds to heal her.

Des made his way up the corridor nursing his cracked ribs and pushed the door to the parking garage open. There, propped against the wall was Anna. Her clothes were soaked with sweat. Des looked closer. Her eyes looked sleepy, but clear. The pox sores on her face looked like they were shrinking.

"I was injected while I was semi-conscious," Anna said, stiffly rolling up a sleeve to display a new puncture mark on her arm. "I think the man who did it, said it was the cure."

"Where's Natasha?"

"She carried me out here and left."

Des walked over and embraced his wife who tucked herself under his arm before loosing her footing in a faint. Des caught her and carried her to their car.

"Did we win?" Anna's eyes looked glazed.

Des showed her the check. Anna spat at it and then rested her head on his shoulder.

"No more games, Darling," she whispered.

*

The creator of the game scratched his beard as he looked down at the screen and the dead players. He scribbled some notes onto the pad next to it and then turned to his guest.

"So, what do you think?"

"You know the game has something," Lucifer said to his host, "So much more relaxing than tempting them and squabbling over their souls in person."

"Yes," the creator said, "This game is a far more provocative test of Free Will. Brilliant suggestion, Lucifer, you have indeed impressed me."

Lucifer smiled, "Inspiration Boss, that's what I do." He warmed a brandy snifter in his hands. "I do prefer it warm."

"Ah, the door opens," the creator said indicating a blinking red light by his desk. He reached over and turned on a monitor. The pair watched as the screen displayed new cars waiting at the entrance of the parking garage. More players were arriving. The creator stretched and cracked his fingers then flipped a switch—activating the loudspeaker.

"Clean-up," he said, "New parties arriving please remove the spent players and place the seating cards for the new arrivals."

Lucifer took a drink from his brandy.

"Cheers."

The creator pointed, indicating a second computer console.

"So my opponent, the deck is shuffled, ready for another game?"

THE COPPER PEOPLE

Ancient Africa is a mystery. We know little before the rise of the great Egyptian and Nubian empires that fought for dominance in that lost time. But there was another people, one much more ancient that might have witnessed the rise of those ancient cultures. Cultures that had not yet discovered iron, yet were so advanced that they might have appeared as gods to the Bushmen whom roamed the savannah first.

It was early. The morning sun had not yet uncovered the shaded slopes of the ancient volcano, whose tired slopes rose above the grasslands beyond. Its long black shadow still extended far west into the savannah, where it ended abruptly as if its sharp edges were cut with a knife. Black, it lay against the bright golden grass tipped with the orange tint of morning's glow, and where the shadow lay it was cold.

Shivering in that cool darkness, Narock of the Khoi-Khoi (Bush Men) climbed through the igneous jumble of lava crust and hard basalt looking for outcroppings of flint. While the red basalt would serve, the gray-black rock he sought made for the finest tipping for spear or knife. This was particularly important to Narock as he was weapons maker for his clan.

Finding the right material was often a matter of close and careful examination of the shards of rock that littered the ground. But this slope was turning out to be a poor hunting ground for the kind of rock Narock wanted. Most of the bare rock was obscured, thickly covered with plants that were rooted into the decomposing lava. Even so, here and there he saw outcroppings of black volcanic glass. It was not as good a material as the flint for shaping, but it was more easily worked from the ground than the red rock.

Narock stopped at one out cropping in the hope that some of the obsidian glass had weathered clear of the lava. It was easier for him when he found rough slivers that were close in size and shape to what he wanted to make. On this day he was looking for pieces large enough for spear tips. Some of the men had broken their points hunting. It was his job to replace them.

Narock scrambled along the low ridge checking the rock as he went, but none of the exposed material was of the he had hoped for. This meant hard work was ahead, as the only way to get new material was to smash chunks out of the cliff face with a large stone and then break that up into sizeable pieces that could be chipped and shaped into what he needed. That was especially risky because it meant he would make noise. Noise often attracted danger and he was alone except for the dog.

Narock paused to watch the small jackal dog that had taken to following him this morning. He tolerated the presence of the animal as it gave him company and its sharper senses added to his protection. For the last few seconds though, the dog seemed especially uneasy about something. It paced back and forth across a small ledge that jutted out from the slope and whined. Narock scanned the ridgeline overhead, but saw nothing. No Lion or leopard stalked the plains below. Narock had seen the worn tracks of a Saber Cat a few days before. Though rare, the cat was an especially dangerous predator, one that would use this broken landscape to ambush the unwary. Narock hoped it had moved on. Out in the sunny grass there were some antelopes. They fed on the grass warily, but showed no sign of alarm. Narock felt relieved. They would not be so calm, if the big cat was around.

Narock reached up to grab a branch of a nearby bush for support, when he heard the dog yipe. Releasing his grip, he turned in time to get slammed off his feet by the marbled coils of a giant snake! It lunged out of its hiding place in the rock and grabbed the dog with the force of a pile driver.

Narock watched terrified, as the rest of the beast oozed out of a brush covered opening in the rubble. The Paleoboa was near forty feet in length, an endless looking nightmare that lifted the doomed dog high into the air. It began at once to swallow its victim without even stopping to constrict it. As it did, another coil wrapped around Narock's right ankle, holding him fast.

Narock struggled to his feet and unslung his bow. He fired his bone tipped arrows into the snake as fast as he could fletch them, but to no avail. The thick overlapping scales of the snake protected its almost three foot thick body like armor. Most of Narock's arrows just bounced off the greasy plates. Those that did stick could not penetrate to the flesh beneath, so the poison they were coated with was useless.

The snake turned its head straight up and gulped down its prey. Narock shivered in terror as the dog's feet and tail vanished down its sickening maw. The body made a bulge in the snake's neck that moved down its throat like a giant pill. Narock stared mesmerized till the dog's corpse disappeared into the mass of the animal.

The snake gaped and readjusted its jaws with a sawing motion that displayed its bloody rows of spike like teeth. Its head lowered as it looked around for more with its unblinking stare. Narock threw down his bow and reached for his knife. The motion was not lost on the Paleoboa.

The serpent turned to him flicking its tongue slowly as it exhaled. The stink of reptile breath on his face, made Narock's stomach turn. He watched the snake's flat head pivot slowly back and forth before him. The Bushman realized that the snake's vision was none to good, for though it had his leg firm in its grip, the serpent acted as if it were trying to locate him.

Narock knew there was no choice left to him, but to either fight and be consumed, or freeze and hope the snake would forget he was there. Narock stood as still as his shaking knees would let him, cursing his chattering teeth as the snake drew near. A tongue tip almost touched him. Narock tightened his grip on the obsidian knife and waited.

Suddenly the serpent struck and its teeth tore in to Narock's left arm like a row of nails being hammered into place! Shock and pain disoriented the bushman. Narock forgot his knife and screamed in agony. Dimly, he felt himself lifted and tumbled as the serpent's coils looped around his body. Within seconds, the air was forced out of his lungs by the sheer power of the snake's constriction. Narock felt his eyes bulging from the pressure. His senses faded from the lack of air. Unless he could defend himself, Narock knew in a very short time he would be following the dog down that awful throat.

He had dropped his knife when the snake struck, so Narock's one free hand clawed at the ground for anything he could use as a weapon. By chance, his right hand felt one of the arrows he had shot. Narock grabbed it and stabbed its poisoned head past his trapped arm into the snake's mouth, stabbing the hole that was its glottis. Blood and saliva flowed from where he pierced it. His efforts resulted in the snake thrashing and biting still harder on his arm. He located a second arrow hanging off the serpent's neck. Narock pulled it out and stuck it in the snake's throat.

Finally the pressure of its grip was too much for him to stand. Narock's fear turned to utter despair. He drifted into unconsciousness as the snake started to swallow him.

*

It was near noon, when Narock reached up to rub his eyes and found that his left arm was no longer trapped in the snake's mouth. His throat was so dry he couldn't breathe. Narock gagged and coughed as he fought to regain the air his lungs had lost. He lay back panting as his body awoke. It felt like he had been crushed into an unnatural posture. Narock carefully flexed his hands and feet and fortunately nothing seemed broken. There was a heavy weight on top of him that stank of reptile. He was still in the grip of the snake! Narock opened his eyes, blinking at the bright sun that blinded him. He could feel the loosened coils of the snake were still wrapped around him. Ever so slowly, Narock turned his head and looked over at the serpent's head and saw that it was lying still with the shafts of the arrows protruding from its open mouth. It looked lifeless, but was it dead?

When he felt stronger, Narock began to slowly lever and pry the rest of his body out from under the snake. Its mass was very heavy, almost too heavy for the tiny bushman to lift. Narock's body was covered in a stinking combination of saliva and blood that had oozed from the snake's mouth. Apparently it had managed to swallow him partially before throwing him back up. From the waist up Narock was coated with slime. This worked to his advantage as, aided by the lubricant, Narock was able to slip his arm out of the straps of his quiver and food bag. Both were pinned under the snake's body. Then removing his hide garments, Narock squeezed and pulled his torso clear of its grip. As he moved to extract his legs, the snake twitched!

Narock froze. The snake was still alive. He could feel the limp coils begin to tighten as he lay there. In seconds he would be trapped again! With a sharp jerk, Narock yanked his legs free of the snake, tumbling backward and rolling downhill before coming to rest a several feet away. At the same moment the snake's head suddenly raised and turned in his direction!

This time, luck was with Narock, as he now rested behind the some boulders below the serpent's immediate line of vision. The wakened serpent made no movement towards him. Instead, it flicked its tongue as it searched its own coils for its lost prey. Narock held himself motionless till the snake finally gave up. The Paleoboa turned back over it's sausage like body and disappeared back into the opening in the jumbled rock.

Narock waited till he was sure the serpent was gone before climbing down the slope as fast as he could. When he felt he had gone a safe distance, Narock paused long enough to relieve himself and whisper a prayer to his gods for allowing his escape. Narock stretched his cramped muscles and let out a painful yelp. His shoulder and left arm were stiff and burned with pain from the snake's bite. There dozens of puncture wounds that now were covered in a layer of drying blood and snake saliva. Fortunately, none of the bites were serious. Revolted by the gooey mess, Narock pulled a handful of leaves from a nearby tree. He scrubbed madly at his body, till he had removed most of the horrible smelling slime. Then the grossness of it overpowered him, his body cramped up and he retched.

Narock was grateful that he had escaped death. The bad thing was that he was still in trouble. In his escape he had lost his food bag, bow, and quiver. Narock shook with terror at the thought of having to go back to retrieve his belongings. But to be unarmed on the savannah was the same thing as committing suicide. Narock had tasted enough of death.

Very carefully, Narock climbed back up to the ledge, taking pains to disturb nothing as he climbed. He located the snake's den. Keeping a close watch on the opening Narock scanned the ledge for his gear. By luck, he found that his bow, quiver and remaining arrows were undamaged. Narock located his loincloth, but his food bag was tangled in the bushes next to the opening. Narock dared not risk going any closer to the snake den. He retreated slowly from the ledge, slinging the bark quiver over his shoulder as he grabbed his bow and again descended. A few feet further down he found his knife and tucked it into his loincloth.

Narock was tired and hungry. Worse, he was thirsty and nowhere near water. Fortunately, the bushman knew that even in the grasslands there was always food available for the wise. With a quick glance back at the lava slope, Narock strode out into the tall yellow grass in search of lunch.

Beneath the roots of an acacia tree, Narock located some juicy grubs to take the edge off his hunger. Some he saved in his quiver for later. The rest he munched as he continued outward. Narock decided it was prudent to give up his search for flint for now and give a wide berth to the hillside. Instead he circled around through the grass before starting back to his people's camp.

*

Towards late afternoon, Narock found a small antelope that was freshly dead. Blood still pulsed out of a small slit in its throat. He looked closely at the wound and marveled over its remarkable clean edges. What could make a perfect cut like that? Narock touched the wound and tasted the blood, pleased to find the taste fresh and untainted by poison. Narock thanked the gods for their mercy. This was a fantastic stroke of luck as not only did the antelope supply meat, but also its hide could be used to make a new carrying bag like the one he had lost. The Bushman drew his knife and began to skin the carcass. As he did, he cut off slices of meat that he could carry with him and cook later. It was never a good idea to stay with a kill for too long, the blood scent would have already attracted predators. So Narock hurried and singing to himself as he cut.

He lifted the antelopes head, preparing to cut the hide just below the throat. When he did, Narock caught the glint of something orange and shinny in the pooled blood beneath it. Before he could pick it up, he heard the sound of human voices. Narock looked up and saw several strange men racing towards him. They were very large, very dark skinned, and very angry. Narock dropped the carcass and ran in the direction of the nearest thicket he could see. His flight went uncontested for the first several yards and then something shiny whistled by and plunged into the earth before him. It was an arrow. Without slowing his pace, Narock grabbed the feathered shaft as he passed. As he straightened up he felt another arrow slice a shallow scratch into his leg. Narock raced for almost a hundred yards before diving head first into a gulley. He looked back and saw to his relief, that he had not been followed.

Narock looked down at his thigh. There was some blood oozing from a long but minor scratch. The flow was minor and the color of his blood coming from it looked good, so he turned his thoughts away from it. Besides, the arrow he held was much more interesting.

The arrow was perhaps the most beautiful thing Narock had ever seen. It was large, almost too long for his bow to shoot. The shaft was of smooth white wood, finely crafted and was decorated with bands of pigment that he guessed from its faint scent might be from berry juice. It looked flawless. The feathers that adorned it were of birds he knew. They were finely trimmed in a way Narock guessed would allow more lift and less wind resistance. They were tied in place with some kind of fiber Narock had never seen. Amazing...he thought.

But it was the arrowhead it self that was the most astonishing thing. It was unbelievably smooth, made of a shiny reddish material that was like glass but not. It appeared like it was on fire. Here and there it was flecked with blue green. Narock ran his finger along the blade edge and it drew blood with ease. No wonder the antelope had died from such a tiny wound. This was strange magic. He balanced the arrow in his hands and stared at it for several minutes before placing it in his quiver.

The smell of smoke drifted into Narock's nostrils carrying the sweet scent of the cooking antelope. He peeked out of his hiding place and saw the

39

strange people's cooking fire. They had chosen to camp on the sport where the kill had been made. "Foolish," Narock whispered.

Narock thought for a moment about starting a fire of his own. He still had his rolling stick so there was no problem making one. The few grubs that he had kept from earlier would make a meal. Night was starting to shade the grass of the savannah. Another hour would supply night's ample cover. Then it would be safe to sneak closer for a look. His curiosity would wait.

The bushman pulled some grass fibers from his quiver and used them to start a small fire deep in the gulley where he hoped it would go unnoticed. He impaled the grubs on a stick and toasted them so they were nice and crunchy. Not venison, but still tasty fare, he thought. As he cooked Narock amused himself by looking at the various animal tracks that were preserved in the sand. There had been many antelopes and a few other herd animals. Mixed in were a few smaller tracks, probably from a jackal. One track though caught his eye. He walked over to it and sniffed. The track was fresh. This was bad news, as it was the pug mark of a Saber tooth. Fortunately the track led away from the gulley. Still, this complicated things.

After eating, Narock left his fire and circled wide around the camp of the strangers so their fire was between him and his hideout. Then he crawled on his belly until he was close enough to observe the camp.

Five men sat around the fire. At least Narock thought they might be men, because they were shaped like him. But their appearance suggested that they might be gods as well. Their skin was darker than his, black like the stripes of a zebra. Their arms and necks were decorated with bands of what looked like the same material as the arrow head. All were dressed in an odd looking white material that covered their shoulders and hung to mid thigh. As he watched, one stood up that had a band around his temples of the red stone. He stretched his arms and walked to the fire. Narock gasped; compared to his height of just over four feet, the man was gigantic. His frame was lean and his face narrow with high cheekbones. The giant turned to speak to his comrades and Narock listened closely to his words in hopes of learning who they were.

The sound of the man's speech played odd but pleasant upon Narock's ears. His language was smooth and rhythmic, so very different from the clicks and grunts of Narock's own language. He could make no sense of it though. Yet without even knowing the words, Narock could tell from the sound that the words the man spoke were angry.

As he talked, the man held up a bag and poured its contents on the ground. Immediately, the others started picking at the pile of what looked like smooth river gravel and talking excitedly. None of the stones looked big enough to work for even a tiny arrowhead. Narock scratched his head at their foolishness. Pebbles...why would they argue over tiny useless pebbles?

Narock was thinking about that when another man rose from the shadows and approached the fire. This man was very strange. Where the other's had skin like ebony, his was light, even lighter than Narock's golden brown. His features were narrow, with a long nose and thin lips. Narock had never seen eyes on a human that looked as cruel as his. This man wore some kind of ring around his head holding in place a stripped drop of the odd material that they all wore. The bits of metal he wore as a necklace and armlets were of a shinny yellow stone with polished bits of green rock set into them. Otherwise his ornaments were similar to what the others wore in design. He was smaller than the dark men, who stood up at when they saw him.

The man spoke harshly to the men at the fire and then raised a stick tipped with a cobra's head over his head. At the sight of it, one of the dark men tried to run. Narock saw more of the pale men rise from the shadows armed with spears and bows. More in fact than he had fingers and toes. One these men threw his spear at the running man, transfixing him through the back. Narock saw the blade blossom from the man's gut as he fell. Immediately, the others reached for their weapons.

The giant lunged for the man who seemed to be the leader of the spearmen. Before he could reach him, two men lowered their spears and skewered him. With a backhanded swing, the giant slit the throat of one of them with his long knife before he fell. The remaining three men stood back to back and were ringed in by the attacking spearmen. Very quickly they were all bloody and on the ground. Narock saw the spears rise and fall several times before the pale men stopped stabbing.

The leader walked over to where the bag of stones had been spilled on the ground. In the course of the fight the pile had been trampled and scattered. He gestured to one of the spearmen who bent and scooped all the stones he could find back into the bag. This he presented to the leader falling to his knees as he held it up with both hands.

The other spearmen gathered the weapons of the fallen. Then they turned to their dead comrade and lifted him onto their shoulders. At a command from their leader the entire group disappeared into the night leaving the rest of the dead where they lay.

Narock waited almost an hour after they left before he dared to approach the campsite. The bodies of the fallen were stripped of weapons and jewelry. The garments they wore were bloodstained but the bushman ignored that as he felt the material. Odd it was like some kind of dried plant fiber or spider web. Narock could not make up his mind. He scanned around in hopes that he might find something to give him a clue to what all this meant.

He walked over to where the stones had been. Most were gone but here and there were some tiny ones scattered around. Then he noticed a glint under the giant. Partially under his body was a large one of the odd rocks. Carefully, Narock slipped his hand under the corpse and grabbed it.

When he held it in the light of the fire the marble sized stone looked clear and greasy. It showed flat edges but otherwise did not look any more remarkable than the clear stone he often found growing in caves. Why would they fight for this stone? Narock wondered and sought to make sense of it. Maybe, he reasoned, the gods had trapped fire in them. The sparkle within the pebble clearly looked like the flame that sometimes fell from the sky. Narock saw a large rock nearby. Perhaps he could test the theory. He placed the greasy pebble on it and using another stone he hammered on it. On the second blow, it split into many tiny clear white pieces, but no fire came forth.

"Useless," he said. Narock sat down and stared at the sparkly bits that were all that was left of the stone. Who were these people? Where did they get the odd orange stone they made weapons from? Narock saw another large pebble. This one was a pretty shade of red. He lifted it and cradled it in his hands. They were so much a mystery.

As he sat by the corpses completely absorbed in his thoughts, Narock failed to notice the soft tread of the predator as it approached him from behind. It was only when he felt its fetid breath on his back that Narock turned...and found himself face to face with the nine inch fangs of the saber tooth!

It was too late to even be afraid. Narock shivered, despairing in his lapse of judgment. "Never stay close to a fresh kill," he whimpered. All he could do was just sit and wait for the huge cat to bite into his throat and kill him, as oblivious as he to the priceless diamond that dropped from Narock's trembling fingers.

SPINNING

There were lights and smoke, the damp feel and sour smell of fresh torn flesh—burnt beyond the taste of any mortal palate. And yes, above the sound of cracking bones there were screams...

Entry from the journal of Jeremy Pane dated August 14th 1948:

There are sounds you hear in the light of day or the dark of night; that either motivate or distract our progress and our thoughts as we make our way through the conscious world. I do not write of the simple sounds and hums that our world normally makes. Not the sound of the sea, or the city, or even the hum of daily commuters on the freeway.

There are other sounds, so subtle... so enticing, just octaves beyond the range of normal hearing. Some of those sounds are of lightness, that make us wake to the day and rest in the cool of night. They are sounds that help us love and dream and create. Beautiful flats and sharps that we never really know, but bask in their love.

There are other sounds, notes that echo in the ear in darker chords. Sounds that make us feel anger and hate that encourage greed, blind ambition, lust and envy that drive men mad and make men rape and steal...and Murder.

Then there are the darkest sounds; those that open doors that shouldn't be opened. The sounds that we really should know and be wary of—but aren't...sounds that shrivel the souls of those fools who tarry within the range of their awful echoes.

I wish to God I had listened.

Wendell Bechham stumbled upon the small village as he drove his new blue van towards Pigeon Ford, Tennessee to attend a music festival. He just had passed the small town of Townsend and was headed Northeast up towards Wear Valley on US 321, when a long line of mailboxes appeared along the side of a dirt road. The tin objects perched awkwardly on rude wood poles that lined the side the highway. Such sights are common in the South, oft passed and almost never noticed. Any other day Wendell would have driven by.

This day however, a trick of the morning sun resulted in one of the mail boxes in the line glinting brightly enough in the light to catch Wendell's eye—blinding him with its glare.

Now what is that?

The car spun out of control—almost hitting a tree before Wendell managed to steer it over to the swale.

Shit, that was close!

Wendell shut off his van's engine and waited for his shaking to stop. As the dust settled, only the trill of a mocking bird and the chirring of a cicada sounded louder than his heartbeat.

Wendell removed his sunglasses and wiped his brow. He looked back at the road he passed through his rearview mirror.

The large amount of mailboxes—set on rickety wood poles, suggested that there might be a small town hidden along the back road. For what Wendell sought, the side road suggested enticing possibilities.

45

Wendell carefully backed his van up, till it was back at the turnoff, made a right onto the corduroy road and immediately crossed a small river that ran parallel to the main highway.

*

Wendell was a student of Rural Folk Music. Not in the capacity of being associated with any particular university or organization. Nor was he a professional, as his sole claim to any background, was the music store he owned. It was more because he was fascinated by the unusual qualities of mountain music and more specifically, the instruments that produced it. He had in fact, become a collector of obscure musical instruments.

It had become his habit to make road trips to actively pursue his hobby on weekends. Often, he would scout the back roads and isolated towns of his native state, in the hopes of finding an old fiddle, a squeeze box, or even a set of spoons.

*

Wendell followed the dusty road which weaved for a few miles before turning due east. From that turn the road sloped down. Through the dark pines that lined it, Wendell could see a small valley and several houses. By his reckoning, he figured he was likely near the border of Smokey Mountains National Park. This town was one he had never heard of, let alone set foot in.

"More promising by the minute," Wendell said as he stopped the van to checkout the town that lay below him. Not that there was much to see. There was a church and several crude wood framed houses. These he ignored for what he sought would most likely be found in the largest building down there. Painted on its front in big black letters he could read the words:

GAU'S GAP FEED AND SUPPLIES.

It was in old feed or general stores like the one before him that
Wendell had found a reliable source of items the items he collected.
Usually these old places had thrift shops, or even just a corner
where people stacked and sold off their excess junk or family
heirlooms. This one was so far off the beaten path that Wendell felt
confident that none of his fellow collectors had been lucky enough
to chance upon it.

"Booty," he whispered and drove down into the valley.

Wendell parked in front of the general store. He stretched,
feeling the cramps that were his huge body's revenge for the
morning drive. Wendell squinted in the bright light as he stepped
out into the sun. Then remembering his sunglasses, he retrieved
them from the dashboard. *Damn its hot.*

Panting heavily, he ducked into the shade of the old store's
awning as quickly as his corpulent body would allow. his pale skin
was already soaked with sweat from the brief exposure to the sun.
He mopped a handful of blonde curls away from his watery blue
eyes and wiped it dry on his pants leg. Wendell paused for a
moment to inspect the coarse white-washed exterior of the building
with its wood shingled roof.

"Got to be something good in here," he whispered.

Wendell heard the sound of the rough wood boards creaking
under his feet, as he climbed up the rickety steps to the door. There
was a statue of a little Negro boy in the grass next to the stoop. It
was the old kind you saw outside of buildings in the anti-bellum

days—one that held a ring to tie your horse to—if of course you had been ridding one. Next to the door it waited, it's black face half hidden by a sparse growth of Azaleas.

The door looked odd and upon closer examination Wendell was surprised to discover that the windows were made of isinglass.

As he entered the store, Wendell observed a long counter on the left side that was almost against the rough wood wall. Tucked behind the counter in that narrow space, was an old man who was seated on a wood crate. He looked up from the paper he was reading and smiled a broken toothed grin at the newcomer. Then wordlessly, he went back to his reading. Wendell began his search.

The front of the store was a disappointing series of shelves, comprised mainly of food items and tack. But experience had taught the young collector where to look. When Wendell walked to the back of the store, he found exactly what he was hoping for.

There was a small enclave where there was lots of boxes and stuff that had to be castoffs that had been brought there by the locals.

In the first box, Wendell found an old Jew's harp and he almost cried out with joy. Next to the harp, he saw a box, which contained several jars filled with nails and screws. Further on, his prowling yielded an old quilt, a plow bit, several old watches and jewelry items, a pair of glasses and some leather scraps.

As Wendell dug through the remnants, he uncovered an antique black satchel which was locked. It looked functional; Wendell tried to pick it up and found it was entangled with an odd looking length of rope. Wendell was intrigued by the strangeness of it.

What made it peculiar was that the cotton rope was woven with multi colored threads. There were bits of things tied to it in a way or purpose that made no sense. There were ribbons and thimbles as well as a few metal can lids that had been pierced and strung onto it, as well as some twigs and what looked like bits of bone.

Wendell untangled it from the satchel and laid the rope out on the floor. It looked to measure about ten feet in length and was terminated at one end by a handle. This had been made by folding about six inches of the rope back and then winding bailing wire around it.

"That be a Spinner son," the old storekeeper said, who was suddenly standing behind Wendell.

"My name's Samuel, son."

"A—Spinner you say? I've never heard of one. What is it for?" Wendell paused, wondering how the old man had slipped up on him. He had hoped to complete his inspection before having to deal with the owner. *Damn...he knows I'm interested. There goes the price.*

Samuel laughed. "What ye do is, ye take a rope and attach a load of doodads to it like this here and ye spins it around Yo head."

"You mean twirl it don't you?"

"Naw boy, ye spins it. Makes a God awful noise it does. Don't they spin where ye hail from?"

"Never," Wendell said. "You mean this is a musical instrument?"

"Well," the storekeeper said as he stroked his chin, "Ye could say that, but there's more to it than jest the music.

"Son...we use Spinners over at the church. Kinda goes with the Sunday singing and such. Makes the words of the Lord a bit more special it does."

"For church music...I've never heard of it!" *This has to be the most unique artifact of mountain music ever.* Wendell knew he just had to have it. None of his fellow collectors had anything like this. It was incredible trophy for his collection.

"Can I buy this?"

Wendell forgot about bargaining. His hands trembled with excitement as he held the Spinner close to him. *Gotta have it.*

"Well I cain't say that I can sell ye this-a-one-" Samuel said taking the spinner from Wendell.

Wendell's heart sank.

"-but Ezekiel, he can do it—That is, he can make you one."

"Where do you find him?" Wendell mopped the sweat from his brow. *Shit, that was close.*

"He lives up by the spoil piles, at the old limestone quarry."

Samuel shook his head.

"I think if yer of a mind to get one, then I best be the one to make the arranging. It's a bit of a rough climb and yer no small man. Hate t think ye get a heart attack or sumptin a fer ya got there. Besides, Ezekiel won't stand for parting with the thing till it's blessed. Confidentially, son, he's a mite tetched. The Lord chose for some reason to suffer the curse of confusion on him."

"I see," Wendell said. "So this...Spinner, it's a religious object."

"Well of course, boy! Spinning is a test of a man's faith, don't you know. Why Ezekiel, he could spin up a Devil when he was young.

"Sacred ropes they are! That's why they all is blessed by the Parson, so it's ok that we can use them at services."

"Ok then," Wendell said, "You can arrange to have one made for me?"

"Sure thing son, ye can pick it up say...next Sunday?" Wendell nodded. *You better believe I'll be back old man.*

"Then we will have you in church Sunday next. Just remember to ask fer Samuel and you'll find me."

Wendell groaned. Spending a morning in a back road's church promised to be at the very least boring. But it meant obtaining the musical find—possibly of the century.

"Ok Samuel, we can do it that way then," he said.

"What about this thing?"

"The satchel?" Samuel picked it up, brushing the dust off it.

"Well son, that's kinda been here for awhile. If I remember correctly; some tourist boy forgot it and never did come back to fetch it home. It's a bit worn though and the lock on its strap is broken. From the weight of it, I reckon there's something in it, maybe a book or something.

"I don't take to no serious reading, save of course the word of the Lord, so I never checked it."

Samuel scratched his head.

"Two bits fer it, son and I think ye might just be getting a bargain at that."

Samuel picked up the Jew's harp.

"I seen ye liked this afore, so let's seal the deal with this—as a gift fer ye."

"Well thank you sir," Wendell gushed, "I almost forgot that."

Wendell took the harp and followed Samuel over to the counter. Samuel promptly put the cash handed him into the drawer of a cash register that looked at least as old as the man was. Then he wrapped the items together in brown paper tied with string.

"Ok then Sir," Wendell said, "I'll see you here next Sunday."

"Ye best remember to be looking for me at the church then, 'cause that's where ye will be finding me."

*

On the drive back to his home in Happy Valley, Wendell thought about the prizes he had acquired.

The antique Jew's harp was a small treasure, but it was not the first Wendell had found. It would of course immediately join the others on his display shelf.

Now the leather satchel—that purchase had been more of a case of curiosity getting the better of him. Maybe the book inside of it was something uncommon that he could sell over the internet, the profit applied to cover fuel costs.

Wendell relaxed his grip on the steering wheel. In his mind's eye, he saw the spinner twirling before a congregation. The folks were singing a gospel song, but he could not make out the words. The air around them was hot and red. The congregation moved and swayed like the beat of a giant heart. Something was happening to the man who was spinning, something terrible.

Good Lord, I'm shaking.

Wendell felt the road go out from under the van. He opened his eyes and saw an oak dead ahead. Pulling hard on the steering wheel, he managed to swerve and miss the tree and get back on the road.

The sweat dripping from his forehead was burning his eyes. Wendell mopped his brow with his sleeve and took a sip from the open soft drink on his dash. The shock of the sweet burning/cold liquid's taste snapping him back from his jitters. *What was that about? Got to focus on getting home.*

No one had anything like the spinner. Wendell shook himself and then laughed at his nerves. *Yeah, can't let myself get too excited over this.* He vaguely remembered hearing something about some aboriginal tribes using a length of rope with an attachment to make sound, but he couldn't remember exactly where. There was nothing he knew of like it in American musical instruments. Wendell made a mental note to research that, just to be certain.

It was just a discovery like this would be a tremendous addition to his credibility and reputation amongst his fellow collectors. Perhaps enough to make them finally overlook the fact that he was an unlettered amateur. It would be good to watch them all eat crow as they stared enviously at his prize.

*

When Wendell arrived at his townhouse, he carried his new acquisitions into his den. Impatient, Wendell tore the wrappings off the parcel that contained his prizes. The harp went immediately on the shelf as planned. He jotted down location and date of purchase on a slip of paper. There would be a more proper ID card for it later.

The satchel, he placed on his work table. A few quick twists with a screwdriver and the damaged lock was sprung. The acid scent of old damp paper tickled his nostrils making him sneeze. Inside, Wendell found the flattened remnant of a very old roll of Life Savers that disintegrated probably decades ago. There was some

Kleenex, a fountain pen that had bled out and a book that appeared to be a journal.

The book itself was bound in red plaid cloth with a black leather spine. It was moldy and partially stained blue from the pen's ink. When he tried to open it, Wendell found that several of the pages were stuck together. He peeled a few pages apart and snorted in disgust. Damn it's ruined.

At this point, Wendell was ready to just throw it away as a disappointment, but as he closed the book, something caught his eye. He quickly thumbed back through the volume till he found what he sought.

There was a page that was half obscured by ink stains, which appeared to contain lines from a song—one unfamiliar to him—as well as musical notes that were printed out in pencil. He could only make out two lines of the score, but it held promise that—if he could salvage more of it, would add a folk song that possibly was new to his list of finds. Donning his reading glasses he read:

Spin it such and you can tell
Poor Boy you spun the...

Unfortunately, the rest was obliterated by ink and mold.

Wendell turned to the inside of the front cover. The name JEREMY PANE was inscribed along with a date; August 14th 1948. The lines beneath the date caught his interest, as the entry had crudely scrawled—apparently written as an afterthought. He read;

There are sounds you hear in the light of day...

The rest of the book was filled with the entries expected of a young man's journal. Jeremy Person had been a student of music. As Wendell read through the few pages still intact, he pieced together that the man had traveled widely thought the Tennessee region just after World War Two.

Jeremy had passed through Sevierville and was on his way South into West Georgia when he had stumbled into the small town of Gau's gap. There was a brief notation about the store. That—combined with the song reference to Spinning, gave Wendell something to worry about.

Was his discovery possibly something that was already known and studied? Wendell anxiously scanned through the rest of the journal looking for clues, but the rest of the pages were intelligible. Only the last twenty pages of the book remained unsoiled and those were blank.

Wendell turned next to his computer to see if there were any references there to Spinning or Gau's Gap but he found none. This just might be a stroke of luck, he realized. His discovery had been previously made by this fellow Pane and for some reason it had never been documented. Yes, indeed, this was a real stroke of luck.

*

Wendell split his time over the next week between working in his music store in Elizabethville and preparing a display case for his Spinner. He contacted his friends and cryptically hinted that he might have something special to show them soon. Several very satisfying Emails shot back in response inquiring as to what this thing might be, but Wendell wasn't talking. Soon enough, he would unveil his prize.

On Tuesday afternoon the president of the Happy Valley Musical Heritage Society, Art Stenmore walked into Wendell's shop.

"Wendell hated the thin faced man whose long nose seemed to sniff out anything that Wendell had found. The man was always whining that those collectables rightfully belonged in a museum and that Wendell should donate his sizeable collection.

This morning Stenmore did not even pause to check the banjo stand for new instruments as he mad his way directly to the proprietor.

"Where is it?" Stenmore demanded.

"Where is what, Mr. Stenmore?" Wendell decided to play it coy.

"Don't play with me, boy, Stenmore punctuated his words by tapping his cane on the floor. "There's talk all up and down the collecting circuit that you might have found something important. What is it?"

"Wouldn't you like to know, Art, but you'll have to wait like everyone else."

"You had better not be holding out on an important artifact-"

"Or what?"

Wendell turned his back on the man, pretending to organize a rack of wood flutes. Stenmore's voice sounded odd, like instead of words, there was nothing but the sound of whirling.

Squirm baby…Boy this feels good.

"Oh, I suppose you'll just sit in your president's chair and moan like you usually do."

"One of these days Bechham I will take action…Damn you!"

Stenmore stormed out the door. In the backroom, Polly Watts, Wendell's only employee called out.

"Looks like the old crud is spinning on your hook, Boss."

"Funny you should say that Polly," Wendell said. He looked over towards the door. *Man, I hope this doesn't fall through.*

*

At last Sunday came. Wendell was up before dawn packing for the trip. He felt elated despite the almost all night jam session he and his group, The Blue Grass Buddies had performed at the local club. Wendell packed his cooler and then on a whim, threw his banjo and guitar in the rear. You never knew where a new tune would show up. Maybe even the rest of the one in Jeremy's book, he hoped.

As an after thought, he went back inside and changed his clothes. Selecting his good suit jacket, Wendell squeezed his huge frame into it and then grabbed a tie. *May as well look respectable. Might help when it comes to dickering on the price.*

Wendell could barely contain himself as he drove down the highway, fighting to keep his speed under the limit so he wouldn't get a speeding ticket—or worse, miss the turnoff. His hands thumped impatiently as he drove.

When at last, he saw the mail boxes and made the right onto the dirt road, he burned rubber for the final miles to Gaur's Gap.

Wendell saw several clusters of people gathered outside the church as he drove up. Off to one side Samuel waved in greeting.

Wendell parked the van and walked over. Samuel met him. In his hands was a new Spinner. Even before the old man handed it to him, Wendell could smell the rich scent of brand new cotton rope.

It is beautiful, Wendell thought, as he admired the green and golden threads wove into it. There was some bone that had actually been scrimshawed with pictures from the Bible hanging from it. There were sea shells and bits of metal tied on with scarlet and lavender thread. The wire handle gleamed with the color of clean red copper.

Samuel grasped Wendell's arm. "Do ye like it, Boy?"

Wendell looked up from the odd contraption that he cradled in his arms and replied, "Its...lovely."

"Ok then," the storekeeper said. "It be yourn. Now what ye got to do now is when the Parson calls ye, get up and spin it fer the congregation. That's when the Parson will bless it."

"Me? Alone in front of the...your, congregation? Man this ain't like playing with my band. I've got the worst kind of stage fright."

"Ezekiel said that be the only way ye get to keep this," The old man said sternly. Wendell could tell the old man was not going to budge on this. *Guess they want to see an outsider make a damn fool out of himself.*

"Ok," Wendell replied. "Guess it's worth the embarrassment."

"There ye go son. It'll be easy, mark my words." Samuel smiled and his gold teeth gleamed bright in the morning sun, like golden tombstones in a red hell.

At that moment the church doors were opened. The preacher entered first, and then everyone slowly filed inside. Wendell found himself seated at the front of the church (in the aisle seat) with Samuel next to him.

An odd old man sat a few rows ahead. Wendell saw that his bald head seemed perched at a strange angle on his warty neck. One shoulder looked unusually high set. Samuel noticed Wendell's stare and whispered that the man was Ezekiel. And then put his finger to his lips as the parson mounted the podium.

The preacher who seemed a jovial round sort gave a brief welcoming speech and sat down. Then a nondescript woman of middle years led the congregation then sang a couple of hymns before he rose again to give the Sunday sermon. He spoke for a few minutes on general topics and then the parson paused in his speech. He looked down at the congregation till he saw Wendell. Smiling down from his perch at the altar; the Parson extended his hands in welcome to Wendell.

"Come forth to be blessed, Sinner!" The Parson said.

"Go ahead, Boy," Samuel whispered as he poked Wendell in the ribs.

Uncertain of what to do next, Wendell rose and walked to a place the preacher pointed to at the front of the congregation. Unwinding his newly made Spinner, he looked sheepishly at Samuel who smiled back encouragingly. Ezekiel looked at him with dead blank eyes but showed no expression. Wendell paused briefly shaken by the deformed face of the old man. *Good Lord, he must have been in a terrible fire.*

Remembering himself, Wendell stretched the Spinner full length out on the floor. Then, lifting his arm above his head, he began to spin it off the ground till it was going in wide arcs around his head like a cowboy's lasso. *I feel like an idiot.*

Then a very odd thing happened. Strange, but delightful sounds started to come from the Spinner, as it picked up speed. The bones and bits caught the air and produced tiny high-pitched notes like those from dozens of tiny flutes. It felt good, the sweet sound of its whirling made Wendell forget his self consciousness. As he spun, he began to feel almost euphoric.

Encouraged by the sound and the approving smiles on the faces of the congregation, he spun it faster and faster, the good feeling increased with each rotation. Vaguely he noticed that the church choir began to sing...

"Spin your rope and make it sing.
Sin and wish for anything,
Spin and hear the Lord's sweet sound.
Then spin and find what you have found."

Wendell became lost in the sound of the thing. He laughed, as the delightful notes that his efforts produced made him giddy. It was like a wonderful drug that just kept getting better and better.

"Fill your ears with sounds of light.
Spin your soul and make it right.
Spin too strong and what you'll do,
Is feed the dark what's good in you."

Wheezing a bit from the effort, but hopelessly caught up in the strangely marvelous sound that the spinner was making, Wendell spun it still faster. The sweet melody deepened in tone, which struck him as odd, as he would have expected the opposite. His arm began to feel heavy. *I wonder how long I'm supposed to keep this up. I'm getting tired.*

With sweat gleaming on his brow Wendell tried to stop spinning, but found that he could not...or would not stop. It was just too beautiful a sound. Gasping for air, he spun it harder and faster!

"Keep spinning boy!" Samuel said.

"Faster...faster..." the congregation said.

"There's the trick and know it too
Spin it wrong and you are through.
Spin it such and you can tell...
Poor boy...you spun the sound of HELL!"

Wendell was feeling dizzy. He was breathing heavily now and his eyes lost their focus as sweat trickled into them. He felt sick, as nausea started to overwhelm the sense of euphoria he had felt before. But he still could not stop the spinning.

Then the room started to darken into a dull ruby color. Wendell at first attributed it to his own failing energy, but then he remembered hid dream.

A strange yellowish purple-black cloud formed above his head, seeming to seep from the ceiling boards of the church. Lost in the wonder of it; Wendell craned his head back. From it came sounds like something hissed and gurgled. There was stench that settled with it. A smell that was rancid like the long dead—yet laced with the bitter scent of acid.

Wendell moaned as he watched something take form in the cloud, something obscene, something unthinkable.

He cried out, but kept on spinning.

Shocked by the nightmare that was forming in the smoke, Wendell tried desperately to turn loose of the rope; but his body would not allow him to stop the Spinner's mad spin. Instead, he found that his efforts to release it only made it spin faster still. Horrified, Wendell watched as the thing in the cloud darkened and solidified. It's face formed a drooling mouth.

"Those, teeth...MY GOD...THOSE TEETH!!" he screamed, as what ever it was suddenly lunged to the floor engulfing his head in its horrid mouth. In bite after spastic bite he disappeared into its acid maw. Trickles of something reddish that fizzed and smelled worse than the cloud emerged dripping from its jowls. The liquid spread out in puddles across the floor. Wendell felt his skin dissolve and burn at the same time. The last thing he felt was his clothing and the Spinner dropping to the floor. Then there was nothing but pain. Then as quickly as it formed, the cloud and the thing disappeared— and Wendell as well.

The sounds of Wendell's shrieks lingered in the congregation's ears for a long while after the man who was both their sacrifice— and their benefactor vanished. Gradually the screams grew softer and then faded.

The church was silent for several minutes...Then Ezekiel and the old store keeper walked over to the spot where Wendell had vanished. Digging thru the pile of torn scorched clothing on the floor, Ezekiel found and removed the new Spinner. He held it up with both hands to the Parson who stood in grave silence at the altar.

The old man asked, "Is this blessed?"

The Parson looked down upon the man and then at the clothing which when lifted, revealed a pile of gold. The Parson smiled at Ezekiel.

"Rejoice! The lamb of the Lord hath been sacrificed. It so be Blessed."

The congregation echoed his pronouncement and then added a scattering of Amen's and hallelujahs.

"Brother Samuel," the Parson said, "You may take a handful of our reward, what is left of the garb and the tools of the lamb to the store. Sell it for your troubles."

The store keeper thanked the Parson and quickly scooped up his share of the gold and gathered up the pile of rags.

Then the preacher declared that the van Wendell had driven would be taken to the quarry where the men folk would take it apart for the scrap metal.

Yes, the Parson thought, the new Spinner was blessed. In being so, it had blessed the town with its bounty.

"There should be some interesting doodads on that there van that might make for a better Spinner," observed Ezekiel, he who was servant of the Lord and once the man who had been called Jeremy Pane.

"Do the Lord's work son," the Parson said, "and rejoice in his wonders."

"Yes," Ezekiel said to the Parson, "The Lord works in marvelous ways to behold!"

THE BORDERS OF VALHALLA

CHAPTER 1

Blood had been the cause of the complaint, and bloody was the reckoning that the northern clans took for their due. The Norse town of Helshig lay dead in smoldering ruins. With axes and flame, the Irish had done their work well, swarming the walls, howling for vengeance owed. What was left of the wood beams that had once supported walls and roofs stood blackened like so many charred matches billowing blue smoke.

The ground as well, was black with soot, save where it was stained red from the slain. The only place not smoldering, was where the blood had pooled too thickly to burn. That was in just one place, the center of town.

*

Ian Macarthur of Dundalk had been truthful in his threats of vengeance. When the Norse raiders took his wife Claire screaming across a saddle to their keep, they left his son sprawled on the turf bloody and dead, long before his man beard had the chance to sprout.

Ian had sworn a terrible vengeance to the stars, to Saint Bridgid, and most importantly, to the head of his boy who lay cradled in his arms. He had pleaded with his cousins of the Clan Airgialla for help...and his cries met willing ears.

The northern clans had massed at Ian's call for aid and so, in a terrible night of wanton destruction, the Irish hordes stormed into Helshig, applying axe and spear to all they could find. In the darkness, bloody deeds abounded as the vengeful Irish glutted their long hatred of the Vikings by freely slaying men and women alike. Even the children were dragged from their mother's bloody corpses and stabbed to death or smashed lifeless against the burning beams of their own homes. The slaughter lasted till near dawn. When the bloodletting ceased, there were none left alive that called Helshig their home. None save the dead to witness the fires that scorched the Norse village with its name into utter oblivion.

Ian McArthur did not recover his bride that night. He learned too late that she had been swept up, not by the swordsmen of Helshig, but by a visiting Viking Jarl who had apparently seen Claire and considered her too rich a prize to be left to the squalor of a small Irish town.

Ian forced the tale from a dying Viking. From his blood foamed lips, Ian learned that Claire was being taken to the Danish isle of Kenburk. So it was that despite an overwhelming victory over the Norse, Ian Macarthur went home to mourn the loss of his wife; for though she was not dead, he knew no one ever returned from the Orkney Islands, save for more raiders seeking Irish slaves.

A bloody vengeance had been won. But, as in so many feuds of this kind, the burden of revenge was now to be passed to someone else to fester and grow.

*

A Raven watched the Norse village burn with a cool eye. He knew and appreciated the inevitability of the cycle of revenge. It was a business he delighted in. Strange thoughts perhaps, for a mere bird, but this raven was not what it seemed to be. Clothed in dark plumes, the trickster, Loki sat atop the pile of severed heads in the center of the village. He laughed with the call of the crow, as he sat and preened his feathers, ignored by the blood-stained Irish clansmen who left with the dawn.

*

Olaf Gale, Jarl of Dubh-lin sat with his nephew, Yelsig the Lean, who was captain of the long ship, Blood Raven. The look of these men was a study of opposites. Olaf was a giant, typical of the Danes his mother came from. Tall, thick, and yellow braided, he had the build of a bull and the temper to match. His nephew was shorter, slender, and dark. The mark of the Mediterranean was on him.

Yelsig's sire had been spent his seed on a Spanish wench named Dulca, whom he had seized from a convent in Cadiz. The Jarl had ridden the girl often and well and as a result, Dulca bore him two sons before she died. Hers was not a happy end.

For a score of years, Dulca suffered the indignities due a house wench in the Jarl's household. When a Welsh arrow took him down, she burned with her dead captor on his funeral ship. It was not through love, or even loyalty. Dulca knew too well the fate of one who balked at joining her master's funeral pyre. Far better to walk the flame, than to suffer the rude throttling death the old women would give her.

Yelsig and his younger brother Gornoff had split their father's holdings between them. Yelsig chose the ship, which was now moored on the River Liffey.

Gornoff had been in Helsig, which was his portion of his father's legacy. Now his black locks blew in the cool Irish air and beckoned to the ever hungry crows from the top of the rotting pile of heads.

This then, was the source of the new grudge, as Yelsig hungered to serve the slayers of his brother in kind. This was a task that meant more to him than just family honor. Gornoff had been close to him and Yelsig deeply mourned the loss. He longed to collect his brother's remains for the proper funeral rites. He journeyed to his uncle's keep and pleaded for aid in his revenge.

*

Jarl Olaf was deep in his cups that night, his thoughts on a Briton maid who waited trembling in his chambers. Though his brain roared with the effects of gallons of mead, he was still lucid enough to understand the nature of his nephew's complaint.

"By the fetid breath of Fafnir, This is sad," he said batting a fly away from his cup. "The boy scarce a score and ten in age and he feeds the buzzards of the Irish.

For the likes of an Irish hussy! Must be something attractive to her, to stand out from the filth she lived in.

"It sickens me, the way these Irish live in their mud and sod huts. They even paint their faces with mud to go to battle!" Olaf hefted his horn drinking deeply.

"Would that I had the cow here, that I could sell her foul carcass to the Saxons for their pleasure." He paused and rocked his hips grossly.

"Maybe I could tarry with her for a bit of fun of my own. Then would these mud men scream for their affront!" Olaf laughed at his own wit.

"Why, Mud Men—that's what they are!"

"Aye," Yelsig cursed, "I wish she was in our hands, so I could choke the truth from her. That would bear good witness to their treachery. My brother did not any a soul amongst them wrong, yet the scum split his skull and then cried because their missing lass were not to be found. Know you who took her, Uncle?"

"Tis my oath, that it was none of my wolves that stole the girl," Olaf swore, "I heard it was a son of Torf-Einar over in the Orkneys that has the wench, and he promises to burn the first ship that comes for her."

"Then the matter is out of our hands, Uncle. But still, the scum that slew my brother need to be reckoned with."

"And so they shall!" roared Olaf slamming his fist on the table. "I shall send my men to that town and slit the throats of every mud man they find. But for now, Nephew, let us drink to your brother's passing, and the blood his axe drank as he went to Valhalla."

*

Shaun O'Brannon walked the path from Wexford with his bow in his hand and his legacy strapped to his back. That legacy consisted of his father's broadsword that had been won in battle with the Danes and then passed to him. A masterless man, Shaun was a mercenary who sold his sword and his skills to the various clans when they warred, or when they sailed the North Sea in search of booty.

Shawn had just returned to Wexford, from a raid down in Brittany and finding the market poor in the Viking town for his trade, traveled west to Denntraige. He had heard the Norsemen were raiding the towns of the region, which meant there was need and profit for a good fighting man.

On this day, his travels chanced to have him come upon a shriveled looking man, who stood baring his path. Shaun paused to take in the view, as the oldster seemed strange to him. To Shaun he looked dead, but he was standing. That the ancient was not a corpse was apparent, only because his left eye seemed to never stop blinking. Its milky blue color was in stark contrast to the brown leathery texture of his face. The oldster was dressed in rags and his left leg was badly twisted. In his left hand, he held a rudely carved staff upon which he leaned on heavily. Shaun nodded in respect as he passed, but the man never moved.

*

As Shaun continued on his way, the ancient ran into the bushes at a remarkable speed for one so old and lame. As he ran his form transformed, growing in stature and aspect to that of a Viking scout. This was no mortal that strode the path in long strides. It was Loki Laufeyjarson; the trickster, the shape shifter, the manipulator. Son of the giants Farbauti and Laufey, he was the Jotun who was craftiest of the Norse Gods and the one scorned by the best of them. Loki knew there was an elaborate game of 'chess' unfolding on Mid-Earth. The Irish mercenary had unwittingly just become a pawn in that game.

A few hundred yards down the road, Loki came upon a small force of North men who just happened to be scouting for Irish raiders. Under the leadership of their Jarl, Lairic, they had originally intended to raid the rich monastery of St. Mullins a few miles back. But the Irish raiders had struck first, and sacked it well. The Vikings had arrived to find the rich coffers already empty and the altars bare. Lairic put the surviving priests to the sword for sport, grousing that there was no booty left to be taken. Now the Norsemen were hoping to catch up and relieve the Gaels of their booty.

Loki was confident that Lairic would see the quick return of his scout as a good omen. His assumption was proved correct by the friendly greeting he received.

"Bornf my falcon, what news have ye?"

"A single Irish knave is carrying a sack of gold from the Christus Monastery, my Jarl. He walks with burdened steps just a quarter league ahead. If we run, we may over take him easily!"

"Well said Bornf!" Lairic cried. "Odin's blood, but I was feeling we would waste our tracks here. Let us catch this Irish devil. This may prove easier than I hoped."

"And so the pawn will meet his game." Loki said. He held back, as the Vikings ran to catch the Irish swordsman.

"The Jarl will drive him towards his fate, to kill the man I wish. One less hero, great Odin, will fill your hall, one less to face me in battle at Ragnarok.

*

At that moment, the real Bornf had his hands full. He had strayed from his path, distracted by a hare that had been remarkably good at eluding his efforts to capture it. Hunger was on Bornf's mind as he ran after the small animal which seemed always out of bowshot. Panting from the chase, the Viking pushed through a thick bush and stepped into the path in directly in front of Shaun O'Brannon.

Bornf's bow dropped, forgotten from his hand at the sight of the Irish swordsman. The Viking looked disdainfully at the tall Gael who was facing him.

"Ye have the look of Irish scum," he spat.

"I do have that honor, sire…of being Irish that is, though I prefer not taking it with the same meaning as ye meant it."

"I care not fool," Bornf said. "Is that not coins jangling from that pouch at your side? If so, give over. It is in my mind to drink good ale in town tonight."

"If yer thinking on me being the one to fill your mead horn, ye best be counting on a dry night."

Bornf shook his head, as the words the Gael spoke annoyed him.

"Give the money to me, wretch and I will kill you easy. Deny me—and the crows will dance on the Blood Eagle I carve on your corpse."

"Fare thee well, good fellow. I do not think you have the right man this day, at least fer the task yer planning. But if it's a dance you seek, then I'm your man. Let's have at it then and see who feeds your grim Odin's pets.

"You mock me, you son of an Irish whore!" Bornf roared and hefted his axe in a sideways blow intended to sever the Irishman's head. Instead, the wild swing met just air. The Gael drew his blade and struck back with an over hand strike. His blade split the North man's shield and knocked him backward. Bornf regained his balance and threw his axe at Shaun who ducked and sidestepped it easily.

"Ye throw it like a farmer, Carl. Your tired of that toy are ye now?"

"I have a better treat for Ye in this!" Bornf said, as he threw down his ruined shield and drew his broad sword.

"Then serve it well," Shaun said, "for my blade thirsts for Norse blood!"

The Viking charged and swung his blade in a powerful two handed blow. Shaun's blade caught it at the hilt as it came down, and the two men were locked in a test of strength. Though shorter, the Viking was built like a bear and outweighed Shaun by several stones. Still, the more slender Gael was no weakling. The struggle proved too intense a test to last long. Finally, it was Shaun who appeared to falter.

The Viking's eyes gleamed triumphantly as he felt the Gael give way beneath him, but that look suddenly turned to surprise as Shaun's sword suddenly released the Norse blade. The Irishman stepped to the side—missing the downward stroke and slashed backhanded, opening Bornf across the belly. As the Viking reached

71

down to stop his guts from spilling forth, Shaun finished Bornf with a chopping blow that bit into the back of his neck, nearly severing his head.

"Tis a sad day indeed, fer ye fellow," Shaun said gazing down on the man he just killed. "You've got yer self slain—

and nary a coin enough, did I have to my purse, fer to make it worth the struggle."

As Shaun wiped his weapon clean on the Vikings shirt, he heard a shout. Looking down the road, he could see a horde of Norsemen running at him.

"Tis time to head fer cover," Shaun said to himself as he retreated, leaving the path to Denntraige. He took off running with great strides thru the heather towards the nearby woods to the north.

"I wonder what they are so hot fer?" Shaun snatched his wine skin from his belt and took a swig without stopping. For the next few days, he would ask the question again and again, as their ongoing pursuit drove him steadily north.

*

Loki watched the chase from his hare-hole in the thicket as Lairic sent his Carls after the Irish warrior.

"Go then Gael," the trickster said, "Go to the sod huts of Dundalk. There you will find ample cause to wet your sword. There be plans besides Loki's afoot this day. It serves the one eyed God's fancy, that those plans be carried out and for I to serve that cause. That is, lest I find cause to trifle with them."

The mischievous God laughed, as he changed his form from hare to man. Then in the midst of his laughter, the sound of his voice changed to the call of a Raven. Black feathers tore the sky, as the dark God took wing toward Dubh-lin.

*

On the roof of the High tower of Dubh-lin keep, two men watched warily, as a crone stirred and spat into the contents of a large kettle which hung boiling over a fire. The old woman laughed, as she added gross items to the stew. Some of those ingredients, made her visitors blanch at the thought of tasting it.

Yelsig, pulled his cloak tight around him and shivered, but not from the cold, while Olaf waited impatiently.

"Are you ready yet, hag?"

"Not so ready me Lord Olaf, that ye can but wait a wee moment more," she scolded. "This pot is for the clumsy guard downstairs that stepped on my foot and then cursed me. I promised him a reward for his rudeness."

She picked her nose and added her findings to the mess. "Tis a fine meal I make to serve him this evening!"

"Enough of that old Mother," Yelsig said. "We seek your wisdom this night."

"Better that, than to serve your other needs. I be too old a mare to foal at your urging."

"Don't banter words wench—lest you find me angry!" Olaf said.

"What have I to fear from a great oaf like you? I, who have scarce as much distance to death's door as a whisper. Cool your fever man...and tell me what you wish of this old woman."

"We seek a means and a method to exact revenge upon the Clans of Airgialla, and the serpent tongued Irish dog that turned them loose upon us," Olaf said.

"We seek your council, Crone, that we may begin our assault with fair omens," Yelsig added.

The old woman moaned and looked upward to the stars. She waited until a shooting star streaked across the sky. From a pouch she wore at her neck, the crone poured some grey powder into the stew she was cooking. She jammed her hand into the pot and screamed in agony. Before either man could move to aid her, the woman held her other hand out to ward them away. The crone's face lost all expression.

"Twice shall be your opportunity, "she said. And two shall be the number of battles ye fight to bring your ends. Of the man you seek, yet another will serve to advance his vengeance and another still will serve to collect your price. Satisfaction shall not be yours in how the deed is done. Yet though you find an end with one feud, it might but spawn yet another."

As the crone spoke, she looked directly at Olaf.

"But know that a powerful God watches over the proceedings and shall move his hand as his amusement wants."

"Great Odin must be watching our fight!" Yelsig said. "We are blessed in being under the eye of the high King of Valhalla!"

"Tis easy to speak of the one eyed god to lead men astray," Olaf grunted, "I think this foul ancient means to curse us."

"She is known as one who has the sight, Uncle."

"I see this crone as a false witch. I would rather you had not sought out such council, Nephew."

"Doubt me then?" The crone lifted her dripping hand from the pot. It was totally unharmed by the boiling water.

"Then ye shall indeed have my curse, king of knaves! But first, I say what the Gods have told me of you!" The crone's eyes took on a malevolent hue. Slowly her hand extended towards Olaf.

"With this hand, I reach out to the servant of Loki. With this finger I point at-" Her words ended in a gurgle, as the knife in Olaf's hand pierced her throat.

Yelsig grabbed his uncle's arm and spun him around so they were face to face.

"Why were you so hot to kill this crone, Uncle?"

"By Thor's blood Boy, I believe she meant to curse us!" Olaf said, as he pulled free and wiped his blade clean on the old woman's garb.

"I had been warned, she was not pure in the Viking blood, but instead half the piss that passes for Irish blood flowed in her veins. She meant to divide us, Lad and I would not have that happen!"

"But she had more to say and perhaps knowledge that might cost us dearly for not knowing."

"Paugh..." Olaf spat, "She spoke in riddles like all these 'so called' seers do. To Helheim, with the likes of her and her kin! I seek not omens and trickery to win my fights." Olaf sheathed his knife. "Cold steel shall suffice."

"Then what do you make of her words?"

"Hah…! Just the foolish ravings of a crone who died later than her time! Me thinks only Skuld herself, knows the future. The Norns speak little of this to the Gods and not at all to man."

"Then what, you have already chosen to attack the Irish?"

"Aye, my reavers have already gathered at my call. This very night they attack Dundalk. Think I would wait for the mouthings of this crone? My wolves raid the country side, as I will it. There shall be none that will dare to raise hand against my authority in this land."

"Would that I was with those you sent to Dundalk. I itch for throats to be cut in my brother's name."

Olaf laughed. "Dear nephew. I like the cut of you!

"I do feel a bit sorry though, that I ended the crone's life—before she could revenge herself. Hah! I love a good jest. Let us see that the guard, who vexed her, gets his dinner."

*

The spears of the Vikings shattered against the moonlit walls of D'un Dealgan, which guarded Dundalk and the molding bones of the great hero, Cuchlainn. With fire and torch, the raiders sought to destroy the ancient Irish fort.

Calling fervently for Odin's blessing, the Vikings clawed their way up the sixty foot mound and hurled their bodies against the rough stone walls—full in the face of the defender's fire. The arrows of the Gaels met them with the ferocity of mad bees, pin cushioning the attackers as they climbed. The Carls climbed and howled as the deadly barrage rained on their fellows.

Finally armor and flesh could stand no longer, in the midst of such torment. The Norsemen, those that were still able, tumbled over their slain brethren as they fell back from the walls. Dozens more of the Vikings died, when the Gaels sallied forth from their blood stained fortress to pursue them. Steel met steel, the retreating Norse despaired that even their mail coats could not withstand the fury of the axe wielding Irish.

With axe and sword, the defenders prevailed, till none stood living on the mound save them. They jeered at the Vikings who dragged their dead of into the night. More than a score of the Gaels had fallen, but more than thrice their number in Norse called for entry this night at the gates of Valhalla.

*

Within the sod and wattle walls of Dundalk, Ian Macarthur watched as the women tended the wounded and bathed the dead for burial. Despite the victorious shouts of his men, Ian knew the Irish had barely driven off the Viking spears. Such was the cost of the defense, that he had not the men to hold back another attack. He prayed that the Norse would not return before help arrived.

Then, as he stood near his men in the village square, a strange man with a sword strapped to his back entered the village through the north gate. The fellow was tall and lean, but powerfully built. Sandy hair sprouted under his steel cap. A dark mail shirt hung to his thighs which were confined by a belt from which hung a throwing axe. He bore the sign of no clan...a masterless man.

A mercenary, Ian guessed. Off hand, the traveler had the look of a Saxon, but Ian could see the mark of his Gallic blood in his blue green eyes. Plans formed in

Ian's mind, as he watched the stranger, plans so audacious, impossible and doomed to failure that they just might work.

Here was a man to meet, Ian decided. Perhaps Saint Bridgid was looking out for him after all. This might be the man to save my Claire.

CHAPTER 2

"Ye see," Ian Macarthur said over a mug of ale to Shaun O' Brannon, "I've take the notion that ye might be a fighting man. By your rolling gait Sir, perhaps such a man as might have known several battles whilst at sea."

The mercenary who had just arrived in Dundalk, travel weary after eluding the persistent Vikings, rested wearily at the table.

"Aye, I have...friend," Shaun replied and winked at the tavern maid as she passed. "I've spilled the blood of the heathen, off the coast of the north islands and along the coast of Brittan as well.

"The north coast is less strange to me, than the children my late wife bore me, bless her soul," Shaun said and crossed himself. Ian did as well.

"I have in fact, raided near Londinium as of late, but the coin earned there took flight with a scoundrel; one who called himself, captain of our vessel. I landed near Wexford with just my shirt and my sword on my back.

I were headed fer Denntraige, but was diverted by a horde of Norsemen that seemed to think I was rich, though fer the likes of me, I don't know why. They chased me to within a day of here."

"I heard they sacked Saint Mullins," Ian said.

"Then I curse them double then, in the name of Saint Bridgid!" Shaun said raising his mug in toast."

"Aye, I'll drink o that as well, the blasted heathen. But now tell me, Shaun, can you navigate those islands ye been to?"

"I have indeed piloted those very waters, friend Ian and likely, I will again. Is raiding the northern coast, what you had a mind for when you accosted me on the street?"

"It was," Ian said as he hoisted his mug and drank the brew in great gulps.

Then I am your man. For my sword drinks deeply when the prospect of money to be drawn from fat priests and merchants is at hand."

"That is not what we are after, Sir."

"It's not?" Shaun wiped the foam from his upper lip with his finger.

"We might be aiming a wee tad further to the north and east."

"To where then would you be headed?"

"To Pomona," Ian muttered from his cup.

"By the bloody hounds of Hades," Shaun shouted, slamming his mug on the table, "what are ye looking to go there fer?"

"I mean to send ye to Kirkwall," Ian said, "to rescue my wife, or slit the throat of that blasphemous Earl, Einar that took her, or both—even as it may suit me!"

"Ye want me to murder Torf-Einar the Bloody over a wench? Ye be daft man! His island crawls with the Norse bastards!"

"Speak ye careful about my wife!" Ian snapped.

"Your wife, dear fellow, warms a Viking bed. Better ye wish her farewell and find a good wench to warm yer loins, than face the icy death the northern reavers bring. They'll carve the blood eagle on your back, fer certain!"

"I'll not be joining you on this trip," Ian said. "Much as I fain would go, I have business afoot here."

"Then ye be speaking of sending men to their deaths, whilst ye rest safe here?" Shaun shoved his stool aside and stood up.

"Aye, I shall and I must," Ian said.

"Then it is not fer me to go, where ye do not dare tread yourself!" Shaun said as he turned to leave.

"Than should I be saying that a man of O'Brannon blood, be not a man," Ian said and turned to his drink, "but instead, a maid that weeps over a little ice and sword play?"

"Curse ye fer the words!" cried Shaun as he spun and drew his blade. Ian rose and faced the Gail.

"If it's proof of me steel ye need Ian then let's have at it! She'll drink any man's blood before he says an O'Brannon would ere back from a fight!"

Ian grasped his companion's shoulders. "Me thinks yer a man of wax, friend Shaun." He beckoned to a tavern wench.

"If you would be so kind lass, place another drop of good ale in this man's mug." Ian smiled wryly. "I'll not be a having a quarrel with the likes of ye, Shaun. My reason's just. Sheath thy blade."

"I will fer the hospitality ye grant me, but mind that I am not a man to be trifled with—or one to send on a fool's errand. So why then are ye sending me and not yer self?"

"I need to help gather the clans and face the Vikings that are raiding our homeland. There will be well enough blood letting here, while you're gone. If the heathens face a thrust at their Earl in the Orkneys, the Vikings may well be divided in interest. That distraction might give us the edge when their cursed Valkyrior come to claim their own on the battlefield. I would that the she-bitches bear a heavy load to the borders of Valhalla."

"Aye that would be a pleasing sight," Shaun said. He sat down and hefted his mug. "So how do ye think to carry it off?"

"Good lad, we are well met this day!" Ian cried. "Drink with me and I'll spell you the details of the raid I have in mind."

Ian cleared a space on the table and traced his thoughts on the table with his wet finger.

"I figure about three or four boats filled with good men might make it up the coast here and cross over to Pomona."

"That is, if we don't run a foul of a Dragon ship."

"I'm hoping ye do, Shaun. It might be fer the better."

"How so, Ian?"

"The luck might come on ye that ye might find a small one. Ye could board and man her. Thus to the casual eye, ye might approach the island looking like a Norse ship returning from the mainland."

"And if luck doesn't give us that prize?"

"Then ye will have to cross the strait as carefully as ye can. Once there, you might find better luck climbing the cliffs on the west shore, as they are likely not to be watching as careful there. Then ye will make it across land to Kenburk. Under the cover of night, plunder the longhouse and recover my Claire."

"What makes you think we can get that close without getting our throats slit?"

"Because, by now they have already sent their Dragons to here, to stop the troubles we are causing. When word of your raid comes back, they will have to head home again. Of course in so doing, they'll be leaving their cities here ripe for our taking."

"Tis a close game your playing, friend," Shaun said, as he tore at a chunk of bread. "But then, there is a touch of madness to the venture I like."

"Saints be praised," Ian said, "I despaired that a man of such stuff as could lead this venture might never come. Yet you be here man and so mayhaps my dear Claire may soon be returned.

"Now then," Ian said hoisting his cup, "let us talk of shares."

*

In the back corner of the pub, a rat scurried about the tables picking up bits of food from the floor. If the men above it could have heard, they would have wondered why the rat chuckled as if its voice was human.

*

The Viking howled, as the knife blade slashed his already tortured flesh. Jarl Olaf had already expressed his anger on his bound victim with his whip. There was hardly an inch of the man—or the stake he was tied to, that wasn't bloody from his efforts.

"Odin spits on cowards that run, whilst there is battle to be fought and men to fight it!" Olaf turned to the cluster of unarmed men who stood before him, shaken to their core by what they were witnessing. The troops surrounding them grumbled in agreement with their jarl.

"This fool was sent to take a small town of the mud men. You had but to follow his lead! Less than a quarter of ye fell there and ye turned tail and ran home!"

Olaf held up the head of the bound man who was their leader.

"Your brother's who fell were men! They feast tonight in the halls of Valhalla. This dog won't be joining them!"

Olaf raised his large knife and swung fiercely at his victim, decapitating him with a single blow. The man's blood sprayed the leggings of the nearest Vikings. Not a man dared flinch.

"I offer him as blota! May the Gods of Asgard, accept him as sacrifice and smile on us!" Olaf pointed his knife at the carls.

"This be what I am offering you, Dogs. My dear nephew Yelsig has a personal score to settle with this Irish scum. Would any of you wish to erase your shame, by bringing him the head of an Irish whelp?"

"Aye!" the voices of the carls rose to pierce the night air. "Aye...Give us a man like Yelsig to lead us and we will burn the town to ashes!"

81

"That is good then," Olaf said. "I hear the sound of men now, where before I heard the laments of sheep. Gather your spears and make haste to bloody your axes on Irish blood. Valhalla may still take more of you to its bosom when the Valkyrior ride. But you, who fall, shall stand with Odin's best!"

Olaf held the severed head of the dead Viking in his hand as he walked forward. He dropped it at the feet of the Carls before him.

"Tonight you are again men. The songs of your victory will be sung for generations. Go now and prepare. Tomorrow, you march back to Dundalk!"

The carls cheered feverously for Olaf and Yelsig as their weapons were returned. Yelsig wondered if the cheering was genuine, or just from their relief of not being slain on the spot. *We'll see if these men can rise and fight when needed. Gornoff my brother, I will spill the blood of those who murdered ye, if the last dog of this rabble must fall in doing so. By the great Thor I swear this!*

*

The clans gathered at the call of Ian Macarthur. The men of Airgialla and Dal-Fiatach came, as did the warriors of both northern and southern Ui-Niell. The Dal-Narade lent their swords to the fight as did the O'Brien's of Dal-gCais. Even men from far off Connacht came to quench their blades in Viking blood. There were men of all rank and manner from the farmers to the west, to tradesmen and villagers from the south. Some were swords men and veterans of many battles with the Norse. Some were reavers and some were lords, whose names were known to all.

There was little organization in the gathering, as each clan answered only to their chief, and each clan insisted their leader should be in command of the whole army. The one thing the Gaels hated, almost as much as the Norse, was the idea of serving under a standard other than that of their own clan. When not vexed by the Vikings, the great families of Ireland quarreled among themselves. No one leader had yet arose to unite them. This was just two years after the great Cellachan of

Cashel raised an army and sacked Dubh-lin. The Irish struggled with the concept of achieving a national identity. So when the call came, the clans gathered, but held to their own fires.

*

Shaun O'Brannon moved about those fires to recruit men to sail with him to The Orkney Island of Pomona. There the one eyed Earl, Torf-Einar Rognvaldsson, kept his Longhouse at Kirkwall. Shaun knew the task before him was nigh impossible to achieve, but his pride had been stirred by Ian's prodding's, and the idea of an Irish woman, captive in the hands of the heathen. The very thought of it rankled him—sparking his desire to act, even without the possibility of seizing rich plunder.

Shaun looked around for masterless men like himself, men whose wildness might drive them to the lengths he needed for the venture to succeed. Out of those who volunteered, Shaun found three score and ten that he felt would follow him to the Orkneys and give good account of themselves.

Carefully, Shaun supervised the fitting out of the vessels that would carry them on their raid. The boats he was supplied with were small and wide. The craft were fitted with, but ten oars and a mast. Each could carry twenty men safely, not enough for a successful fight on the open sea against a dragon of fifty warriors—which also had the advantage of superior height—but they were small enough to chance slipping through the straits between the Hebrides without being spotted.

As the sun rose over the Dundalk inlet, Ian brought a priest to bless the venture. With prayers to Saints Patrick and Christopher for good winds and tides to carry them, Shaun O'Bannon's four boats sailed from Ireland north towards the Hebrides and to the Orkneys beyond.

*

The Vikings, under the leadership of Yelsig the Lean marched across the Irish countryside driven by the need to return to Dundalk. Beneath their chain mail, which covered them from head to calf, each man's heart burned with the anger and humiliation of their last defeat. These men had a grudge to settle, and only Gallic blood would quench their hate. Equally driven was their leader, as Yelsig had sworn a blood oath to the mighty Thor that the men of Dundalk would be stacked on the deck of his brother's funeral ship as sacrifice to the Gods.

As they marched the coast road near St. Patrick's island, Yelsig noticed a Viking in the lead was walking strangely. Before he could ask the problem, the man fell dead with an arrow in his chest.

"By the blessed Mary—Attack!"

From out of the woods on either side of the Vikings poured hordes of woad painted Irish warriors, so close at hand that Yelsig could see their blue faces, wild with battle lust. Most were naked, save for their kilts and leggings, as they detested wearing body armor. They charged with no semblance of order.

"Form a square!" he yelled as the first of the attackers drew close. Yelsig ran him through as the Viking next to him split the man's skull.

"Plenty for everyone!" the Carl laughed and turned to another Irishman who flung a spear at him. Yelsig swung his round shield in time to stop the shaft. Then the full weight of the attackers hit.

Yelsig was knocked backwards by the press. He slipped, as hands reached to tear his shield aside. A dirk in a woad covered hand pushed through and gashed Yelsig's mail just above his buckler. Infuriated, the Viking slammed his shield hard upon the man's arm-breaking it. A spear lunged through at his face. Yelsig's sword separated the spear and the hand wielding it from its owner. As the man fell, the Viking rose, stepped forward, and planted his foot on the Irishman's throat, crushing it.

Yelsig swung his broad sword in wide strokes hacking savagely at the woad men before him. In his fury, he became lost to sanity in a berserker rage. Flinging his shield into the teeth of an attacking warrior, he changed his grip and laid about

84

him, swinging his broadsword in great two handed blows. He scarce noticed when a spear grazed his thigh, or when a thrown Irish axe flew out of the press and knocked his winged helmet off. Dimly, he was aware that the Viking next to him fell and that another took his place. In his madness, all he could see was the bloodied face of each victim as his sword took deadly toll.

Then suddenly, there were no more men in front of him to kill. The Irish retreated into the woods dragging their wounded. Still lost in his fury, Yelsig bellowed and started to charge after them and his own men raced to stop him. Briefly he fought their restraint till the madness left him.

"Patience, Sire," he heard a voice say. "Like as not, they will be back."

Yelsig turned to his men. A quick count confirmed twenty dead, but dozens more of the lightly armored Irish lay scattered in the grass. Most of the Vikings that were left standing bore wounds that would need tending.

"Reform the men," Yelsig said to his lieutenant, Gothor. "These Woads are not from here. Look at their kilts. There is more than one clan here. This was not just the locals looking for a fight. The clans must be gathering in force. We will have to return to Dubh-lin for reinforcements."

Yelsig looked back at the woods as movement caught his eyes.

"But not yet. Gothor—form square!"

The Irish charged again, only this time the Norse were ready. From behind the shields of their comrades, a volley of arrows flew into the tightly massed ranks of the attackers. It was impossible to miss, so the feathered shafts took a deadly toll. It proved too much for the men of Erin to stand, so they retreated back to the trees yet again.

Yelsig directed his men to head back to Dubh-lin. The Vikings maintained their formation carrying their wounded within, to the chorus of taunts and insults from the Irish in the woods. A few tried to press it further by attacking the Viking rear guard, but Yelsig's archerers soured them on the idea.

Yelsig knew that his plans for vengeance would have to wait. Right now, he needed to hurry back to Dubh-lin to warn Olaf. This was looking more and more like the Irish were gathering for a major attack. Dubh-lin was the most likely place, since the Viking hold there was, but briefly reestablished. Olaf would need time to reinforce his keep. The Jarls in the Hebrides, Iceland, and even Norway could send help, but how soon they would arrive was up to the Gods.

*

Jarl Torf-Einar sat by the great fire that burned in the center of his longhouse. By his side, his son Thorfinn Skullsplitter played with a comely blond wench, who squirmed on his lap. A Carl approached Einar and indicated that he had a visitor.

"Bring the man forward and serve him ale," Einar said. "I am in a giving mood this night."

At his words, the Carl returned to the door, which blew open by it self. A tall man, his form obscured by a dark cloak and slouch hat, came in from the snowy darkness. The fires of the great hall seemed to grow strangely dim and odd whispering sounds invaded the silence.

In spite of himself, Einar shrank from the sight of this figure. There was something terrible in the manner of him, like death and worse, walked with him into the hall.

The room fell silent, as all within the hall waited to see what manner of man or what the stranger was.

"Who are you?" Einar's voice sounded small. Surprised, his son turned and looked at his father and then the stranger.

"Who is this man, Father?" Thorfinn drew his blade. "What makes you tremble so?"

The cloaked figure made no pretense at bowing, but instead came and stood at the feet of the Viking. Cold, the one eye that peered out from his hat was, like the sea before a storm that stared at the Jarl. When he spoke, the whole room vibrated from the power of his voice.

"Lo...mortal! You know who I am. And boy, you may yet live to know why I am here!" The slouch hat tilted back. Einar gasped at the empty socket that was revealed.

"Son, lay down your sword," Einar hissed. "Clear the hall."

"For this stranger, Father?" Thorfinn felt afraid, but not so much that he forgot that he had plans for the girl whose wrist he held tight. He hesitated, his hand still on his blade

"Do it boy!" Einar shouted with murder in his voice. Thorfinn released the girl, but held on to the sword. He motioned to the guests and servants to depart. In seconds, the hall was empty.

Thorfinn looked down at his father and asked, "I as well?"

"Sit boy, for what ever is said here, I'd have you be a part of it."

"What is so important about this traveler?"

"Have you no eyes my son!" Einar said. "Look at his face! I fear we are in the presence of the great one, himself." Einar turned to the stranger, his voice hushed to a whisper.

"You are whom I think?"

The stranger nodded. Einar shrank back into his chair breathing heavily. Thorfinn also sat down, his mouth gaping in wonder. "Great...Odin."

Einar gasped, "What do you wish of us?"

The cloaked god rose to his full stature and then reached forth with arms that seemed to fill the great hall. A wind sprung up whirling around him like a cyclone. In a booming voice he spoke.

"I speak of war to the south. I speak of my cities being burned by the followers of Christus and flaxen haired women butchered in their beds by Gallic rabble."

"I had not heard of this Lord Odin," Einar said meekly.

87

"Listen you well," the god said, "for now the ravens feast on the bodies of warriors that come to Valhalla begging for their brothers to avenge them! The Norns have been busy. Living men must replace those whose thread hath been cut!"

To Einar, the voice of the God seemed to vibrate through his soul in its awful basso. "Why seek me, oh great one?"

"It pleases me mortal, for men to war. It pleases me more to see mine own children win against those who serve the whelp of Israel that seeks to overthrow me!"

The god's face grew darker under his slouch hat. So the one eye glowed like a blue diamond.

"The cities that have been built in my honor must not fall to the blasphemers! You Torf-Einar, be closest to give succor. Go you then, to the land of Erin, Where Jarl Olaf is beset by the raging clans. Go there and wet your blades for my glory in Irish blood!"

The longhouse was rocked by a whirl of air that flowed through it, almost like a gale. Einar put his hands up before his face to block the wind and screamed. When he lowered them the god was gone.

Einar sank back into his chair and waited till his shattered senses returned to him.

"Thorfinn, how many Drakkars have we in port?"

Ten ships are here my father," The red haired Viking said. "Half are just Tjue-sesser (twenty oars) but there are five Drakkars of thirty oars or better."

"That will have to do, Thorfinn. We can send near two thousand men to Erin. You must go, as I feel weary as of late. The duty requires a strong man and you are the greatest of my sons."

Torf-Einar smiled as an idea came to him. "This, we must do before two suns set. I wish our fleet to set sail before any call comes from Jarl Olaf."

"Why Father?"

"I can at least guarantee that the fool will owe me dearly for my unsolicited aid. A debt owed can pay well later."

"You are wise, Father," Thorfinn said, "But what then, of the strange man? Do ye think he really be great Odin?"

"You have eyes, Boy," Einar growled, "Though not a brain to hold your tongue. Do not seek to question a God when you are before him. We must sacrifice this night, so not to offend him further. Make preparations!"

*

In the darkness outside the Longhouse, the great cloaked figure stood. The cloud filtered moonlight scarce revealed the changes, as the giant form shrank and changed to that of Loki the Trickster.

"Well spread, the discord I've sewn this night! Lord Odin, it is your work I that I hath turned for my pleasure. I made this war! That two should meet and one should fall. Is that not the way of the world? My game continues." Loki faded into the night mist.

"Your move great king."

*

The fog that had settled in the channel was as dank and gray as the hair of the great wolf Fenris. It hung low and thick on the water, making all with in it appear as shadows. It was a time of great risk for the four boats that made their way northward in the predawn hours of the Scottish coast.

Shaun knew this was the most dangerous part of their journey. Rocks and enemy ships looked the same in the murky dark. Shaun knew that wise men would moor and wait for the fog to lift. Desperate men, like those he led, risked pressing on.

The boats moved forward as quickly as Shaun dared in single file, lest one might veer from its course and run aground. The bow of each boat was tied with a length of rope to the stern of the boat ahead so that none would be lost in the dark. Shaun stood at the bow of the lead boat, straining his eyes for any sign of enemy, or of land.

"Tis, the breath of Midgard," a crewman uttered, "The serpent protects the lair of the Norse."

"Nonsense," Shaun answered. "Don't be giving in to old wife's tales and heathen beliefs. Day will come within the hour and burn this mist from our path. See there, the fog brightens with the promise of sunrise. Here and there, clear patches of sea became visible. Cheered by this, Shaun accepted a water skin offered to him and drank deeply of it. A few minutes more, the Gael figured and he would be able to get a bearing. With luck, less than one more days sail would place them close to the Orkneys. Then he would moor off one of the small islands and wait till night.

"A serpent, by me mother's grave!" a crewman shouted. "Do ye see it, Lads?"

All hands looked to portside. The helmsman of the second boat called out that he did as well. Then all the crews were shouting and pointing.

"Quiet fools!" Shaun hissed at his men, trying to silence the noise, but it was too late. Out of the mist the head of a dragon ship emerged just behind the second boat.

With no time to avoid it, the third boat crumpled as Dragon ship rammed into it at full speed, instantly swamping the vessel. Those men, who were not killed outright, struggled in the icy water and tried to grasp at the oars of the dragon ship. A few of them made it out of the water only to be speared or shot by the Viking archerers. By their shouts, Shaun could tell that the Vikings were as surprised by the encounter as he was.

"Cut the rope!" Shaun yelled. The dragon ship continued to move forward. As it did, pulling his boat backwards towards the battle. The men in the second boat fletched their arrows and let fly at the Vikings above them. Then the two ships were pulled along side of each other. Men leaped from the Norse ship into the teeth of the Irish spears. Several Vikings were slain as they jumped, but there were far too many on board the dragon ship for the defenders to hold out for long. Shaun could hear the fourth boat was engaged in battle on the other side as well. Sickened, he knew there was nothing to be done for the other boats in his small fleet. The battle was already lost. There was but one chance for the men in his boat, and that was to get away fast.

Quickly, Shaun moved down the boat climbing over a crewman whose throat has been pierced by an arrow. Taking an axe from yet another man whom had fallen, he struck hard at the tow rope, severing it and freeing his vessel. Then he yelled to his men over their protests to get to rowing.

Shaun steered the boat towards the thickest fog bank he could see. Fortune was with them, as the dragon ship was fouled by the Irish boats on either side of it. Behind it, Shaun saw a second and then a third dragon ship emerging from the fog.

"Do you want to die with yer brothers?" Shaun pointed to the other craft. "Lay too it lads, and pray Saint Christopher guides us clear!"

Soon, only the sounds of battle were left to tell the fate of the other boats. Shaun scanned the seas ahead and saw a small island.

"There's our cover," he said softly, "Lower the mast. We'll hide there, till this fog clears enough to make way."

Shaun checked his crew. They had lost two men to arrows and three more were wounded. That left him with fourteen men in condition to carry on. Not enough for a full scale raid, but maybe enough to rescue the woman. As his men rowed, he addressed them.

"We just got beat good and proper, Lads. To the south of us now, we have a fleet of dragons that know we are near. To the north, there's a maid of Irish blood held captive. We can hide out here and try to crawl back to Erin, or sneak into

Kenburk and maybe get our throats slit fer trying to rescue her. But then, we might get lucky and walk out with some Norse gold.

"I think it proper that all say what they feel on this, fer if we go, we must be agreed to the plan."

Shaun waited as the men talked amongst themselves and finally one (whom the others elected spokesman) replied.

"It seems to us, that our path home is blocked and our trying to go there now, might not be of much use. As it stands we are dead men the first time a dragon finds us. Captain, we will follow ye where ye lead us. Tis better to die fighting the heathen, than to hide like rats."

"Good then," Shaun said. "I think we should hole up here for a day or two, till we're sure no one followed us. Pomona is but an hour's sail from here. When it is safe, we will steal into Kenburk at night and rescue Claire Macarthur, or send as many Vikings to their grave as the fates allow."

As they rounded the small island, Shaun was relieved to see no dragon ships. Beyond the island was another to the east whose cliffs shown brightly in the morning sun.

"There she is lads. There's Pomona on the horizon. There's where our fate lies...and may Saint Bridgid make it a good one at that!"

*

The Irish forces gathered in a broad field near Dubh-lin to await the Viking army that was fast approaching from the south. Close to five thousand men blocked the road to Dundalk, the men of twenty clans had risen to the call. On hand were the Ui-Briuim, the Oirghialla, and the fierce Dal-Riata. On the right flank waited the men of Connacht. Ian stood with the men of Airgialla at the center. To the left of him, the Dal-Cais sharpened their axes along side the men of Uni-Neil.

The Vikings from Dubh-lin had gathered reinforcements as well. Blond Grenner of Iceland stood with Halfdan Longlegs—who was son of the King of Norway. Enian Thorsblood had marched with his men from Limerick and Baldric had come with his Danes from Wexford.

Thorfinn Skullsplitter had not wasted time seeking out the boatload of Irish pirates that escaped from their chance encounter. Instead, he had continued on and moored as quickly as he could with his two thousand Carls at Dubh-lin. Thorfinn took up a flanking position to the Irish right. His brother Arnkel who had been visiting in Dubh-lin joined him.

The Vikings formed ranks, presenting a solid wall of shields and spears to the Irish. At a signal from Olaf, the Norse line moved forward.

At one hundred yards, the line stopped. From the Irish ranks, a voice called out. "Baldric, ye heathen, have you the stomach to fight a man of the Osraige?"

Baldric replied, "Is that you Cedrick? Long have I waited to split your skull with my axe."

"Then come at me man!" The Gael stepped out from the Irish ranks.

Tall Cedrick was, and lean as well. He wore no armor save his shield, which sported a spike from its center. In his other hand was a light axe, similar to those used by his cousins, the Dal-Cais.

Baldric was shorter than the Gael, but thick in girth. He wore a plain steel helmet with a nose guard and a mail drop. Beneath his fur vest, Baldric wore a shirt of fine Spanish steel mesh. He too sported an axe, save his was of the two handed kind. Bare armed; he walked forward swiftly to meet his old enemy.

Baldric struck first, aiming a blow at Cedrick's head. The Irishman ducked and swung upward with his axe slicing through the fur of the Viking's vest, but glancing of the steel beneath. Baldric countered with a back hand swipe that caught Cedrick in the shoulder with the flat of his axe driving him to the ground. Then he brought it around his head in a wide arch and smashed down—cleaving the Gael's shield in twain and breaking his arm. Roaring with triumph, the Viking raised his axe for the kill stroke.

A sudden movement to his right distracted the Viking. Cedric seized upon this. He reached into his belt for his dirk and made a desperate throw. The knife caught Baldric in the throat just below the chin strap of his helmet. As the Viking fell, Cedrick staggered to his feet and rushed forward—splitting the Viking's skull with a downward stroke of his axe.

As he pried his axe from what was left of Baldric's helmet, Cedric saw a small rabbit scurry away from the fight.

*

Down the field, other champions dueled as well. Oddly, most of the combats had gone in favor of the more lightly armored Irish.

"There are bad omens in this," Yelsig said to Jarl Olaf. "That our best should fall so easily, speaks of witchcraft. Mayhaps, the Irish Christus has cast a spell on this fight."

"Nonsense boy," Olaf said, "Me thinks our champions have fattened themselves too well on Irish meat and ale! Let's have at it, and may Odin look with favor on the throats we slit."

On Olaf's command, the Viking line advanced. The Gaels, who looked to capitalize on their success, ran to meet them. At fifty yards the front line of the Norse dropped shields allowing the archers behind them to fire a volley. Their arrows took heavy toll of the Irish who returned fire from their back ranks, causing little damage to the heavily armored Norse. Then the two lines surged forward and met. The air was filled with the sounds of screaming men and splintering wood. Though the Irish were more numerous than the Vikings, the heavily armored Carls pushed the men of Erin steadily back—except for on the Viking left flank.

Thorfinn Skullsplitter saw a Gael in the midst of the fight, who was laying down Carls with his great sword like chord wood. The man was dressed as a chieftain and wore light mail over his tunic and kilt.

Thorfinn charged through the press so that he came to stand before the blond Gael, who upon recognizing him saluted the Dane with his sword.

"Greetings, Conner of Connacht," Thorfinn said, "My sword awaits you."

Men nearby on both sides ceased their combat to watch the champions fight.

The Gael struck first with his sword, slicing a wing off of Thorfinn's helmet. The Viking stepped back a pace and threw his own axe to the ground choosing to draw his own long sword instead. The two men exchanged hammer like blows with neither one gaining the advantage.

Then from nowhere, came the brush of black wings against Thorfinn's face— temporarily blinding him. The Irish chieftain struck low, laying open the Viking's left leg.

As Thorfinn fell to the ground, a giant Viking with but one hand, stepped over him and stuck with an impossibly big axe—splitting the Irishman from shoulder to waist.

The Viking turned to look at Thorfinn who shook his head to clear his eyes. When he looked up, the giant was gone.

"The God of battles," He whispered, "Great Tyr hath saved me this day!

Thorfinn wondered as his men carried him back from the fight. *How many gods fight as men this day?*

*

Ian Macarthur found himself being pushed back by the Viking spearmen that advanced foot by foot over the bodies of the Irish. They had fought desperately, but their efforts proved ineffectual against the Norse of Dub-Lin, led by Olaf and Yelsig.

Calling on Saint Mary to protect him, Ian charged forward followed by a dozen Gaels. In the distance, he could see a dark Viking that looked to be a leader. "Dear Mary," he prayed, "let me take that Viking's head before I fall!"

*

Yelsig saw a cluster of Irish who were cut off from the rest. They fought savagely, these men, following a madman armed with a sword that seemed to slay a Viking with every stroke. This man seemed familiar to Yelsig and within seconds he knew why. The warrior was the mayor of Dundalk, Ian Macarthur, the man he had sworn to kill.

"Stand clear and let me at him!" Yelsig roared, and elbowed his way through his men. For a just a moment, he lost sight of the Gael and then he had broken through his ranks and stood before him. But it was too late. The Irishman lay dead with his blade buried deep in the chest of a Viking.

*

The uneven battle raged for another hour, before the Irish broke and ran. Many chiefs and carls of the Viking host were dead on the field, but thousands more of the Irish had fallen.

On a hill overlooking the battle, Loki perched in a tree disguised as a raven. Silently, he cursed Odin, who had sent the War God Tyr to offset his plans. The Vikings won this day which meant Odin's throne in Asgard was secure for now. The mischievous God fumed over Odin's interference. But Loki knew there was more mischief he could do this day.

"Odin," he said, "I may not have achieved your fall this day, but I have damaged your holdings. Another will rise from this isle. I will guide his victory and drive your precious sons from this land. Soon Ragnarok will come and you will find far less of your dear humans to aid the fight."

Loki looked carefully to make sure no God was watching him. Then he flew along the tree line north towards the Orkneys.

96

Late that night, the one remaining boat of the Irish raiders made its way into the harbor at Kenburk with muffled oars. Under the cover of a rocky outcropping, Shaun O'Brannon beached the boat and made his way to a place where he could see the Viking stronghold. He took note of where the store houses were situated and also of the longhouse where Claire was likely kept-close to the watchful eye of Earl Torf-Einar. As he had hoped, there was only a single dragon ship in port.

"We're in luck," he said to the men. Most of Einar's men are gone. That means fewer swords to deal with.

Splitting his men into three groups, Shaun took his own party and worked his way through the town in the direction of the longhouse, while the others searched the slave quarters for the missing woman and other Irish slaves. The third group set out to scuttle the dragon ship.

In the darkness, a Viking guard had his throat slit and another was stabbed at his post, before Shaun's group made it to Einar's house.

The Gael was surprised to find the Earl's longhouse almost empty. He crawled carefully past the great fire in the middle of the house to find Einar lying asleep with his arm around a dark woman, who was of a race Shaun did not recognize. Carefully, he put the edge of his blade to the throat of the Viking and poked him.

"Where's the girl?"

Einar said nothing. Shaun poked him harder and cut him. No blood flowed from the wound.

"For the love of Christ," the Gael next to Shaun cursed, "The man is dead!"

The dusky girl next to Einar woke and screamed when she saw the Irishmen. One of the men hit her on the head to silence her and then Shaun and his men ran for the door. The sounds of shouting Vikings and hard fighting broke the silence of the night.

A group of Norsemen stood outside the longhouse blocking Shaun's path to his boat. Yelling his war cry, the Gael drew his sword and charged into their ranks swinging wildly in a rage that was pure murder. His men followed and soon the ground was littered with the dead and dying. Of the combatants, only Shaun and one man of his party remained standing. Shaun could hear the Gaels from one of the other groups locked in battle with the Vikings.

As he paused to listen, an arrow flew from the doorway of the longhouse, piercing Shaun through the shoulder. He saw the dark wench they had left behind, fletch another arrow. She let fly and caught the remaining crewman in the back as he tried to run. Then strangely, she just stood there and laughed.

With an oath, Shaun tore the bloody shaft from his shoulder and staggered off in to the dark. With the sounds of slaughter behind him, Shaun joined those of his men that had scuttled the dragon ship. They raced to reach their boat with Several Vikings chasing after them.

*

The dark girl reached over to Einar and roughly kicked him. The old Viking had died in his sleep of a heart attack.

"So Alfdaur, your Norns have spared this warrior the red death I would have served him, despite my manipulations. Small matter, as the Valkyrior still shall not chose him for Valhalla. He will rest, unable to help you in the great battle to come. For now, I must hide, lest ye discover my hand in this. But another day, I will return to vex you, Odin."

The girl's features shrank into that of an owl, which flew off into the night.

*

Within his chambers in the tower of Dubh-lin, Jarl Olaf sat on his bed talking to Claire Macarthur as she combed her red locks.

"He is dead then?"

"Aye he is, Lass. Yelsig pointed his corpse out to me when the fighting was over. A pity, the boy really wanted to cut the blood eagle on that man's back."

"So...what of the boy then?"

"He has returned to sea—intending, he said, to explore beyond Greenland. So we can consort freely now, without him knowing that it was I that had you taken from that fool husband of yours. Tis better, for I would not want to slay him to keep our secret."

"Aye," Claire said, "Enough have died this day to feed the ravens that gather in the heather. I think it time to rest. Time enough there is now, for the bruises that foul beast of a husband laid on me, to heal. By the Blessed Virgin, I was glad when you discovered his cruelty.

"A strange oath to my ears," Olaf said as he stroked her hair. "Is that of the Christus the Irish worship?"

"Does this anger you?"

"No, my little dove," Olaf said.

Claire smiled.

"Let me tell you of him then, and of his ways."

*

In the darkness outside, an owl hooted as it preened the salt from the North Sea off its wings. The way of the Dragon Lords was ending in Ireland and with it the rule of the Norse Gods. Another generation would walk this land, till a leader would rise to lead the Irish against this—and the other Viking towns. Boru would come and the Norse standards would be driven forever from Erin.

Loki laughed as he perched on the sill and watched Jarl Olaf, who listened to the words of his lover and took the first steps to embracing Christianity.

Odin and his northern Gods were fading from the emerald isles. The seed of the God's final destruction was securely sewn. Loki listened, as they talked with satisfaction. Odin was a God not fond of the giants, whose blood Loki shared. So, what did he care that they should end?

"A good night's work," Loki whispered, looking back at the lovers, "For there sits one more warrior, whose path will never cross the borders of Valhalla."

APOTHEOSIS

It was the Great White Way...sort of.

Manshanker Productions Inc. was located in the same city as that icon of entertainment, that boulevard of dreams, Broadway, except the brownstone building that housed it was several blocks away—and in the wrong direction.

The old Hanhiem Theater was in fact, so far 'off Broadway' as to almost merit another off in its description. A tattered remnant of a different—older age of glitz, the sad building was lost, tucked deep into in a backstreet, half hidden behind a billboard that was pitching laundry soap; about as far from all the glitz and glamour as a place in New York could get.

Its present owner/director, one Bernie Manshanker, an ex song and dance man veteran of Vaudeville, did not see it that way. Instead, he mused that the same air that filled the lungs of the great performers, who danced and sang for legends like Cohan, Berkeley, and Ziegfeld, drifted down from that glimmering street and filtered through the back alleys to his little theater. There the particles of recycled greatness that had passed through the lungs of such as Fanny Bryce eased the doorman Fred through his latest bout of smoker's cough. The breath of its autumn chill made the Manshanker chorus line shiver as they rehearsed, as surely as it raised goose bumps on the Rockettes just blocks away. There was magic in that air...Bernie believed it.

But in recent years that magic had been lacking. The house's take was scant as of late, the stage too often bare. The Hanhiem's octogenarian musical director, Ed Neggely was spending more time napping in the orchestra pit than conducting his musicians. Even the box office girl had taken to playing solitaire.

Alphonse Blesianet, the choreographer was having problems with keeping his dancers. Salaries were way behind. Mrs. Blesianet's home cooking was all that was keeping the chorus line from leaving.

"Thank God actors eat," Alphonse said to Bernie as he stepped into his office. The little man sat on his chair with his shoes, resplendent in white spats, propped up on his desk. A small cloud composed of cigar smoke rose from behind the copy of the newspaper he was reading—like whiffs from the peak of a small volcano.

"What's that, Alphonse?"

"More money demands from the cast. They are demanding their back wages."

"They expect to get paid?" Bernie dropped the paper, scattering cigar ashes as he bounded to his feet. "What... are they not artists? Doesn't the love of the craft mean more than just a small delay in the cash flow?"

"They haven't been paid in four months."

"But they have been paid this year."

Bernie scowled and tipped his ashtray into a nearby wastebasket. "Feed them more pasta, they'll never submit to starving."

"Uh... My mother says her pension won't be able to support her cooking for them much longer. We need to get this new play up and running soon, or we will run out of noodles and lose our cast."

"Too late, Alphonse," Fred the doorman said as he walked into the room.

"What are you doing off your post?"

Fred shrugged and removed his hat.

"Mr. Manshanker, the dancers just walked out. Except for the drunk who sleeps in the box above stage right, the place is empty."

"There's a drunk sleeping in a seat here and he hasn't paid for a ticket?"

"I'm not sure, Mr. Manshanker, but I think his snoring isn't offending anyone."

"If we don't have this production up soon we aren't going to have a cast," Alphonse said.

"Or a theater," Fred added.

Bernie stepped from behind his desk and picked up the paper.

"We have a problem, gentlemen, but I think I might have a solution here in the classifieds. Read this."

The small shop nestled in a back alley off a shoddy street in East Harlem stank of old spices and mold. Alphonse examined the various stuffed animals and bottled substances of questionable origins on the cobwebbed shelves and grimaced.

"Ick…this place is full of dead things."

"What atmosphere!" Bernie threw up his arms, in so doing nearly decapitating a mummified rat. He took in a deep breath.

"What atmosphere, Bernie? This is a voodoo shop."
Alphonse pointed at a row of stuffed heads behind the counter and squeaked.

"Are those real?"

"As real as I be, man," a voice said from behind the counter.

A very tall figure rose from the shadows behind the cash register with the effortlessness of a ghost. His greasy slicked down hair reflected the light of the single naked light bulb that dangled above much like a polished ebony knob on a cane. From his extreme gauntness, Bernie wondered if the man had been exposed to long to the formaldehyde fumes the shop stank of.

The giant's long dark face seemed to split in half as he removed a pair of cheap sunglasses and his large white rimmed brown eyes opened wide.

Alphonse blanched, "You are the, uh…proprietor of this establishment?"

103

Bernie looked up at the man who reminded him of a National Geographic special on Egypt he once saw. As greased as his hair was, the man's skin contrasted. It looked like dry parchment. Bernie wondered if a mummy's skin looked like that.

Adding to his uncanny appearance, he was dressed in a clean black suit. Its somber shades relieved by the presence of a stick-pin. The effect was disturbingly corpse-like.

"I be one Mashtaka, the proprietor of dis place. You de man who say you want to talk wid me of de walking dead?"

"Zombies, you mean?" Bernie chomped on his cigar.

Alphonse noticed Mashtaka's stick pin was a gem cut into the shape of a skull. It seemed to be winking at him. He shrank pack crossing himself several times.

"Dat word be so Hollywood, man. I prefer to call dem recycled people...More modern, you tink?"

"Uh...yes, so you think you can supply enough working...uh 'stiffs' to supply my need?"

"So let me get dis. Man, you telling me serious dat you want to staff a Broadway production wid my people?"

"That's the ticket," Bernie said.

Mashtaka stared at Alphonse who in turn tried to hide his three hundred pound bulk unsuccessfully behind Bernie. The choreographer's small curled moustaches twitched nervously.

"Good lord, sir. It wasn't my idea." Mashtaka's stick-pin leered evilly.

"Well, it be right strange to me, as dem dead live by dey own rules, and dat not always de way of living man."

"But you can animate them, and get them to perform?" Bernie tapped his foot impatiently. "They at least have got to be as good as equity players."

104

"Me no-know equity, but I tink we can do that ting, but best be careful, dem dead, dey no like too much disrespectin."

"Yeah, but you don't have to pay them," Bernie said mopping his brow with a hankie.

"Jess me, man." Mashtaka smiled a smile beneath his pencil thin moustache of pure gold capped teeth.

"Of course, sir," Bernie said, "Now, would you like to have your services charged against shares in the production?"

It was two days later, when Bernie emerged from his office sniffing. There was a smell in the air that was very unpleasant. Bernie tucked his head inside the men's room but it wasn't coming from there. Before he could call the janitor, Fred came walking up.

"Mr. Manshanker, there's some weird jig with greasy hair along with a bunch of people that look like stiffs gathered at the stage door. Want I should shoosh them?"

"No Fred that would be Mr. Mashtaka with our new cast."

"You sure, Boss? They don't look like union players to me."

"Not your problem, Fred. Send them backstage, so I can have a look see."

"Gee," Fred muttered as he headed for the door, "and he was complaining about one smelly drunk."

With some effort, Bernie managed to get the sixty odd zombies to line up in five rows. With a lot more, he got Mashtaka to understand what he wanted them to do. Alphonse looked at the covered buckets Mashtaka's bald headed assistant was carrying.

"What pray tell, is that?"

105

"Raw meat, it keeps they attention." Alphonse squealed and retreated several steps. Bernie grabbed him and pushed Alphonse back onto the stage. A quick look confirmed the choreographer was too shaky in the knees. Bernie decided it was time for him to take over the audition.

"Ok," Bernie demonstrated doing a quick buck and weave, this is a simple dance move. Let's see who's got talent here."

Ed got the orchestra to play a sprightly little number from a classic show. As he did, Mashtaka began to mumble a chant. At first nothing happened. Then first one, then the rest began to jerk in time to the melody. Bernie watched, his critical eye already picking out the hoofers from the duds.

Alphonse scratched his chin and pointed out one zombie that seemed more coordinated than the others.

"He might do, and about thirty of the others, but I don't know. They stink something awful."

"So...we set up a couple of fans offstage and open the windows—"

"But Bernie, they are so obviously rotting."

"—and turn down the footlights, the audience won't notice if it's dark enough."

"But what about our star? Candy is not going to like this."

"Pan a spotlight on her, and get her to show more cleavage. One look at those maracas and maybe the audience will forget she can't act."

"And—"

"If they applaud, she'll be happy an' keep her trap shut. Do I have to think of everything? Look, whatever comes up we can handle it. Now, let's put these, uh...kids through their motions."

"Ok...then," Alphonse said as he stepped on stage. Zombie eyes stared at him hungrily, a few growled, some drooled. Alphonse looked down a Bernie in the audience and cringed.

106

"Uh, ok...Girls in one group, boys in another and step-two-three-step-two-three. The zombies danced to Alphonse's direction, faltering at first, but then stepping with more energy.

Mashtaka walked the line stuffing chunks of beef into each undead mouth he passed. Alphonse shivered at the sight, but kept up his direction.

A couple of hours later, the combined efforts of Alphonse and his staff had resulted in working out an acceptable looking dance number. The zombies shook as they did a spin, and several even survived doing a split. The choreographer managed to cull the number down to twenty eight that could dance and still looked reasonably human.

Bernie twirled his cigar and smiled. It was time to see if they could sing. A stage hand walked down the line giving each zombie a copy of the sheet music. The undead examined the pages with a great deal of curiosity. Some even managed to look at the music right-side up.

"At least they aren't eating them," Bernie whispered to his choreographer.

The first rasp that rose from one dead throat made Bernie hope for a tenor, but when the chorus tried the libretto, the anguished groans that issued from the undead players dead tonsils and withered lungs were just too discordant. The air filled with exhaled dust.

"I think we will need to fill in with at least some legitimate actors," Alphonse said coughing. "We might be able to talk Candy Clinton into getting a couple of our other singers back, if we give them an advance."

"How's your mom's pension going to handle that?" Bernie said scratching his head. "Maybe we can send for take out or make box lunches. Think they'll go for that in lieu of pay?"

"Candy was doing a good job of chewin her lip when I saw her last. Said her costumes were feeling a bit limp. The right food and I think some of the holdouts will crumble."

107

Bernie tapped his toe to the sound of the orchestra. Maybe things were finally starting to work for them.

Alphonse arranged the remaining zombies into formation. There were twenty eight corpses in the finale, all strutting their stuff in one long can-can line. Up came their left legs kicking out in unison towards the audience, hard and sharp.

Only twenty legs came back down. The remaining limbs flew into the orchestra pit in a bizarre volley. When their right legs lifted, the eight amputated zombies crashed to the floor and three right legs spiraled into the apron.

Bernie looked down and saw the conductor shoving a disembodied leg off his music. Another limb kicked spastically, caught in the pit net. Bernie slapped his palm to his forehead.

"Neggely, can you bring that leg up here?"

Bernie counted the casualties. Seventeen zombies still stood…kind of. Six were wobbly and two clung to the runners, ready to fall.

"This isn't gonna work," Alphonse said.

Bernie called Mashtaka over. "What's with these rubes? They'll never make it past the matinee."

"De dead, dey don't last long. I tell you so. I don know you be wantin this much from dem. You be needin new blood for dis dancing stuff."

"New blood eh, you mean like replacement zombies?"

"Yeah, like your blood—dancer folk, dey be easier to train fo dis."

Bernie shuffled his feet—deep in thought. The show was in jeopardy. They had to have a solid chorus line somehow, but live dancers at this point were just more than the budget could handle. There was no choice; he knew it even as it disgusted him. Bernie shuddered at the thought of what this might mean, but he was a showman born and bred. He sniffed at the rose on his lapel and then shook himself. When he looked up there was an air of grim determination on his waxy face.

"We could always advertise in the trades, see what comes to audition."

"My word," Alphonse gasped, "You aren't suggesting grabbing live-"

"Naw, but they might know some dancers who are close to starving. Well... we might get to them before the coroner."

"That's outrageous!"

"Alphonse, we must have something to work with, or the show will fail and I will have to close the doors here. Let me think...Maybe my cousin Meyer—"

"The Mobster," Alphonse wrung his hands. "Bernie, can't we just dig in our pockets a bit more and get...Equity players?"

"AL, you know we're broke. If I shell out to get better zombies, we still don't have to pay as much as for the live ones. With the living, we got to pay em scale."

"Oh well," Alphonse sighed fanning himself with his ascot, "Try the zombies again and pick what you will...as long as they're not the cute boys."

Candy Clinton sat in Bernie' office a week later, filing her nails in a vain effort to look sophisticated. She wasn't succeeding. Her bola looked ratty and her short hemline could not hide the wear and tear on her garter belts. Not that anyone was paying attention to her dress—except Alphonse.

"Being an Equity rep n' all," she said, "I had heard you, Mr. Manshanker, was puttin on this show with actors not union. Scabs, Not on my watch, says I. I don't act for nuthin...neither do the people I work with."

"My dear, we are on the up and up. Just stick around for the afternoon auditions. We are bringing in special talent."

"They better be carryin cards or I'm walkin," she pouted.

"They will Miss Clinton," Bernie said and on the aside to Alphonse, "Any chance they get her for lunch?"

A half hour later, Mashtaka showed up with the replacements. At first glance, Bernie felt a chill go up his spine. These obviously were newly dead zombies. The life smell on their clothes was still faint. Most of them had the look of professional dancers; some were even still garbed in leotards. Their dead eyes focused ahead with a sinister stare as they strode grim and silent towards the stage. One looked up at Bernie as it walked down the aisle. Its eyes looked shadowed—dark...evil.

Mashtaka led the silent parade up to the stage, arranging them again in lines, as he chanted soft verses that sounded like the hisses of serpents.

Alphonse shook as he stepped onto the stage, shooting Bernie a damning look that said "I know where you got these!"

Bernie himself gasped, when one of the female zombies trailed by. He recognized her as an understudy he had tried to lure away from a follies review. No doubt about it, Mashtaka had chosen his replacements well, these zombies were pros.

Ed Neggely started up the orchestra with a slow ragtime melody. Alphonse used it to put the line of undead through some simple dance steps. The chorus line strutted smartly with hardly a quiver.

"Thank-God—they're-still-fresh," Bernie said, his hands clasped over his heart.

In response to each command Alphonse gave, the zombies danced with almost mechanical efficiency. After a few minutes, he broke them into smaller groups and tried more advanced routines. Every pirouette, every lunge and slide, all that was demanded of them were executed to eerie perfection.

"Fantastic!" Bernie cried. "Now bring in the live talent."

Candy and a couple of very nervous looking actors stepped onto the stage. The zombies watched them but did not move, but their eyes looked hungry.

"Ok," Alphonse said, "I want you to take your places below the curtains."

The actors moved to the front of the stage. Candy stepped forward and began to sing her solo. The zombies groaned in harmony. She looked back at them, confused, but kept on singing."

"A real trouper that one, eh... Mr. Manshanker?"

"Yes Fred, but alas, she's an expensive one." Bernie watched Candy as she continued, wondering if she would keep her voice as a zombie.

"She's got no clue as to what they are, right boss?"

"You got it. Thank heavens she's blonde."

Bernie sat back in his chair and watched the rehearsals progress. All the bits gradually fit together; zombies, actors, musicians, stage crew. He pulled out his tin pocket watch and was pleased to see the performance was running true to time. This time he had a winner, yeah, it was that good.

Opening night was blessed with clear skies and only a slight nip to the air. Important guests were coming to see the show, Bernie's cousin Meyer had seen to it. There was a strong smattering of black ties, spats and tails in the audience. There was even an unguarded critic or two moping around. *Well,* Bernie thought, *we'll give em a show to remember.*

Backstage, Alphonse was approached by Leo, the head of wardrobe as he passed the dressing room.

"How do you expect us to costume these things? One of them just bit our best seamstress."

"Mashtaka said to throw some raw beef from those buckets over there at them; it'll keep them calm till we're ready."

"Dear me, Bernie," Leo said, "If you're going on the cheap with the talent, you should at least feed them before my girls have to work on them."

Leo walked back into the dressing room pausing at the door. "And give them mouthwash too." he said and closed the door.

From within, Alphonse could hear his voice, "Anyone for Sen-Sen? Gee Wilma, I hope Bernie stocked up on band aids."

Opening night, the stage was ready, the costumes cleaned and fitted. Bernie looked at the stage, the audience; magic was ready to be made. He stepped of the stage and ducked into the orchestra pit to speak with Ed.

"All set here, boss," the withered conductor said. His white collar look spiffy, his bow-tie was straighter than ever. *Good omens...*

"Fine Ed, I'll have the house manager bring up the stage lights at rise as you're finishing the overture. Then hit the opening number for all you're worth. It'll be the thing that sinks or swims us. After that it's all up to the audience. If they don't walk out by the second act, we may have a hit."

Bernie climbed out of the pit and slipped backstage as the house lights dimmed. Crossing his fingers, he fumbled for a cigar. Then remembering his twisted digits, he uncrossed them and lit up his smoke.

The overture played with great fanfare and then the curtain lifted. A single spotlight fell on to stage center, highlighting Candy Clinton—dressed in black tights loaded to the hilt with rhinestones. As she broke into her song, a second curtain rose to reveal twenty eight dancers dressed, in blue and gold spread in a large semi-circle. Candy sang;

"I am a girl from small town Indy,
My name is Joan, but they call me Annie..."

The zombies danced with uncanny perfection, ringing her and the two other principles that joined her. A murmur of approval rose from the audience.

"It's going to work," Bernie whispered to Alphonse. "A Tony, I should at least get a Tony for this."

The zombies began to twirl in an intricate formation around the actors. They alternately ducked and rose as they spun past the leads. Bernie could hear light applause. Things were going well indeed.

Between acts, Candy cornered Bernie for a moment. These dancers are sure lookin sharp, but I don't like the way they're lookin at me. I'm not that kind of girl, you know."

"Relax my darling; we got two acts in the can. If we can keep the Z—dancers under con-uh, don't worry…I saw a critic, he wuz dazzled by you."

Candy racked her brain to make sense of Bernie's words. *Control?* Then the thought vacated her mind, replaced by his other comment. A critic had noticed her. Candy was happy again.

As Bernie walked off, the starlet stood lost for the moment her perfect bowed lips relaxed into a smile as she twisted a blonde ringlet in her fingers.

"Dazzled..." she sighed. "I'm a star!"

Two acts gone and one left to go. Bernie was thinking of press releases and options. Alphonse watched from backstage and thought of real restaurant food. Fred watched from the entrance with a Lucky Strike in his hand, dreaming of getting an actual paycheck.

Candy sang what had to be the show stopping hit of the production. Bernie saw a critic scribbling madly in the fifth row. Meyer saw him and signaled thumbs up.

"Ten more minutes and it's in the bag," Bernie whispered. "Almost there."

Then as the closing number tolled of the final seconds of the show, a zombie in the front row missed a step. Instead of returning to its place in line, the zombie turned and bit off the hand of the male lead. Instantly the chorus line reacted to the spilled blood and swamped the injured man tearing him apart—spattering his blood and guts into the orchestra.

The musicians stopped playing and began to retreat from the pit. Several zombies jumped in after them clawing through the netting and slashing at the artists as they retreated. Bernie cringed when he saw a bassoon player get his throat torn out. A trombonist was impaled by his own instrument. In seconds the entire string section had met their demise.

Bernie heard a scream. Candy Clinton galloped by him headed for her dressing room. What was left of her garments was in rags, allowing Bernie enticing peeks at her ample figure as she passed. Not far behind her, four male zombie dancers were in hot pursuit."

"Don't worry dear," Bernie called as she passed, "I understand they're mostly gay."

Candy got the door open just as the horde landed on top of her, biting and tearing at her exposed skin. The squirming pile fell through the door slamming it behind them. Bernie could hear her screams from within.

"Is that?" Alphonse peeked out from behind a curtain where he had taken refuge. His face looked gray.

Bernie nodded.

"Oh dear," Alphonse said and ran for the men's room. Half way he tripped over a disembodied hand with a zombie attached. He squealed jumping back

114

to his feet. Then he reached his sanctuary. The zombie never stopped chewing. Bernie heard the lock click. Alphonse's squeals continued from within.

Below, the zombies had climbed out of the orchestra pit swarming the front rows. There was a fierce battle going on between the zombies and some of Meyer's friends who were peppering the undead with a variety of hand guns with limited success. One man in pinstripes was torn to pieces even as he unloaded his Smith & Wesson 38 into a grinning zombie face. A dowager, heavy with pearls laid helpless in the aisle, her petticoats no protection against the thing chewing on her legs. Another woman was trapped, pinched in-between two of the undead as they ate her brains.

"Alphonse," Bernie said knocking on the men's room door, "They're eating the audience. Is that kosher?"

From within came a groan, this time all too human.

"Bernie, we forgot to feed them between acts!"

The battle in the audience was winding down. Most of the people had fled. A few fought gamely with the undead but it was clearly the zombies that were prevailing. Bernie walked out on the apron and watched the uneven struggle.

Then at the entrance, Bernie saw Fred and Mashtaka. The tall Haitian was chanting loud and strong while Fred kept the zombies at bay with a folded newspaper.

"Naggstra hamu vas tres mortem Gagamoth," the voodoo man said.

The zombies stood up dropping their victims. Tall and straight, they became rigid like statues. Then, one by one, they crumbled to dust.

The surviving members of the audience wasted no time retreating out the exits.

Bernie climbed down from the stage, passing Neggely, who was staring at a cello that was hopelessly smashed.

115

"Ah, such notes you played..." the choreographer said and wept.

Bernie surveyed the damage. Half the orchestra was gone. Here and there a patron or an usher breathed their last. Blood and programs lay scattered or smeared on the floor and seats.

"I guess a matinee tomorrow is out of the question."

"Hey Bernie," Cousin Meyer daintily stepped over a couple of his departed associates, being careful not to get blood on his spats.

"Yes?" Bernie answered noticeably wilting. He knew what his cousin was capable of.

"You should' a told me your last act was a bang-up; me and the boys would have packed more heat."

"Sorry Meyer, we kind of lost control of the cast."

"So I see. You know, it ain't too healthy for a show if you bump off the audience, makes for bad turn-around. Now I ain't gonna hold this against you because you went on the cheap. To be honest, several of the stiffs here weren't on my long life plan anyway. Just the same though, next performance, warn me so's I can stock the audience better, if you get the drift."

"Uh...sure thing, cousin."

"That's my Bernie," Meyer said slapping him lightly on the cheek. "Now excuse me, I have to pay a special visit to someone. The boys can use some of them instrument cases. Looks like the owners won't mind."

Go right ahead," Bernie said.

"Gus, Joe, grab the fiddle cases. Bernie, it's been swell." Meyer walked over to a slightly bloody blonde.

"See ya kid."

"Bernie shivered...and then almost jumped out of his skin when a rough hand griped his shoulder. The owner of the hand was the voodoo master.

"Thank God, it's someone uh...alive," Bernie whispered.

116

"Mr. Manshanker," Mashtaka said, "You no feed de undead too good. Dey be hungry for man flesh. Dis mess be no fault of mine. I lose much money in destroying dem. Much money it cost to make more now."

"Uh, can't you harvest anything from these?"

"No sir, Mr. Manshanker. De bodies here too ripped to last long. Not neat like either. No sell to good when dey guts hang out."

There was a commotion at stage left. Candy emerged from her room tripping over a piece of scenery. Her body was scratched and her costume reduced to scraps of cloth. She plopped down on the stage her feet dangling over the apron.

"Anyone got a smoke?"

"Sure doll," Fred said and he walked over and lit one for her. Candy took a long drag and stared at the mess.

"You were wrong about the dancers, Bernie."

Alphonse emerged from the men's room wringing his hands. He stared down at Candy and shuddered.

"Oh...dear."

"If this show goes on I want a new contract," Candy said.

Bernie looked down at the bodies lying on the floor; it was like looking at a grotesque jig-saw puzzle. Near his feet lay parts of a mangled figure that looked familiar.

"Good Lord, that's Charles Charleston. Curse us all, we had a real big time critic here and our cast ate him!"

"Some people would call that a favor," Fred said from the stage.

Bernie lifted a note pad from the dead man's hands. He flipped through the wet pages as the impact of what had just happened finally hit him. Bernie clenched his fists, letting out a cry of anguish.

"Why...why did it have to happen on opening night? It wouldn't have been too bad on tour."

"Just the breaks boss," Fred said.

Bernie held the pad up to hide the tears of guilt on his face. Convulsions wracked the small man's body as he walked back to his office.

Mashtaka looked around him and then straightened his collar.

"Doan know 'bout you cats, but I be leaving."

"Me too," said Fred. Alphonse wrung his hands and shrugged.

"Any chance you'll be passing a bar?"

The next morning the trio returned to the theater. The police had been there as evidenced by the chalk outlines all over the floor.

"That's the last time I drink something called a Zombie," Alphonse groaned rubbing his hand across his Fedora, flattening the brim to his face. Mashtaka tried to look cool behind his dark glasses, but his processed hair was hanging limp over his face. Fred looked disheveled, but then Fred always looked that way.

Candy was asleep atop the remains of the piano in the orchestra pit. Fred nudged her awake.

"Not now," she said, "Roll over and go to—what!" Alphonse gripped her arm and nodded towards the office.

"Candy, did they arrest Bernie?"

"Uh...No, Bernie told them a gang of bootleggers tried to off their competition who's was enjoying the show here. There was a couple of guys in pin stripes the cops recognized so they bought it."

"So where's Bernie?"

"Sitting in his office for all I care. My costume's shot and my hair is a mess...Are we getting paid for this?"

"Of course…of course my dear," Alphonse said patting the hand he held. Then he released it and dashed off to join Fred and Mashtaka who were already headed backstage.

"Boss…hey Boss, You in there!" Fred banged on the door. From within, Bernie's voice shouted, "Enter."

Mashtaka, Alphonse and Fred looked with horror at their employer. In the midst of a stack of bloodstained papers strewn all over the desk and chairs Bernie was smiling.

"God I love this city!" he cried jubilantly as he pointed at the papers. "LOOK, it's Charleston's notes...and over there the Hemlock Review and here's VARIETY."

"Oh no," Alphonse said.

"Mashtaka," Bernie shouted, banging his fist on the desk top, "Get more Zombies, Neggely, more musicians. Gentlemen, we're a HIT!"

THE STORY OF A HEAD

Chapter 1

It was nineteen twenty eight when Brother Person and Jack Bristow set off on their memorial journey into Melanesia in search of salvation by spreading the word of the Christian God to the heathens.

They never returned.

*

Three years later, Doug Masterson sat in a cheap bar on the trinket coast talking to a dealer of island curios about a stuffed head that looked very familiar.

"You see, Monsieur; the quality is profound, unusually well done for these things."

Messer Francoise lifted the head from its case and handed it over to the American seated across from him. The rich pungent fumes of preservative spices filled the air, overpowering the stale barroom smell.

"I say…it looks like a white man's head." Doug said as he examined the curio's face closely. "It hasn't shrunk very much either."

"That it is a white man's is what increases its value. This is no trade copy; it is genuine, collected of the island of Baki-Ki in the southern reaches of Melanesia."

"Balls, man...How'd you get it past the authorities?"

"My cousin, he works for the local police, he's got pull."

"You mean he knows the right people to bribe."

"So it has always been in these parts." Francoise said simply, "How do you say-"

"It's who you know," Doug said. "Any idea who that poor wretch was?"

Masterson had a pretty good idea, but he wanted the Frenchman to confirm it.

"Does it matter so?"

"Only that the price is five thousand American dollars if you answer correctly."

Francoise's eyes popped. Taking a swig of the raw brandy that was before him, his eyes narrowed in suspicion.

"But Monsieur, do you even have that kind of money?"

"I know someone who thinks that it's important enough that five G's would be your cut—that is, if it is who I think it is. That is my highest offer."

"Let us not play games, Monsieur," Francoise said, "We both know whom this noble artifact belongs to, but, I am curious, American. While I consider your offer for this fine head, I should like to know what you think you know about it."

As you are aware, Messer Francoise the story of the head started three years ago...

Chapter 2

Person and Bristow contracted the services of the tramp steamer LANGDOON SAITE. She was a small ship, scarce more than a banana boat in size. Its compliment was twenty two able hands, and a bastard of a skipper named Turug who was part Mali.

They sailed their ship into the warm waters of the South Pacific in search of lands unknown to modern Christianity. There Person hoped to find an island suitable for the spreading of their faith, one not contaminated by missionaries from other denominations. Aye, it was for a virgin island they sought, one where the savages would be easy to mold...or so they thought.

It was on the night of the fourteenth of August when the lookout spotted the cursed black form of an ancient volcano rising above the waves. Bristow was set upon checking it out so they steered a course intending to seek moorage beneath its grim slopes.

We settled her in at in a cove to the southwest of the volcano's peak. Grimley, the lookout said that he saw fires near there.

Person was excited. He said we had a real chance of finding innocents there to teach the word too. Curse him for an idiot. The captain warned him that it might not be a good idea to set ashore till morning, but Person would have none of that.

"Let us greet them on the shore, so the light of dawn may show upon us as their new friends."

"Me think you be long pig by tomorrow," the captain said.

"Nonsense," Persons said, "There has been no cannibalism in this region for decades."

"So, you say, Preacher," Turug said chewing on a cigar stub. We land you tonight then. I send a couple of armed men with you. Maybe they keep you out of the pot." Turug pointed at me.

Personally, I thought it sheer lunacy, and started to object, but the captain ordered me to go ashore with three other swabs and the two clergymen. I saw the hate in Turug's eyes as he said it. He never forgot our quarrel over that dame in Singapore a few years back.

We set ashore in a longboat packed with bibles and trade goods. The sky was cloudy with only patches of light from the quarter moon above. Cold was the spray of that water on our bodies as we rowed. But Person stood at the bow with his bible clutched to him as if it were a summer day. Lord protect us from such fools as he.

We made fast to a large rock near the island, the beach being too rugged to land our craft safely. We carried the preacher's gear from the boat on our shoulders to the shore.

Dammed if Person didn't break out in prayer the minute he set foot on dry land, his thin reedy voice scaring the hell out of the monkeys in the trees. The imps scattered and screamed in reply to his pronunciations.

"Shouldn't we be quiet, Person?" I put my finger to my lips. "Such an unfamiliar noise might scare the natives."

"There is no fear to be had in the voice of the Lord," Person said. "Rather the joyous noise will bring them forth for salvation, such as lambs in the field."

It was at that moment the buggers jumped us.

Bristow bought it first; I think it was some kind of dart that flew out of the darkness and caught him between the shoulder blades. Then a spear took another of the crewmen. One poor salt, I think it was Jaylong, ran for the woods. I heard him scream something awful. Then Grimley went down with an arrow through his leg.

The heathens poured out of the forest screaming like demons, their naked bodies covered with white paint. Person had his brains jellied by a club. I saw the other two crewmen fall under the mass of attackers. There was naught to do except make a run for it. I near made it to the boat, when I felt their hands on me. I swung and shattered one fellow's teeth, before they grabbed me and forced my head beneath the waves.

*

I awoke vomiting salt water. When I recovered my senses, I found myself tied to a stake across from Burke, one of the two sailors that were

123

overwhelmed. He had a leaking wound in his gut, so I knew he was done for. Grimley was tied to the other side of me.

My head hurt like hell. My wrists were already raw from hanging from the ropes that secured them to the stake. Bad as I felt, worse was to come.

The scene before us was one to chill the blood of any man jack that would dare lay eyes on it. The bloody heathens had taken the bodies of our crew—stripped, gutted, and hung them up like sides of beef. There was a big fellow near us, whom I guess was the cook, who sliced up the bodies taking care when carving what I guess was the choice cuts. These were cooked on large spits from which the people would cut slivers to eat as they sat chanting around a large bonfire. There were male dancers with strange costumes who gestured with obscene movements. The women drenched themselves with the blood of their victims before submitting to unspeakable acts of depravity with the men. If Persons was alive, he would have called the scene an orgy of the damned.

Several natives ran over to Burke and tore him from the stake. I averted my eyes, but his screams told me what they did to him...and what I was certain they would do to me.

Sometime late, after midnight I guess, they stopped their chanting and the cannibals—one by one—drifted off to sleep. Grimley stared at me, his fear making him look so much like a cornered rat—his yellow teeth were clenched in a look of pure madness. Shortly after that I succumbed to exhaustion. I fell fast asleep, too spent to care what happened next.

*

They caged Grimley and me. For a week we lay in squalor, as the children of the damned tribe poked at us. Little food was offered and less water. Mostly they gave us a kind of beer they called Guto-kaki. I did not find out till later when I saw them make it that the mess was fermented grass, coconut juice, and human blood. Lord, if I knew what was in that devil's brew, I would have never touched it.

Grimley suffered far more than me. Eventually his wounded leg began to fester, and the stench of his rotting flesh became intolerable. One night I awoke to the sounds of a struggle. Grimley was gone. Lord, I heard his screams as they butchered him.

I think I lost it then, my mind cascading into madness. I cared not if I lived or died, only that I should not be roasted on that awful spit, to be devoured by savages. I huddled in the darkest corner of the cage, waiting for my turn.

A little later, one of the heathens—a child—brought me something to eat. I stared into her large brown eyes and asked myself, "Could a people this terrible produce such an innocent?"

The girl smiled when she offered me the meat, steaming hot on a sliver of wood. I knew what it was, but I was starving, so I ate hungrily of the cursed fare—not caring that it was human meat I consumed. Call it fear…or hunger, I knew not that I was damning my soul for the act. Oddly, instead of feeling sick, I relished it. Rather than being repugnant, I found that it was fair good to the taste.

After that night, the savages gave me the freedom of the village. As soon as I was able, I sneaked over to the shore. The natives did not care. The ship was long gone.

They were curious about me, being as I must have been the first white man they had seen with blond hair and blue eyes. It fascinated them; they would often come to me and stare and to touch it. It was for this reason, I think, they spared me.

The chief, a rather stout individual adorned with feathers and bones, visited me on one occasion leaving a young female with me; I suppose to service my carnal appetites. May my dear precious Angela forgive me, I did eventually make use of his gift, and in return, the heathen wench cooked for me and cared for the lean-to I built.

I was to spend several months with the cannibals. They treated me with respect and even a little awe. Eventually, I learned a few of their words, and that is how I can tell you of their interest in me.

One surprise was that it seemed the wench, whose name was Koona, was brought to me to father a child. I guessed the village wished to embrace me into their family by making me a relative.

Reassured that their intentions were no longer hostile, I settled into the islander's routine, fishing and hunting with the men and doing odd chores for the villagers, in hopes of improving my value to them. They seemed to appreciate this and when it became obvious that Koona carried my child, a large celebration was planned. I was told that every clan on the island would attend in my honor. Finally, the big day came. I was presented with Koona before all the chief's. They seated me in a place of honor at the feast.

We danced that night, before the same fire pit my companions had been murdered and cooked at. What did I care, for my life as I knew it was gone, and a wilder more savage existence had become my fate? We celebrated the birth of my child in the most base and earthly way till near midnight, drinking Guto-Kaki and eating ourselves into a stupor. Somewhere in the midst of it, I stumbled back to my lean-to with Koona and fell asleep.

*

It was close to dawn, as the sky outside was gray. I awoke to a noise outside. Koona was missing. Before I could stand up and don my trousers, I felt something hit me on the head.

Chapter 3

Masterson shivered as he finished the story. The American held the head in his hands, his fingers examining the blonde hair, the tightly sewn eyes, and the scar of a brutal wound in the back of the skull.

"Now you understand." Francoise said.

"Understand what?"

"That you, the last survivor, Monsieur Masterson...You were saved from the pit till last. Yours is the head we bargain for, No?"

"Dear God, so it is," Doug said in his oddly disembodied voice. The Frenchman leaned forward staring at the ghostly headless trunk before him.

"Now you truly know the reason you seek its price."

Francoise paused for a moment to study the amber fluid in his glass. He rubbed his chin as if deep in thought.

"That is an interesting story, Masterson; one that is especially ironic— considering the nature of our meeting tonight. I think though that under the circumstances, your offer is alas, too small for my sentimentality to be superior to my financial needs. I should think ten thousand dollars will suffice as the proper price for disposing the possession of this cranium to you."

"Damn you for a thief with no soul," Masterson growled, "That's twice my offer."

"Tis far better to have no soul, Monsieur...than to endlessly wander the Earth with no head on one's shoulders."

"But, as you can see, Frenchman," Doug said pointing to his ragged clothing, "I carry no such funds upon me. Say—half that and I will place my mark on a contract, my wife paying upon presentation."

"Ten thousand American dollars...and no less, Mr. Masterson, unless you want me to toss it to the sharks in the bay. Then you will always walk this plane in torment."

"For pity's sake—"

"No less!"

Masterson rose to his feet, his neck pumping dark blood from its severed top. It seeped down his shoulders thick and bitter scented. If there had been a head and eyes above that torso, the Frenchman knew what their expression would be.

"All right then, if you'll have it that way, then I'll sign a note and my dear wife Angela will pay it when you present it to her!"

"It will be suitable," Francoise said handing Doug a pen, "Just sign this paper and we're done."

The bloody thing that once was Doug Masterson signed the I.O.U. the pen clicking in his boney hands as he wrote.

"God's curse on you, for the deal you dealt this night, Frenchman."

The apparition rose, tucked his head under his arm, and walked from the back room, out through the bar. Men, who saw the abomination, clutched their hands to their breasts and prayed to God that such should never be their fate.

*

The Frenchman sipped his brandy as he watched Doug leave.

"Alas, you are still doomed my friend. Retrieving your skull will not save your soul."

The Frenchman folded the I.O.U and stuffed it in his pocket. He would contact Angela Masterson later and collect his bounty. Francoise lifted his glass in a toast to the ironic.

"It is not often," he commented wryly, "That a man balks at paying the price of his own head."

A VISION OF DEATH

(Author's Note: This story was written originally for an anthology of Poe stories. The style of punctuation and word usage is crafted to reflect the writing style of Poe and his contemporaries.)

"I shall entertain at this time to note the details of the decline and eventual passage from God's Earth of my celebrated patient, one: Edgar Allen Poe. A poor soul who was an occasional resident of our fair city to whom drunkenness and calamity had frequently visited themselves upon…"

> *From the diary of Judith Arnold; nurse under the employment of Dr. John J. Moran.*

Under personal invitation, I–your humble servant, E. Poe—had taken the occasion to visit the home of a certain Mr. B— in Richmond. He had heard some word of my fame and had requested the pleasure of making my acquaintance. For this I had been invited to join his circle of friends in sharing an 'occasion of merriment'. Acting upon this I spent the first –of several nights as it turned out—at his home in the role of 'honored guest.'

His home was unusual for the area as it was built in the Spanish style, having stucco rather than brick walls. He had explained to me that the house—which was old—had been built by a Spanish slave trader in the last century, who had resided in it for some forty years. The house had achieved somewhat of a sorted history as its cellar had been used at that time to house the unfortunates that were newly imported from Nigeria for the slave trade. My understanding was that several of the poor wretches died there while awaiting sale. The present owner had acquired the house after the trader—a Spaniard by the name of Garcia—whom sadly had been plagued by misfortune—had ended his miserable existence by suicide.

Mr. B—had taken the house because of its convenient location on the east side; just to the south of the three bridges that crossed the James River. This allowed him ready access to his holdings, which he could see from his back porch. These occupied one of several warehouses on the west bank.

Mr. B—was a portly man of some means, whom (fortunately for my needs) was taken to providing lodging in his home, for persons he referred to as 'Interesting Characters'. It was his pleasure to spend each evening engaged in collecting clever stories and witticisms from his guests, for which he in turn, supplied ample refreshment from his extraordinary wine cellar.

As my manner of dress precluded me from accepting various invitations, due in large part to my lack of an acceptable frock coat or other refinements, I had come of late to find this house a bulwark against the dismal atmosphere of Swan's Tavern where I might otherwise have spent my nights. Mr. B—seemed to have no misgivings about the casual apparel of his guests; and so I felt it an opportune place to sequester myself on those nights that were not spent with my beloved Elmira. As I was feeling the scourge of fever that night; I choose to abandon my fellows and to instead take refuge within the confines of the large wine cellar below. There I sought privacy and drink. In this enterprise, I was not entirely to succeed, as my privacy was soon intruded upon by another of Mr. B-'s guests.

The fellow who joined me was a rather callow lad, who went by the name of Reynolds. The young man fancied himself a poet and actor, but for all his Herculean efforts at the task, I found him dull and lacking in skill. His metaphors and similes were devoid of any true merit. Particularly since his poetic verse mimicked somewhat the form and manner of that detestable fool Emerson.

As to his aspirations for the theater; I feared that his efforts would also be futile. His physical presence was less than satisfactory for his other endeavor—as he lacked both bold good looks and presence. His long gangly figure would never serve him on the stage—in spite of an overwhelming enthusiasm. One such as he could carry a spear, but not an audience. His were the hopeless dreams of a child not gifted with the talents or abilities to achieve them.

Still there was a certain charm to the youth and because of this I suffered his presence. Reynolds was much taken to dreaming and I found his flights of fancy somewhat stimulating. As to how much the ready quantities of wine helped—I dare not say—but it may have been substantial.

Reynolds who was a comely youth, despite his gauntness, had chosen that night, as well, to occupy the wine cellar. His occupation (in part) as refuge from the civilities that was going on upstairs—the other was to seek out my company. Being fortunate in this endeavor—he had (in fact) chosen to share my location. Having found me, he abruptly deposited himself on the floor where I was sitting propped up against a keg of Van Zeller Port. He seemed quite clear headed—which to me felt strange, given the location where we had found ourselves. I for one was at my usual destination—that is to say— well into the hands of Bacchus—the result of having managed to make a reasonable impression upon a bottle of Claret which I had brought with me to my refuge. A draught from this I offered to the young man and he drank deeply before returning the bottle. He then sought to make light conversation with me.

"Master Poe," quoth he, "I thank you for the hospitality of your fine Claret. I had to escape from upstairs, as the politics that were being endlessly debated there were overly tiresome to me. I hoped you would not find my company here too boorish."

I indicated that I was indeed willing to suffer his presence—for as long as he did not plague me with questions about his literary aspirations. We sat a while in silence, engaged in the judicious enterprise of draining my bottle, till the weight of the silence became unbearable to the young man. At last he could stand it no longer; and so to stimulate conversation, he suggested a diversion.

"As you are a man of imagination—I wonder if you ever see things in the walls," he said absently.

I asked, "The...walls?" My alcohol fogged brain not quite understanding the young man's statement.

"The walls, can you see pictures in them? I can Sir—if I try make out faces and beasts if I concentrate upon it. It is an amusement I learned as a child, that I have on occasion partaken of; to pass the time on nights such as this one."

"You mean a game then, Reynolds? A passing glance at a line or shadow to trick the imagination—as to seemingly portray what is not there?" I laughed at his suggestion, "That sport would more better suited to one who has dealings with the Chinamen—and who dwell in their parlors chasing the dragon."

Still, I was forced to admit that the time spent in the wine cellar had become tedious in spite of the aid of the bottle of Claret. The relief of a diversion such as the young man proposed could contribute to improving our present situation. With this in mind, I undertook to learn how this game was to be executed.

"It is quite simple," my friend said. "Just gaze at the wall and see what your imagination can make of it." The young man waited for what he obviously thought would be my immediate success in this new venture. In all fairness it might be said that the capacity to gather my wits into such a discipline was somewhat lacking. For a brief span—maybe minutes—I could see nothing. Then slowly my sotted brain managed to make out a shape from the cracks on the wall. It was the profile that to me appeared to be that of a cat. Having determined that this was what was expected, I made the youth privy to my discovery.

"Very good Sir!" young Reynolds replied and then applied himself to the sport. "I have it then…A monkey!" he cried as he pointed at a particularly grainy portion of wall to our left. I squinted at this and—sure enough there were indeed some cracks that had a simian aspect to them. This I confirmed to his eminent satisfaction. Then I returned my stare to the masonry as it was again my turn to indulge.

I fairly lost track of the time as the game went on for hour after hour—such being more for the state of our drunkenness than the appeal of the exercise. Finally, I noted a particular section that was seemingly like the face of an old acquaintance of mine from some years past. At first it was just a few lines, but then as I looked closer—I could make out the features in sharper detail. "Why," I cried, "That's old Mrs. Harper!"

"Really—" Reynolds replied. He sounded sleepy and I assumed that he was well on his way to unconsciousness. "And whom might that be?"

"She was my landlady some years back. As I recall, she died from the effects of too much liquor some years ago."

"Sadly met—friend Poe," My sotted companion mumbled and then lapsed into unconsciousness.

Strangely, I felt an odd sense of invigoration with my discovery; as I felt compelled to further my explorations of the cellar walls. Slowly at first, and then with increasing regularity, I began to catch images of other people. Some were sharp and clear, other were but shadows that hid in the recesses as if waiting to emerge. What did seem strange about these visions was that every face I knew—belonged to someone who had died! Somewhere, in the course of my discoveries; I must have finally succumbed to the effects of the Claret, as when I awoke—as from a seemingly deep slumber—I was back in my rooms at Swan's Tavern.

I recovered my senses with no sense of recollection of my manner of transport there. I rose and washed mechanically in the bowl by my bed as my mind—for reasons I know not— still dwelt upon the images of the night before. That it had been a singular experience there could be no doubt. While what I had seen in some ways troubled me, I was still caught in the almost "mesmeric" fascination that had driven me to the discoveries I had made. Eventually my mind cleared enough, that I—fool that I was— decided to dismiss the night's events, as being the results of suggestions acted upon by a feverish and inebriated brain.

I was to give one last lecture on this day, to be concluded before making my arrangements to leave Richmond. The affair went well and profitably, which was a relief, for now I had the necessary funds to travel on. I took the time free to me that afternoon, to write my dearest heart Elmira and thus implore upon her to write to me in Philadelphia. I asked that she address the post to E. S. T. Grey, but not to sign the letter—lest it be that I did not receive it.

That night I spent with the Talley's. It was an unremarkable evening, though Susan, a young lady with a delightful imagination, at one point had observed a meteor in the sky as we said goodnight. I happily showed her a letter I had received from Griswold, who had presented himself as available to act as my literary executer. This pleased her and she applauded my good fortune in this matter.

As the next evening was free, I decided to again take advantage of the Spanish house and its hospitality. As fate would have it, young Reynolds was absent. So—on a whim, I again retreated to the wine cellar, with the intent to resume my activities of the previous visit. This time I found it was easier to call up images from the wall—as I had not yet reached the state of intoxication that I had—on the last occasion. Again I saw the stern aspect of Mrs. Harper displayed in the stucco, and also that of the Patterson boy, who had drowned in a boating accident when I was young. There seemed to be a host of new faces however and I eagerly sought each one out in turn.

This I pursued for some time till I saw a face that was painfully familiar. As I stared at the image, I realized—to my shock—that I was looking at my poor dead brother Henry.

"My God!" I said aghast at what my eyes beheld. I strained against the impossibility that was staring me in the face. It had to be imagination. But there could be no doubt. The profile—the chin—the hair, what lie could be so clear in detail as what my eyes were now telling me? Henry, my lost brother who had died of consumption, sadly portrayed there on the cursed wall before me. I looked close into that anguished face and I could almost smell the sickroom odor. I saw the sweat pour off his pallid features—all of this and more—captured with the rough grain of the stucco walls. And then; as my mounting horror seemed to choke the soul within me—he

136

spoke! Or at least he seemed to, for there was no sound. Just the movement of his lips, and the wild hopeless look in his eyes!

At that point I think I swooned, for when I came to my senses, I was seated on Mr. B—'s comfortable couch surrounded be he and some of his fellows. The man had apparently produced some smelling salts for my awakening was abrupt.

"Heavens Sir, are you all right?" His rich basso voice was laced with a degree of urgency. "We heard you cry out and then found you senseless on the floor!"

"Quite so—" I lied. For who would but think me mad for what I saw. "I am afraid that I slipped and just cried out as I fell."

"Well Mr. Poe, you gave us quite the scare. Perhaps you should sit with us a while. Mr. Brandon is telling us about some fascinating politics in Charleston." I smiled graciously at my host and set about trying to make the sense of my latest visions as I gave lip service to the political argument around me. It was indeed strange that the wall (that I had inspected so closely the evening before) should reveal new apparitions that had not been there previously. To have my poor brother's features so cruelly displayed upon that cursed stone face—pleading with me and suffering so— it nearly tore my heart from my breast; with the pain of it. That night I determined never to return to the Spanish house and its abysmal cellar.

The next two days were spent with friends. But the pleasant diversion into the warmth of good company failed to dispel the morbid curiosity of the place which haunted me. I found myself drawn into endless speculation as to what I had experienced on those two nights. And yet, there was something else. I found my thoughts returning to someone else, someone that was so dear and so long departed.

137

So despite my misgivings, once again I found myself knocking on Mr. B—'s door. The gentleman was pleased to see me in better health then my last visit and so allowed me access to his home and guests.

"It is sad though Mr. Poe," my host gravely announced, "That I have the misfortune to inform you that your young friend, Mr. Reynolds has met with calamity and was found dead in his apartment this morning."

"How could this happen?" My senses were rattled by the news. My host could not speak with certainty about the details, but it seemed that the tragic end of my young acquaintance was deemed possibly of a sinister nature, as it was reported that his rooms were in disarray. Though strangely, there seemed to be no marks on the body to indicate the exact nature of his demise.

This revelation cast a somber note to the night's festivities and so without much trouble, I was able to slip from the parlor and escape down to the cellar undetected. I resumed my vigil and thus engaged, I stared at the wall for some time. But there was little solace there as I saw nothing. Its white surface still bore the same cracks and creases that I had seen before, but they lacked the cohesiveness that gave my fancies form and life. Religiously, I kept to my station, propped against the keg of Port; yet the secrets that the wall kept, were jealously hidden from my view. For hours I sat in frustrated silence and finally, in desperation pleaded and begged for some sign that the visions would return—but it was to no avail.

At last I gave it up, and rose dejectedly from the floor—stone sober and weary beyond what my frail constitution could take. I walked away from my tormentor and began exhaustedly to ascend the stairway.

"Mr. Poe!" a voice called out softly. Holding fast to the stair rail, I strained my ears to hear more. Forgetful of my diminished condition, I rushed back down to the cellar and faced the wall. Frantically I pressed my ear to it and suffered the cold stones embrace as I strained to listen. Strained and heard no more save my bitter breath, for I panted with the excursion. But it had been enough. For that call that had teasingly caught my ear, I had recognized. It was the soft clear tones that issued from the mouth of poor young Reynolds!

I waited for what seemed hours more by the blank expanse of the cold cellar wall till finally I took my leave. As I did, I had the unnerving sense that I was being watched by something, as if a presence lived within the stucco wall.

I spent the next day completing the final preparations for my trip. I decided that I would spend my last night in Richmond visiting my friends the Mackenzie's. This would also allow me the latitude to use this one last night, to further my investigation of the cellar of the Spanish house. With that in mind, I once more knocked upon the door of Mr. B—'s home. He greeted me in his usual jovial manner and pressed upon me that—since this was to be my last night; I should partake the activity of presenting a reading of one of my more gruesome (as he put it) tales. I selected The Tell-Tale Heart for my selection—as for some reason it seemed clearer to my memory than the others. So for a substantial period of time, I impatiently awaited my appointment, as I listened to the mediocre poetry of a fellow named Randolph. This went on for what seemed an intolerable interval. Then we heard the political posturing of another man—I think his name was Bingham. Finally my turn came and I related the cursed story quickly as I dared. My host seemed to take pleasure in this presentation; for he was loud in his praise at the conclusion. I had but scarcely sat down, when each guest in turn, applauded me and complimented my work. But I was not there for praise and soon made my excuses to withdraw to the cellar. My host inquired about the time I had been spending there; and I assured him that it was my intent in seeking out this peculiar solitude in order to create yet another horrifying tale. In fact, I had, I told him, all but completed my exposition. This seemed to satisfy the man, though he looked suspicious. Reluctantly he consented to my absence and sent me on my way. As I left the room, I could hear him comment to the others about the peculiar eccentricities of writers (and of myself in particular).

This time I came better prepared for my limited exploration of the walls of the cellar, having armed myself with another bottle of Claret—similar to the one I had consumed with poor Reynolds on my first evening. I confess that it was there as much to fortify my courage, as anything else. I further aped my previous visits by placing myself again at the same station held— that being on the floor with my back against the keg of Port. Thus satisfied at the exactness of my recreation, I sat and waited as I drank the Claret.

I did not have long to wait this eve; for soon several of the familiar profiles began to appear. First a few (placed in random fashion) and then facsimiles appeared in greater numbers as if all were engaged in a contest to be in view. I marveled at this for a while, but then I grew impatient. There was someone I desperately hoped would lend her countenance to the press of faces. That was the features of my long lost Virginia.

Anxiously, I surveyed the faces—of which there were hundreds now— hoping to find that sweet profile. For hour upon hour I watched the dark parade of figures that appeared and then vanished upon the pale walls as if the gate of Hell had opened and each poor soul came to this place—as if it were a window—to gaze upon me sitting there. I was about to give up hope when finally, my patience was rewarded. I saw emerge from the press, the one I sought!

"Oh my sweet angel Virginia, my beloved Sissy; at last portrayed on this tragic field!" I looked at her lovely round face so graciously enhanced by her black curls—oh saddest of tortures! For now that I could see her—I desperately wanted to speak to her. To this end, I called softly to this sought after apparition, in hopes of gaining her attention; and—God's Mercy—she seemed to hear me! She seemed to reach out as if to touch me, but her forward motion was stopped by the barrier of the walls surface. Sissy looked at me as if pleading desperately to be released back into my arms. Then—from out of the press of faces—a vile black hand shot out and seized her!

Screaming her name, I lunged at the wall but the hand pulled her back. I could hear laughter that taunted and tormented me. Furious, I slammed my body into the cursed barrier, my hands scratching and pounding on the wall—till I tore the skin from them and left bloody stains on the white plaster! I screamed and gnashed my teeth till my mouth was foaming—but for naught. My angel, my darling Sissy was gone. I collapsed upon the wall weeping in my agony, till I collected my shattered senses enough to pull myself away.

When I returned to the rooms upstairs, my host greeted me. "I say, Mr. Poe; you look the worst for wear. Might I pour you a brandy?" I consented and shortly there after sat with the large man in his study.

"I sent my servant to watch over you. He heard your screams downstairs and informed me of the nature of your laments," my host began.

"I fear Mr. Poe," he said gravely, "that some misfortune might befall you if you continue this vigil you are keeping. That cellar dear friend—was the site of many abuses against the slaves that were boarded there. Some say that it has the curse of some lost African Witch-Man on it, but

I'm not taken to following that nonsense. I do know that it seems unhealthy to you and because of this, I will have to ask that you do not return. I fear greatly for your safety, Mister Poe. I will not have you come to harm here. Seek out this other lady, Elmira—as I believe the dainty creature is called. Place your heart with her. The dead must rest with their own kind sir, as your love must rest with the living."

With that he bade me to leave, and escorted me to the door. He wished me well and as I passed I could feel his hand slip something into my pocket. He then called for his coach to ferry me to my lodgings. I rode home in silence; but my head was filled with the horrifying image of my sweet Virginia's terror as she was dragged from me. Once back in my room, I threw myself upon my bed and slept—not unlike one who was dead.

I awoke the next morning at noon with my head pounding from the effects of the claret. Shortly my memory beckoned the return of my experiences with the horrors of the night before. I had found the vision I had long sought—and found it horrid. My illusions of my beloved Virginia waiting for me in Heaven were shattered by that cursed view. In that bitter moment, life had become repulsive to me, as the bitterness that ate at my soul would not find peace with what I had experienced. I knew that madness would creep into my brain and rot what was left of me if I allowed it. I had to forsake the vision and forget what I had seen.

I determined that the light of day might offer the succor I needed. To advance this theory, I took it upon myself to take a walk in hopes that this tonic of my divination would help me to resolve myself with the past night's events. In that it was at least partially successful, as my spirits were calmer by the time my evening activities came due.

I made use of some of the money Mr. B—had slipped into my pocket by indulging in the luxury of a carriage ride to the Mackenzie house; where I spent a restful evening partaking of their hospitality. They expressed a reluctance to see me leave Richmond, fearing for my health. Dr. Carter, who was a family friend, suggested that I should take a lengthy sojourn back in the south after my affairs in Baltimore and New York were concluded; indicating that it might restore some of my lost vigor. But I knew now, that I had to leave Richmond—possibly for forever. So I said my parting speeches and betook myself to the parlor. There I said a sweet goodbye to my dear sister Rosalie and then left.

As I found myself feeling the pangs of hunger, I took dinner in a restaurant on Main Street, where—during the course of the meal—the realization struck me that I had accidentally made off with Dr. Carter's cane. I resolved to send it to him, but in the course of conversation with two acquaintances that joined me briefly, I forgot about this and—after stopping to purchase a few items for the trip, carried it aboard my boat for Baltimore. I watched the lights of my beloved city disappear and braced myself for the tasks I need to complete in the next few days.

When I finally retired below deck to my cabin, I felt assured that I had left the sadness behind me. Thus absolved; I decided that at last I would get a good night's sleep.

I slept for at least a few hours, till I suddenly awoke to the tedious sound of my own watch ticking the time. But why should this familiar sound rouse me from a sound sleep? I stared at the clean whitewashed walls of my cabin and watched the shadows form and move upon the walls. In my mind, I fancied that they assumed shapes—But no! I dared not let this happen.

"But—why not?" I thought. The cursed house with its obscene cellar was miles away now. I had escaped its cruel grasp. Why should I care now for a simple flight of imagination?

It was then I heard the sound. It was a small kind of tapping that rattled low and soft to my ear. I wondered about it for a moment—could it be an apparition?—and then I realized what it was. The strange sound was the chattering of my own teeth! The humor of it took hold of my senses and I laughed like a madman. Eventually, my spirits calmed and reassured of my mind's counterfeit—I resolved to go back to sleep and—in a brief time—my effort was successful.

After another (was it an hour?) I again was awakened. For a few seconds I wondered what it was that had disturbed me. Then, before my fuddled mind could recall—I heard a voice!

"It must be just a crewman on late watch," I assured myself, "or perhaps the young couple who occupied the next cabin was indulging in late night gossip." I lay still for awhile congratulating myself on my deduction—and it happened again! A high feminine voice called out; a voice that had a faint, but definite lisp.

VIRGINA! By blessed God, I knew that sound. Anxiously—I waited to hear again that dulcet call that was so familiar to my ears. My sweet love, my Sissy had followed me on my trip. But no my shattered sense of reason insisted—Virginia was dead and buried. It could not be her. It was then, that my fearful eyes saw her aspect upon the wall of my cabin. There!—her face portrayed in shadow—It was her!

I watched helplessly, as she stood with hands wringing in anguish, so lost, so untouchable. Could any sight be more cruel? I was helpless to succor her—or to hold her tear stained face in my embrace. My soul screamed with the torment of this vision. "Why Virginia—why do you follow and torment me?"

Then, (when I could stand it no longer) I reached next to my bed and lifted a bottle of cheap whiskey that I had purchased before boarding. To what Hellish depths my torment sank, I know not. Hungrily, I drank the fiery brew till Virginia's screams disappeared and the entire world went black into sweet oblivion.

When I again awoke, I found myself upright, the result of being supported by a man who identified himself a Mr. Walker. Upon asking the day and state of affairs, he informed me that he had found me in a gutter dressed only in my breeches and a thin shirt—which upon my inspection I determined was not my own. As to more information he was at a loss. Mr. Walker suggested that I must have disembarked in the state of dress I was found in—due to excessive drunkenness, for I was without baggage or even a penny to call my own—save only for the Malacca cane that even now I gripped tightly in my hand. The gentleman assumed that I had been transported and used by pollsters to cast multiple votes—as there was an election going on, and I had been found near a polling place—Ryan's 4th ward.

I found that I was in a truly sorry state—I was shivering, and quite unable to stand up on my own. I expressed my gratitude to Mr. Walker and pressed upon him the need to contact my friend Dr. Snodgrass and inform him of my dilemma. This he readily agreed with and sent a messenger to the doctor shortly after he had conveyed me to his own home.

I do not remember much for the next few days, as my fever and delirium seemed to cause me to drift back and forth between the conscious and unconscious world. I remember Snodgrass examining me and requesting if I had knowledge of where my belongings went. Another time I heard his associate, Dr. Moran questioned my sanity, as he disclosed to Snodgrass that he had heard me speaking to spectral and imaginary objects on the walls.

During a brief moment of wakefulness, I inquired about the state of my being. Dr, Snodgrass informed me that I had been found on Wednesday and that I had been unconscious for two days.

I informed him that I had left Richmond and did not know how long ago that was or even if my baggage had made it aboard. Then he said a peculiar thing. He asked my wife's health. In my delirium, I wondered if he had also seen my sweet Virginia. I replied that I thought I had left her in Richmond, a response for which the doctor looked upon me strangely. I would have said more save that I again blacked out.

I awoke to the darkness of night in a small room I did not recognize. By my bed, a small candle was burning on a poorly crafted wood table. I found that I could not move my arms and soon realized that it was because two nurses had held me fast—for how long? My body was soaked with sweat from fever. My mind cleared and I asked the time. The younger of the two nurses, whose name was Judith answered that it was late, near ten. I had been in delirium for many hours.

I relaxed upon the bed and absorbed the atmosphere of the room which I soon realized had to be within a hospital. It was small and plain with just a crucifix above the headboard to give it decoration. The nurses who guarded me spoke but little. Yet there was not silence in the room, for I soon found that my head rung with the sound of strange voices. I looked from one nurse to the other and saw that neither one contributed to the sound, which rose from everywhere, as if a multitude were trying to speak at once. Bravely, I smiled at the young women who held me, and upon seeing my calmer state, they released their grips upon my arms. A sense of anticipation lightened my spirit, because I knew now that somehow with the sound, that in some short time my beloved must come for me.

I gazed at the dim wall of the small room and very shortly thereafter, the candles flickering light revealed that indeed—she was there. Ah, Virginia, plump and lovely as I remembered, she was standing with her arms reaching out to me. I called to her and was elated to find that she smiled back at me. I knew it then, that my fevered brain would soon find rest. I half rose to reach to her, but my strength was not equal to this. "My lovely Sissy," I whispered.

Then suddenly—the dark hand with its cruel taloned fingers grabbed her yet again! She screamed and called to me as she disappeared into the rough fabric of the wall. I could see her struggles as her poor body was clutched within the fiend's grasp. I tore my sheets in frustration. "Reynolds!" I cried. "For God's sake—why did you show me this path of pain and torment?" For my cries and pleadings, there was naught but cool silence and a low deadly laughter that tormented my soul.

It was then that I saw it. As I looked deep into the wall, the thing emerged from the shadows—its horrid voice calling to me. I could see the face—that had so long hidden its dark bestial profile from me. I shrank from the dark brooding eyes that were ringed in white chalk—the wasted countenance that spoke to me of the grave.

"Do I know you, fiend! What has Hell sent to call me?" The horror of its hideous aspect shook what life I had left into fragments that crumbled as I felt my shattered soul being drawn in deadly fascination to the cruel face on the wall. What demon from Hell greeted me here?

147

But wait—no, the face grew still clearer—I could now make out its painted Negroid features it bore. They were clearly those of an African slave. It spoke to me as if whispering from far away.

"Do you not recall the first place you saw us, we who are shades that passed from the mortal thread?"

I nodded my head and answered. "Yes I do. It was that accursed wall in Richmond."

"Cursed is right," the apparition said. "Remember that dismal place was a holding cell for slaves brought from the dark lands of Africa that were ours. We poor creatures were lost—Lost to home, to family—to country. Amongst them was a Juju man of great power. He used his magic's to create that in that wall, a window where he and his poor suffering kin could see the souls of their loved ones—and thus gain a measure of succor from the Hell they were stolen and sold to. I am that juju man—or what Hell has allowed to continue of his spirit.

You have stolen a look into a gateway—a path that souls take to journey towards Heavens rest—or Hells torment. It was your insufferable need that called your sweet Virginia back—Back to bear the pain of your longing. That is not right, white man, for your woman's place is in Paradise. For such as you and I—a different fate beckons us."

As I struggled to understand his meaning, his visage began to fade. I thought that I heard my brother's voice cry out but, the sound was lost as darkness enveloped first the savage—then me.

I had hoped in my folly to be absolved of my sins, but now I knew that it was not was not to be. My efforts had borne bitter fruit. It was not Heaven—but Hell that beckoned to me to come home. My Virginia truly was lost—as well as any hope for my soul's redemption.

I cried out in despair—and the darkness cared not as it took me. I gasped for air and was rewarded with none. I felt smothered, as Death cocooned me within its despicable cloak. I cried out once more in anguish and with my last forced breath uttered, "Lord, have mercy on my poor soul!"

The last night, Mr. Poe seemed tormented, though by what, or how I am left but to guess. It was clear that in his delusion he conversed with something neither I, nor my fellow nurse saw or witnessed. At the end he cried out and struggled as if something held and choked him. Then he spoke his final words and expired, to be taken into the tender bosom of our Lord.

A final note: when Mr. Poe's body was taken to be cleaned for burial, it was found that buried within his bedding was concealed a small object. How it got there, I am at a loss to say. However, upon examination by Dr. Snodgrass it was determined that this object was a cheap wooden bead— of a kind commonly given in trade for African slaves.
Judith Arnold; October 8[th,] 1849.

JASMINE IS THE SCENT I LOVE...

"There is something about floral scents that adds freshness to the dank wetness of an alley. More so, on a rainy night like this," Cleo says as she crushes her victim's crotch with her spiked heel.

He sees her figure offers as a stark black shadow against the reflection of the neon white gleam of the streetlights in the puddles on the asphalt.

"You know," she tells him, "it so hides the smell of the freshly dead as well."

Cleo sticks her tongue out at her victim. It's double pierced and hanging from her lips like a dog's in heat.

"I like Jasmine, Don't you?" The pain she is causing is making her horny. Purrrrrrrrr...

Her victim cringes and stares at her with eyes that are almost shut from repeated contact with her six inch heels. He is small and very ordinary in an I-just-stopped-to-pick-up-something-from-the-drug-store kind of way. Doesn't matter; He's rat meat now and he knows it. As he sits and shivers in his own urine, he whimpers.

"What's that fool? You gonna tell me that you can access that ATM and get big bucks to save you?"

Viciously she groin kicks the man again.

"Not what I'm after tonight, Sweet Meats. Right now I'm here for pleasure."

*

The sound of screams is not an uncommon one in the backstreets. People hear but don't listen, people know-but don't tell. No one comes near to the wretched puddle of what is left after Cleo finishes. It makes no sense to get involved. It's just the way of the street'.

No one cares, as the tall black shadow wipes the gore off her spike heels on the corpse she leaves for the cops to find.

*

Cleo scowls, her little sister is waiting as she walks into their flat, pausing to throw a cheap watch and a wallet on the coffee table. The wallet looks thin.

"Not much out there?" Jenna's question is to Cleo's back, as she removes her halter top and heads for the shower.

"Just some dumb fuck that made a late call at the Rexal. Hardly worth the damage he did to my shoes. He was kind of squishy."

Cleo silently curses her self. Yeah, you dumb bitch, why didn't you go for the extra cash? You knew we needed it.

Cleo grimaces as she checks her bloodstained clothes before tossing them into the hamper by the bathroom. She steps into the shower and turns on the hot stuff. Cleo says something else, but the sound of water and steam masks the words from her sister's ear.

Jenna shrugs. She knows her sister is getting too heavy into the 'kicking ass' thing. That shit could draw attention even here in the French Quarter. She pulls the money out of the wallet and counts it. There are blood traces on the cash. It is becoming too obvious that money is not the most important thing her sister is after.

Cleo emerges from the shower and towels off, pausing only to scratch at the panther tattooed on her shoulder.

"Don't do that!" Jenna says, "Jeanue said it would infect or something."

"The shit itches, but ain't it a cool cat?" Cleo dries off the head of the Black Panther. Its eyes glow a cool yellow in the light.

151

"Jeanue said Kitty is my totem, and he should know. He's into that magic stuff. She's my power and you know...well, you've got to feed the kitty."

Jenna stares at it, marveling at the detail. Jeanue, the Haitian over at the parlor is a master with the needle. His are the finest inks, the most detailed art. Jenna's own body bore several examples of his skill.

"So it's done now?"

"The last part was finished this evening, like just before I saw this creep. Damn Sis, I can almost hear it purr!" Cleo looks at the wallet.

"Crap, I was hoping he was carrying enough to pay for this. Hand me that shit sis."

Jenna passes her the joint and then reaches into the little box on the coffee table and pulls out another. As she does, a bit of watery red catches her eye.

"Fuck, Cleo, you opened it up. That panther is bleeding."

Cleo dabs at the blood with her towel.

"Naw, this belongs to the creep. Thought I washed it all off."

"Better be careful girl. You might get infected or something."

"Sure Sis," Cleo says and spreads herself across the couch. Droplets of water fall from her body to stain the couch. Cleo is beyond caring. She is asleep.

*

Two nights later Cleo walks the strip looking for hookers to roll. Luck's not with her, as word is out that she is a predator.

"Kitty is hunting," she coos.

A couple of pimps had been heard discussing how to off the tall redhead, and had even gone as far as offering a bounty; but the truth is, nobody has the equipment to act on it. She's 'Queen Tiger' and nobody messes with that.

Cleo walks off the strip, and heads into the backstreet tenement sections, hoping to catch a cheating husband, or some other fool that would slink around at this late hour. The fog is rising from the sewers and Cleo reaches into her jacket for her perfume to mask the stench. Jasmine always brings a sense of calm to her. She spritzes a bit on her collar before returning the bottle to her pocket.

A movement makes her turn and look. It's an alley cat, who looks at her with wary eyes. *You recognize of the same breed of cat.* Cleo sings softly, "Kitty-Kitty."

Up ahead, she sees a young couple necking on a balcony. Too high up to be a good target. The guy's hands are fumbling with the girl's bra. *He's to busy to care.*

So instead, Cleo goes to the vehicle parked in front. *Must be his.* She runs her hand along the hood. It is still warm. From her jacket, Cleo pulls out a long tool. This she inserts into the door of the car and twists. With a sharp click, the lock breaks. She looks up but the guy is still into doing the girl. It's safe.

Once inside the car, Cleo laughs. The young dude necking upstairs is a dealer. Under the seat there are several bags of blow. That at least is worth the trouble, she reasons. Cleo harvests the stuff into her pockets and the roll of bills that was there with it. The night had suddenly turned profitable.

She gets out of the car and stretches. Cleo feels an irritating soreness in her shoulder.

"Fucking tattoo...still itches." she growls and then marvels at the sound. It was very 'Cat'.

"Damn! That sounded good," she laughs. Then she stops and looks upstairs. The sound of her voice might have been heard. The dealer upstairs probably has a gun and there was no sense in facing that down. Not when there was plenty of good flesh to eat.

Why did I think that?

It's quiet, so Cleo walks back into the shadows keeping low. Before too long, she's back on the strip. She finds a newsstand she can shelter near. Safe under the shadow of its overhang, Cleo pulls out the roll of bills and counts them.

"Good, Mama your rent is cool for the next few. I can take this shit home and Jenna and I will party."

Cleo directs her tracks to a cab. The driver knows her—and her reputation, but he has good safety glass behind his seat and a loaded Glock beside him. He drives her home and accepts the crumpled bills she tosses through the slot without comment. Cleo departs the cab at her building, goes upstairs, bathes and falls asleep in her room.

Cleo dreams of cats and blood. In her sleep, she purrs low and easy. On her shoulder, the panther stands guard.

*

The music beats with both a loudness and monotony that rocks the senses of the redhead, as she dances mechanically to the band. Cleo did not feel all that in the groove. The guy her sister has fixed her up with is a loser and not even worth the quick trip to the bathroom of the club for some action. Cleo feels hot, itchy and uncomfortable. She decides it is time to book. She leaves her date on the dance floor, flipping him a finger when he protests. Jenna follows her.

"What's up Sis, you dumping the guy?"

"He's limp, Jenna. Besides, I feel wasted," Cleo says as she applies more Jasmine to her skin. She cringes because it burns.

"Your shoulder still bothering you Sis?" Jenna takes the bottle.

"Like, you really need to see a doctor on that, Cleo. Let me look."

Jenna pulls the black jacket clear and gasps.

"Shit, there's blood on your jacket. That rash looks bad-and it's spreading. If you want, I can get George over at the free clinic to get you some salve or something."

"Then I better go out and raise some funds. Even their medicine costs money," Cleo says. In the back of her mind she senses Kitty is awake.

"You sure you shouldn't just go home, Cleo?" Jenna touches her sister's face, "You look sweaty."

"Our bills don't get paid, Jenna!" she snaps, pulling away. "Unless I do this, we have to go back to peddling your sweet ass!"

"I could do that..." Jenna says in a small voice.

"No way Sis, I don't want you getting some disease." Cleo says, slapping her sister on the side of her head.

"Ok Sis, like I'm sorry OK?"

Jenna cries. She's scared and Cleo feels like shit.

"Yeah, me too, Sister Bug," Cleo says and pulls her jacket back on.

"See ya around two maybe. Gotta feed the kitty, ya know."

Cleo kisses her sister's cheek and then ducks out of the bathroom towards the back of the club.

*

The street is wet, which suits Cleo fine. That means less people will be out there to see her. She walks down the street unzipping her blouse to show more cleavage. *Ok creeps, the bait's out and I'm ready!*

Cleo walks down the street like a cat on the prowl. Shaking off her tiredness, she adds some wiggle to her walk. *Gotta look like a pro.* Sure enough, Cleo gets about two blocks when a SUV pulls up and the passenger window rolls down.

"Hey, bitch, want some action?"

Cleo looks into the window and there is this guy, kind of Italian looking and dumpy. As he talks, the guy wipes his hand across the greasy black hair that he is obviously vain about.

The creep looks like he has cash...*Cash for Jenna.* Cleo smiles.

"Some place private, honey, I don't want to end the night in jail."

The guy opens the door for her, quickly shoving some magazines onto the floor. Cleo notes that they are pornographic. *Warmed up are we?*

Cleo laughs as she sees the embarrassment on the Italian's face. He knows she's seen them and is uncomfortable.

"It's OK honey, I look at those too. Doesn't it get you...hot?"

She turns to him, making her blouse open wider. "Let's go play," she purrs.

A few blocks down, the Italian guy pulls into a blind alley and parks. His hands have been busy the whole time and Cleo lets him explore. She is tired and distracted by the itch, which seems to have spread to the side of her face. Unconsciously, she scratches and her fingers feel damp.

"Let's do it against the wall," she says, pointing at the brick wall outside, "It feels too hot in here."

The Italian shrugs and pulls her closer.

"Outside, Ass, I mean...honey," Cleo says and jerks open her door. The guy, looking sheepish, fumbles with his pants as he gets out of the SUV. His zipper is down and Cleo sees him tuck himself back in. Creep...

Then he's got her against the wall and has his hands inside her blouse. Cleo gets ready. A growl rises in her throat.

"Damn bitch, you're wet!" The guy says and pulls his hands out. In the dim light of a street lamp he can see they are bloody."

"What the F—" he says, grossed out by the mess. He looks at her face, and his expression betrays his shock.

Cleo decides she has had enough and brings her knee up hard into the Italian's groin. He stumbles back against the wall. She spin kicks him in the head but the blow feels weak to her. *Not enough...*

Cleo feels pain now like her whole face is raw. Her legs feel like the bones aren't right. Something (sweat?) gets in her eyes. She hears the SUV back out of the alley and tear up the street.

"Kitty...Kitty..." she moans as she falls back against the brick wall and slides to the ground. *It's not nice to scratch.* Cleo tries to scream, but the pain is too much and the taste of blood is heavy on her tongue as she feels it drool from her mouth. *Got to feed Kitty.*

*

Jenna arrives at the hospital and is directed to the morgue. Inside the clean white room, she sees a gurney with a bloodstained sheet covering someone.

"I have to warn you miss," the coroner says. "She's quite a mess. Odd, this is the second case like this I have seen this week."

He hands Jenna a mask.

"Don't touch anything or we'll have to quarantine you."

"What do you mean Doc?"

Jenna braces herself. She knows this isn't going to be pretty and the fear is making her choke.

"I really shouldn't let you in here, possible flesh eating bacteria," the coroner replies.

"We had a man brought in last week whose body was almost consumed by it."

The coroner takes Jenna by the hand and says. "Miss, you might want to think of other means of identifying your sister. Otherwise, we will have to go on dental records. We do have her wallet. That's how we found you."

The coroner pulls up the sheet. Jenna gags at the smell and the fact that the body has no face-just hamburger. Her hands look raw.

"Does anything look like your sister?"

Jenna looks at the body on the gurney and turns to the coroner.

"That's not my sister," Jenna says. "Look at her shoulder. The cat is gone."

"What cat? Look, are you sure? There's no finger prints left on her. We really don't want to spend the money on DNA testing some homeless-"

"Look at her right shoulder!" Jenna says. "There should be a panther tattoo. My sister had a rash there too and this girl doesn't."

The coroner lifts the body from the examination table and wipes the blood away with a tissue. The pale white skin of her shoulder is clean and unblemished.

"Guess your right," he says. "We'll keep looking."

Jenna walks out of the morgue feeling relieved. Cleo is out there somewhere, but at least she wasn't there. Jenna sobs as she thinks of the body back there on the gurney. *That poor girl, what a horrible way to go.*

Jenna feels dirty, so she pulls out her sister's perfume bottle that she borrowed. She spritzes some and rubs it into her skin. *Jasmine is always so fresh.*

Jenna walks with her hands clenching and unclenching as she runs her nails over her itchy palms. "Kitty-Kitty," she whispers. In the back of her mind she hears it.

Purrrrrrrr...

PARTS IS PARTS

Lenny could hear the Parts Carts coming down the damp rough cobbled road from the front. He licked his fingers to remove the grease from the bucket of leftover fried chicken that had been his lunch. Food breaks were where you got them in this detail.

He chucked the basket with the rest of his meal into the trash and donned his plastic gloves as the first body cart drove up.

"Hey Lenny," the driver said. "Slim pickings in the pumpkin patch today. Gonna make pumpkin pie out of this? Looks more like Pizza."

To illustrate his point, the driver hefted a bloody head. Its yellowish skinned face was slashed into bloody tatters. "Even kind of looks cheesy, don't it?"

The driver laughed and unhooked the cart from the line he was towing. Most of his load was going to the med station closer to headquarters. Lenny ignored his prattle. The cart men always seemed to have the worst sense of humor.

"Leaving me the tailings again, Bosco?"

"Naw, these are harvest fresh. They just got too itchy on the battlefield."

Lenny waved the driver on and then checked the load. The carts were always presorted, so what came back was usually better than what was left on the field. This one was loaded with craniums. Some heads were only partial, others nearly intact. The 'best' still had faces...kind of.

Lenny sorted through them, his sharp eyes looking for the most salvageable skulls. Most were just bloody pulp, with barely a brain. One with remarkable blue eyes caught his stare. The eyes still were clear, almost living.

159

"Pretty damn fresh," he observed, "Must be a non combatant."

Civilians occasionally got caught up in the fighting. When one was recognizable, it was supposed to be sent back to its family. However, with the shortage of fresh material, few—if any, made it to that point. Lenny tossed the head onto the conveyor that led to the hospital tent.

The rest of the heads were unsalvageable. Lenny marked the cart with a red 'X'. Those skulls were to be ground down and sent off to be sold as fertilizer.

"One way or another, ya serve," he muttered.

A cart full of torsos came next. Sticking out of a butt at the top of the pile was a hand posed making an obscene gesture. It seemed Tory over in collecting, had a sick sense of humor.

*

It had been like this for the last six months. The 'Zombie War' as some called it, was fought endlessly. Days and nights of combat, who cared? Since humans no longer fought, casualties had become meaningless. Just patch em back together and send them out to meet the enemy's next wave of rebuilts. Problem was, with no human combatants, the supply of spare parts was getting scarce.

The governments had tried for a while, scavenging graveyards for replacement parts. This worked, till families started cremating their love ones to keep them off the battlefield.

Lately, the forces sent out from either side were so worn, rebuilt, and patched that it was a hard guess to tell which limbs had fought on which side-and how many times.

*

Dr. March tapped Lenny on the shoulder.

"How's it going?"

"Shit, Doc…this is getting depressing," Lenny held up a severed leg. "You can see the stitch marks on this thing. It's been out there at least twenty times."

Grayish ichors dripped down from the once finely muscled stump. Lenny tossed it back into cart, cursing when it splattered black gore on the doctor's white shoes. The doctor bent and wiped it off with a Kleenex, cursing at the stained laces. Embarrassed, Lenny couldn't think of something, so he said,

"Ever notice how it kills the shine?"

The doctor said nothing. When he stood up, he turned his attention back to the cart. So many pieces in the leg cart were fragmented and rotting that it looked nothing more, than like a large pot of spoiled stew. The stench of it was even worse. Dr. March reached into his pocket for the menthol salve he always carried. He applied some to his own nose and then offered it to Lenny.

"No thanks, Doc. It just makes the smell worse when it wears off."

"We may need to just write that load off, Lenny. Any luck on the other carts?"

"I found nine good craniums between the two earlier cart deliveries. That gives us thirty four for the day."

"We may make quota, if their all salvageable."

"Hey, remember this guy Doc?" Lenny held up a head, wiping the gore off with his pocket hankie. In life, the man must have been good natured and probably well liked. Even though huge scars crossed his face like centipedes with oozing legs, the cheerful smile on his once handsome face still remained intact.

"1139-Joe," Dr. March observed. "Look how the stitching held up from the…what was it? Oh yes, the forth time we used him. Good solid material there. I think we can use him again."

"Good, I'll send him to prep with the others, Doc.

161

Behind the carts, came the others. The Zombie troops filed in, torn battered frames staggering along, most being minus an arm, or upper torso. *Chassis looking for new parts,* Lenny decided.

No different were they than the car he was rebuilding at home. He thought for a moment of his beloved T-Bird. It was things like that which kept you sane. Lenny flexed his hands like he was steering her, hot and new on the road. Easier to fix than the dead things he sorted.

Lenny puffed on his cigarette. *Shit, here comes the junk.*

The last lot of zombies to stagger by was by far the worst. These were far gone that there was nothing to them, but a line of walking hangers supporting remnants of parts to be scavenged. Even minus the head, they were still animated to the point where they could be stood up and sent home. Some of these wrecks were nothing but ragged skeletons, dusted with Zombie Powder to keep them animate. Chain-linked together, they were lashed to one of the walking dead with a still intact brain, to act as guide.

As they marched past, Lenny saw one with just half a spine and two legs. *Who would waste Zombie Powder on that?*

One of the cart drivers called over for a smoke. Lenny lit him one and flipped it. The driver, through long practice, caught it on the fly.

"You know," the driver said, whose name was Bucky, "This would have been over years ago, if they hadn't taken away their guns."

Lenny thought about that. "Bucky, the brass stopped giving the zombies weapons capable of firing, because they said it wasn't cost effective to have them armed. You know bullets alone won't kill. Besides, they couldn't prevent them from shooting civilians and officers they stumbled upon." Bucky laughed.

"Hey man, I know a couple of bitches I'd love to see ride zombies."

162

"Too messy for me, with those clubs they carry. And the metal talons attached to their fingers, just too much shredding to for me to enjoy."

"Shit Lenny, I just gave my slut a skull cap. Man is she gonna freak, when she finds out what it came off."

For protection, each zombie was sent out to battle with a skull cap to shield the brain area from damage. In a fight, that cap had to be removed before a kill strike could be delivered. Lenny had stacks of those caps. He had heard that the discards were sold on line as soup bowls in Asia. Lenny debated testing it out, though the idea had the ring of an urban legend. He could use the dough.

"Shit Bucky, even if they had guns, we still would have to piece em back together. I got a family at home that needs this check, so I'm not pissin' about ending this war soon."

Lenny heard screams from the operating room. Chucking the arm he was holding he raced for the tent. Before he got there, Lenny knew what he would find. Sure enough, when he and Bucky burst in, Lenny saw Dr. March and his assistant trying to pull a zombie off what was left of the scrub nurse. Zombies rarely bit and this one was no exception. Still it was amazing how much flesh could be torn off a living human by their metal claws. The nurse was more than gutted, she was practically shredded.

"F—king-cross-stitched-piece-of-junk!" March said as between the three of them, they managed to pull the zombie off its victim and strap it back to the table.

"Damn it, Lenny, did you check the tattoos to make sure this was one of ours?"

"I thought I did, but some of them are like, pretty necrotic. It makes it hard to read the numbers off their rotting skin...it turning black an all."

"Well, you let one get through. This just cost me a good scrub nurse."

"Sorry Doc," Lenny knew he had screwed up. But then an idea hit him.

"But hey, we can use her for replacements, right?"

March looked at Lenny evilly, "You cold blooded moron, she's got family. They'll want her remains."

"For...what, so they can cremate them?"

"It's their legal right."

"Screw that, Doc. Look at the line outside. I say parts, is parts. We can rebuild at least six fighters with what's left of her. How long has it been since we've had new meat, Doc? Dammit, I call this opportunity."

Voicing a prayer under his breath, the doctor paused. Then he turned to his other nurse. "Strip her down and wash her, Miss Chappell. Give her jewelry to one of the matrons." The doctor lowered his voice.

"Ok Lenny. We'll say she wandered too close to the battle and got eaten. You better hope that flies."

Lenny nodded and then bumped the driver who was staring with interest in the dead nurse's boobs. "Come on, Bucky." Lenny said as he grabbed his collar and dragged the man outside.

"She was hot, man."

"Your one thoroughly f—ked up dude."

"Naw man, just know a good piece of ass, when I see it. She is hot. Did you see those smooth legs? You could run your hands from here to there on them."

"Wasn't looking at it, Bucky, I..." Lenny paused in mid thought. *Smooth?*

*

It was kind of embarrassing for sure, when Lenny walked in and slipped a 'C' note to Miss Chappell. At first she didn't get it and got pissed off about not being that kind of girl. Then Lenny told her it was for her college's limb. The nurse lost it and barfed under the table. Still cash, was cash. She carved the thigh to Lenny's specifications. Chappell questioned him with her eyes, as she wrapped what was left of the thigh in plastic and placed it in the refrigerated satchel Lenny carried.

"God, I don't want to know," she whispered as he went out the door.

*

The last zombie tottered a bit as it staggered into formation to be returned to combat. When the line moved forward, it stalled. Lenny kicked it in the ass and it restarted, following the rest.

The doctor emerged from the operating tent. He looked tired.

"Did we make thirty four, today, Doc?" Lenny sat astride his Yasuki 2098. Its chrome sides were speckled with gore.

"The doctor nodded. "We made quota...barely."

Lenny adjusted the grips on his motorcycle.

"Uh...Lenny?"

The Doctor was staring at him hard. Unconsciously, Lenny ran his hand over the cycle's saddle bag.

"Lenny, by any chance do you know what happened to the scrub nurse's left thigh? That driver that was with you was looking at it."

"Bad news there," Lenny said, "it turned out there was a tumor in the bone. Had to chuck it."

"The doctor shook his head and turned back to his tent where he kept his booze. It was obvious that he did not believe it. "Better run it through me, if you see something like that. You could be mistaken."

"Will do, Doc," Lenny said. He hated lying to the doctor. He knew Dr. March could check the nurse's records, if he chose to. But he wouldn't. They had all been through too much for it to matter.

But it hurt Lenny's pride to know that. Worse, it made him look like a sicko. Lenny knew sometimes men, like Bucky for example, took home

165

'souvenirs' for entertainment, while they watched their videos. But he had a different need. This part might just fill it.

*

Lenny ran his hand over the hood of his classic T-Bird. The lacquered finish felt like cool sex, to his exploring hand. He looked under the hood. Its spotless beauty made him sigh.

"Your one hot lady," he said.

She was almost complete. He had scavenged the funds to recover the rearview mirror from a collector in Fresno. It gleamed like gold and silver in the work lights. Now the only flaw remaining was the steering wheel. Its leather covering was old, stained...worn out.

"Gotta fix you, baby," Lenny said. He opened the case and laid the thigh on the table.

Lenny had tried for months to find the right quality leather for the job. None of the catalogs on, or off line, carried it. Lenny measured the skin of the thigh and smiled. Even with shrinkage, there was more than enough.

"Well, parts is parts," Lenny said as he began to cut.

SUNLIGHT

The heat of the day was incredible, even for a shady street in this small village in Kenya. It was one of those cloudless nightmares of blinding sunlight that when combined with a deadness of atmosphere, could fry the sweat off a man's body in minutes. The dust that was almost always shifting on the dirt road lay like flat powder for lack of a breeze to stir it.

Even the flies, the constant torturers of the African savannah, seemed to realize that it was just too hot to even attempt to trouble even the scruffy old dog that was tucked into the darkest corner of the corral at the entrance to the town. They sought their own relief, by gathering in the dark corners of the shabby tin shingled roof of the hotel, which was the tallest building on the street. It did not help that the straw and mud shacks that made up the village were all white-washed and so reflected the sun with an eye burning brilliance.

It was one of those days when no one ventured out from the dubious coolness of the shaded doorways to walk the deserted streets. Most the men sat grimly waiting for the relief of late afternoon under the slow twirling ceiling fans that hung from the ceiling of the only bar in town. As they sat and drank, the men told stories and pretended not to feel the heat.

There was however, one person, a lady, whom at this particular moment was standing out on the street. Though the woman was white, and with no escort, she commanded no interest from the patrons of the bar. The locals would have told you that such a sight was no surprise, for she was a foreigner and as everyone knows, foreigners are prone to eccentricities. However, it seemed like no one even noticed she was there.

From the look of her, you could tell she had come a long way on foot. This in itself was also not surprising, as the nearest train station was just over six miles from town. Her appearance though was remarkable.

167

At over six feet in height barefoot, the woman was tall even for a foreigner. Her very thin frame was clothed in what was once a white lace dress that could easily have passed for a wedding gown. Now it was torn and soiled as if she had rolled around in the dirt. She appeared young though her disheveled state made the determination of her age difficult. On a better day you would have noticed that her hair was blonde and curly. Now it hung in dirty ringlets, except where the sweat and blood had matted it to her skin. The lady's cheekbones were high and the large blue eyes spoke of someone who was used to the more polite atmosphere of high society. Now her eyes showed only extreme weariness, and something else...Fear.

*

Rousing from his nap, Mulumbe sleepily looked out from his table at Jamaal's Bar. A Wakamba, he was from a hunting people, masters of the bow. He was shorter than most of the men around him as they were Bantu. Though he had come to live in this border village, he still retained the skills his father taught him on the Savanna.

He saw the woman alone in the street. He waved to her and signaled that she step inside. The woman stared at him, but did not move. Curious at the woman's reluctance to come in from the heat, Mulumbe roused himself and began to study the odd stranger.

Easily, he read the woman's story from the tattered image she presented. She had been afoot for quite a while. Obviously she had either fallen off the train or had been separated from some group venture into the wilds for which she was not dressed. The blood in her hair and clothes suggested that the thorny brambles that littered the savannah had done their work. Mulumbe guessed she was likely in shock.

Mulumbe wiped the sweat from his smooth ebony face and considered the situation. The woman obviously was lost. How and where she came from would have to be determined. That she (or her family) had money, was assured by the presence of a cameo at her throat and a large gold ring that looked to be of no small value on her hand. How she had made it to the village without being robbed or falling victim to the slavers, the rebels, or the lions, spoke of better than normal luck.

168

The Gods favor this lost one, he mused.

Here then was opportunity. Not in the sense of any altruistic leaning, but more in line with the possible reward that might come from a grateful family, or friends of this lady in trouble. Mulumbe quickly finished his drink, flipped a coin to the barkeep and then smoothly moved thru the crowded bar till he reached the street...And found himself alone.

"Hey young son, what you do there in that sun?" Mulumbe turned to see his friend Kirakangano, an ancient Masai who was standing in a nearby doorway, shading his eyes from the glare. Though his traditional red blanket hung from his gaunt frame like from a hanger; at nearly seven feet in height, his raw muscular frame was still impressive. Kirakangano had one peculiarity though. On his head rested a tall stovepipe hat that his father had received as a gift from a missionary, many years ago. The old silk hat never left his head. That hat was a rare concession to the 'white world' that had so dramatically changed his home.

"Why for you hanging out in dis heat?" The old man's English was heavily flavored by his Masai accent.

"I came out to see the tall white lady that was here. Did you see where she went?"

"I see nobody but one hot Wakamba. Come friend. It be too hot for men to stand. Let's go back to my kraal and drink."

"All right my friend," answered Mulumbe in Af-Maxaa, the lingua-franca of the region. "That is if you'll stop trying to kill my ears with your English."

Kirakangano looked at his friend and shrugged. Then he answered Mulumbe in the same language. "I have to keep practicing if I am going to keep track of my affairs. There is way too much foreign influence around here, son."

Kirakangano bent and scanned the dirt road, his eyes squinting against the sun's glare. "There's not a track here that looks right for a white woman. Are you sure you haven't been drinking too much of that cheap beer they serve in there?

"Not I, old man, just stepped in to drink something cool, so I had an Orange Coss."

169

Mulumbe shook his head. "I saw her clearly, a tall blonde woman with blue eyes. She was standing here! Don't you be telling me I'm seeing Bantu ghosts, or something like that? She must have turned down a side street when my back was turned."

Kirakangano laughed and throwing his arm around his friend's shoulder turned him toward the road from town.

"Now see my friend that is the problem. Drinking that foreign sugar water is not for a man. It dulls your senses, and now you let a pretty girl get away.

"Come now; let us be off to where I can share with you a man's drink! My wife has been too friendly lately and I tire of her. Perhaps later, you can work off that passion with her and take your mind off your own lost lady."

Mulumbe laughed and smiled at his friend. A foreigner would have been shocked at his suggestion, not realizing the old Masai was being polite and even paying special homage to his friend by offering to share his wife with a non Masai 'outsider'. Kirakangano laughed, slapping Mulumbe on the back. As the old man began to spin a story the two of them left for the Masai village a few miles to the south of town.

*

Kirakangano was a rarity among the Masai in that he had allowed a certain amount of western comfort to invade his home. He had evolved an affinity for German dark beer which he bought with funds raised working with Mulumbe as a guide for tourists. Kirakangano regretted the fact that he did not have refrigeration (or for that matter any electricity) in his hut to cool the beverage, so they drank his beer warm. As they did, Kirakangano regaled his friend with more tales of his exploits as a Moran, as the young warrior/hunters of the Masai are called. Mulumbe had heard most of the tales many times before. What made them enjoyable was that Masai did not lie about such things. Mulumbe sat and listened to the stories, marveling at the feats of pure courage that the moran had performed as a matter of course.

Kirakangano had a claim to fame that was a remarkable distinction even for a Masai. He was one of the very few Moran still living that could claim the title of 'Melombuki'.

170

This highly sought for honor could only be obtained in a lion hunt. A man proved his worth exhibiting his courage by grabbing and holding a lion by the base of its tail, until the other moran could finish it. A moran that held this title had to be willing to fight anything.

As he listened to the old Masai's story, Mulumbe pulled a pack of Tick-Tacks from his pocket and offered one to Kirakangano, who politely refused. "Still not used to our food," the ancient commented nodding towards the gourd on the ground in front of them that held a mixture of cow's blood and milk, which was the staple of a Masai diet.

"It is the after taste that I don't care for. It tastes a bit like a dead frog." Mulumbe shrugged and stretched—his arms his hands scraping the top of the low roof of the straw and mud hut. Kirakangano laughed and reaching for the gourd took a long drink before handing it to his wife to refill.

"It grows strong men though. Look at me! Seventy four summers and they still won't feed me to the lions." Mulumbe nodded respectfully.

The Masai had commonly left their aged out for the lions to dispose of until recent years, when the government made the practice illegal. Still, sometimes grandfathers and mothers disappeared into the night and everyone knew that was just the way of things. Men of Kirakangano's age were rare among the Masai.

*

As the sun set, Mulumbe bade his friend goodnight and left the kraal to walk back to town where he had rented a small house. He had planned to leave earlier, but found it impossible, as Kirakangano always managed to find a good excuse for telling one more amazing story. Darkness was not the time to be alone on the savannah and so Mulumbe hastened on his way. In the distance he could hear his friend and his wife laughing and realized that maybe the old man wasn't so tired after all.

The temperature was still warm, but the cool night air was starting to take the edge off the heat. Mulumbe began to whistle to himself as his steady tread made short work of the distance home.

171

It was times like this he thought, when the stars were just coming out from where the Gods kept them safe from the day, that he wondered if in fact they might be cruel. They came out and teased men with their beauty, distracting them, when it was time to be alert for the dangers of the night. Mulumbe decided that they must be feminine as they were tricksters and tempted men with their wiles.

He stopped suddenly, roused from his thoughts by the sound of a low guttural cough. There was a lion near by. He listened patiently, till the sound of movement gave him its location. Mulumbe smiled then, as he knew it was moving away. *Sweet night ladies...You did not get me this time.* He looked up and gave a wink to the wicked stars above him. Then he continued home.

Sleep came slowly to Mulumbe that night and brought strange dreams.

Somewhere off in the distance he could hear bells. He strained to see, but the mists over the savannah had not yet burned off with the light of day. Mulumbe could hear men's voices, foreign and strange. The words were unfamiliar to his ears. A frog jumped past his foot to land in the litter clumped under an acacia tree. He followed its track and there in the thorny branches close to the ground was a bit of ribbon. It was shredded and its pink color had been stained brown with the color of dried blood. He reached for it and then realized that he could not remove it with his hand. Mulumbe fumbled in his pockets till he found a pair of long scissors. They were dull and rusty but he knew that he had to cut the ribbon free. The sense of danger was strong upon him and he sawed...and sawed...and...

Mulumbe awoke to sound of scratching on his door. Groggy, he rose from his bed and staggered to the front window of his house. Looking down he saw an old dog chewing at the fleas that irritated him. His hind leg was twitching at the itch and as a result was scratching the door as well. The Wakamba yelled at the dog and instantly regretted it, as

172

his head began to throb with pain. In a low voice he cursed the Old Masai and his warm beer. This was going to be a major hangover.

Mulumbe stumbled to the small refrigerator that occupied one wall of his single room house. Inside he found a can of Orange Coss that was half empty. He quickly drank it and then remembered that he needed to find an aspirin. Mulumbe searched the small cabinet next to his bed, but only found a bottle of cough medicine that someone had left. Shrugging his shoulders, he decided that it wouldn't hurt if he drank some, so he tipped the bottle and immediately started to choke and gasp. The bottle contained alcohol and it was well over 100 proof! Mulumbe reached for the pitcher of water next to the bed and poured it over his face. He groaned feeling the impact of his now fully awakened senses. "If I had a rope, I would hang myself."

Mulumbe headed for the door, pausing only to grab and put on his sunglasses. Even so, the bright daylight he emerged to was enough to make him wince.

After taking a few seconds to gather his composure, Mulumbe walked over to the hut that served as a pharmacy for the town. The proprietor of the shop was a fine featured Somali, descended from the nomads that came to this region. He was different from his Bantu customer's in that his hair was soft 'jilec' as opposed to their kinkier 'jareer' hair and coarser features. This allowed him to feel a certain sense of superiority over his clientele.

Mulumbe did not care for the man, but he still did business with him, as his was the only supply store in town. Mulumbe needed the store to fit out his Safari business and it was the best place to find news and customers. It also was an outlet for the woodcarvings his family made for tourists.

Mulumbe searched the shelves till he found a pack of headache powders. From the storekeeper, whose name was Bakumba, he bought an Orange Coss and used it to wash down the powder. Tossing his change on the counter, the Somali motioned towards the bulletin board by the door.

"There is an American couple coming here from Nairobi in a few days that want to come to Masai Mara and then go on safari south near the Tsavo River area. Maybe you and that crazy old Masai friend of yours can make a few shillings."

"Minus of course, your usual percentage...right, Bakumba?"

The Somali nodded.

"Well then," Mulumbe said, "They will want to see lions so Kirakangano and I had better do some scouting. Maybe we can show them some cheetahs, if they are still hunting that brushy area near the lava flows. The ladies always seem to like them best."

The Somali shook his head. "What ever they like," he said yawning. "Too much sun out there this time of year. You boys are welcome to it".

Mulumbe picked up his change and left. *Too city bred this Somali,* he thought. *How could he not understand the feel of open savannah, or the taste of clean air?* Lost in thought, the hunter started towards the Masai kraal to find his friend.

*

The next few days were spent arranging for the American couple's safari. First Mulumbe made a trip back to his house, where he checked his inventory. The right cam furnishings were necessary, those that were suitable for soft foreign tastes. Then the foo had to be arranged, which was Bakumba's part. The Wakamba went to the corral and make sure his lorry was fueled and ready and also to rent a second vehicle. Then Mulumbe and Kirakangano drove out to the site to check on the flow of game animals and to make sure the river was passable. Finally, a quick check was made to make sure Bakumba had the 'small items' that were essential to the trip, like extra film for the couple's cameras and the small toiletry and grooming items that Americans always seemed to need but usually forgot on these kind of trips. By the time the couple arrived on the Nairobi train all was in readiness.

*

Mulumbe waited at the station, which was little more than a straw covered out building, for the train to arrive. He wore his best tan safari jacket and shorts. On his hea

the pith helmet was clean and straight. His brand new sunglasses sharply reflected the light of the bright African sun. Only his callused feet were unadorned, as he never wore shoes.

The old train pulled into the station and Mulumbe was happy to see his friend Jamba, who worked on board smiling and waving at him. Happily he returned the greeting. Jamba pointed at the cars ahead and signaled 'two'. Understanding, Mulumbe shot a quick 'thumbs up' which was returned. Then Jamba ducked back into the train.

Quickly training his eyes on the steps of the forward car, the Wakamba saw three village men and then a Bantu girl step off the train. Sunlight reflected of the trains chrome trim. Mulumbe blinked. When his eyes cleared, he saw a woman on the step. Tall and blonde, Mulumbe recognized her as the woman he had seen in town. Her eyes looked lost. *Strange,* he thought, *no one is trying to help her.*

"Mr. Mulumbe?"

The Wakamba turned around to see the young couple he had been looking for standing in front of him.

"You're our guide?" The man was smiling and extending his hand. Mulumbe shook it and then when offered, the lady's as well. Mulumbe shot a quick look back at the train. The tall woman was gone. With other matters to attend to, he dismissed her from his mind and turned his full attention to his guests.

The man introduced himself as Ben Sheffield. The lady with him was his wife, Angie. Mulumbe looked up at the Americans, looking for any clues that might mean special needs would be required. Ben was average looking and dark of eye and hair. Angie had hair the color of honey and was very pretty and plump. They were dressed in the usual safari 'white hunter' outfits, though Ben made it clear in his message that they were only interested in photography.

Mulumbe quickly guessed that they were city people and this was they're first real adventure as a married couple. So much the better, they would be easy to manage. All he really had to do was to be entertaining and show them some animals to photograph. From

175

the spoor he found in Masai Mara, he knew the cheetahs were still hanging around. Mulumbe knew that having that extra treat probably would result in a good tip on top ⟨ his regular fee.

The Sheffield's wanted to spend a week. The money Mulumbe would make from th would help cover his finances for the better part of a year, along with the qat his family harvested from the wild Mirra plant. Like many families in the region he subsidized hi income with this popular local narcotic.

After explaining to the Sheffield's that their camp was already set up for them, Mulumbe drove them into town to let them shop at Bakumba's. On the way, he filled them in as to what they should expect out on the savannah, dropping helpful hints abou those 'extras' they might need. After some shopping and Bakumba's version of a safar lunch, the Wakamba drove them to the Masai village.

Kirakangano arraigned for some tribal dancing to entertain them. Later, the two gui took the young couple on the long trip out to the camp to spend the night. From there i would be another day's travel to Mtio-Andei. From there they would set up operations Tsavo National Park. Mulumbe had hired a Somali woman to cook on the trip and whe they arrived at base camp she was well into preparing dinner.

*

After the meal, Mulumbe sat down and talked with Ben Sheffield to find out exactl what the young couple hoped to see. The good news was that they were not looking fo anything in particular, just the usual game animals. Mulumbe noted that Sheffield seer more interested in impressing his young wife than anything else, which made things easier. Mulumbe knew just how to accommodate that. He relaxed at his good fortune, they were pleasant people. The next week would be fun as well as profitable.

Later, after the couple had turned in, the Wakamba sat alone by the fire oiling his ri a .475 Jeffery #2 double barrel express, that his father had received as a gift from an o white hunter. Though a skilled archer, he always carried it with him, as it was very

176

reliable in a tight spot. Mulumbe fell into a rhythm as he polished the barrel and his mind wandered over the events of the day. Slowly, his mind drifted further.

Mulumbe was standing at a campsite barely visible in the predawn mists. He heard a low grunt, quickly followed by something tearing at the canvas of one of the tents. There was a startled cry...and then the tall woman emerged through the front flap. Looking back at something inside, she screamed and ran. Clutched in her hand was a long pair of scissors. In the distance, for now the location changed, he could hear voices calling in a foreign tongue. A man in odd fancy clothing ran rapidly past him calling a name. It was strangely inaudible, as if the sound was being heard from underwater. This seemed right as the taste of muddy water and (blood?) came to his lips. Mulumbe started to choke. Something was pulling him to the bottom. He opened his eyes and-

Kirakangano was shaking him. "What's wrong with you man? I come back from the woods and see you almost falling into the fire. Have you been chewing qat?" The old Masai looked into Mulumbe's eyes and turned pale. "Your eyes man, the pupils are like pin pricks. You're soaked with sweat. What is wrong?"

"I do not know, my friend. I have seen her—the Wazuka, and she has come to me this night!"

"Who?"

"The tall woman!" Mulumbe gasped.

"What woman? There is no one here but us. The others sleep in their tents."

Slowly as if shaking himself out of a bad trance, the young hunter related the details of the dream. As he listened, the old Masai's expression drifted between awe and concern.

"Young friend," he said, "Indeed a ghost has come. I know not why this Wazuka has come to trouble you, or what we can do about it. It is unlike any in my people's legends. Perhaps it is because she is foreign.

"I think we should find out what she wants. Perhaps when we are through here, we should find a Lamba man and tell him. They are wise about these things."

"And very expensive," Mulumbe said, as the terror of the dream started to subside. The old Masai laughed, but the sound of it was hollow.

"My friend it is not an easy thing to deal with. Maybe we will figure out a better way to handle this."

"I hope so," Mulumbe said. "I wish to be rid of her."

"That we will handle, my friend," Kirakangano said slapping the Wakamba on the back, "Now maybe I should tell you of the time I fought the elephant."

*

Five days later, Mulumbe was driving the Sheffields north of the rolling Chyulu hills towards the river near Makindu. Before he reached the town, he left the road and headed west towards the river. He knew of a shallow crossing that would save them time. As he traveled, Mulumbe communicated with Kirakangano, who had taken the second vehicle and gone ahead to scout by radio. They had heard of a stray elephant herd that had been sighted up near Amboseli Park and were hoping for a last photo opportunity before driving back to Masai Mara.

It had been a good safari for Mulumbe. First they had gone to North to Tsavo East. The rolling scrub land had offered some great shots of buffalo and lions that were easy to find. After that, he had driven the couple over to the famous Tsavo river bridge. The cheetahs had moved from the lava flows, but fortunately Kirakangano (who was scouting ahead) located them near the Tsavo River itself so a detour was made. Then they drove south to the lava flows in the west part of the park.

The young couple was well satisfied with the many photo opportunities that Mulumbe and Kirakangano had found for them and they were generous in showing their gratitude. As for the Wakamba guide, the horror of a few days ago had been forgotten in the camaraderie of the successful trip.

178

As they reached the river, Mulumbe hopped out of the lorry and checked the trailer. The river at this point got about waist deep, so he told the couple to pull their legs up, so they would stay dry. After making sure all was secure, Mulumbe jumped back into the lorry and they drove down the shallow embankment. Carefully plotting his path, Mulumbe drove into the water and started across. Then the hunter saw a pair of eyes and a nose surface a few yards to the north of their position. There was a large crocodile in the river, but Mulumbe knew the reptile would steer clear of the vehicle.

Suddenly, the Wakamba saw a white hand emerge from the water! Startled, he turned to the right and the lorry jerked—hard as the front wheel settled into a deep hole. Franticly shifting gears, Mulumbe tried to gun the lorry to get it out, but he was too late. Water leaked into the engine causing the vehicle to stall. They were stuck.

Mulumbe climbed out of the driver's seat and sat on the hood of the lorry to ponder their situation. Extracting the vehicle from where it was fouled was no big deal. All he had to do was stretch the cable from the front of the lorry, over to the nearest tree, secure it and then turn on the electric winch. The powerful motor was more than adequate to the task. The problem was that crocodile. Where was it?

The Sheffields in the back of the lorry were busy talking about options. Mulumbe knew that he had to do something fast as the heat and flies would get to them before too long. It was only about 20 meters from the bank. He would have to wade that distance quickly before the crocodile lost its fear and decided to have a go at him.

There was a large Acacia tree close enough to the bank to fasten the lorry's cable. He could winch the vehicle to shore with it.

Mulumbe motioned to Ben and handed him the rifle, indicating that he should fire at anything that should approach while he was in the water. He then pointed out the switch on the dashboard that would start the winch.

Scanning the river, he hopped off the lorry and started to wade rapidly towards the opposite bank with the cable in hand. The Wakamba made his way carefully, as the sandy bottom had pockets where a man in waist deep water could suddenly sink up to his neck.

179

Mulumbe was almost across, when a movement to his right caught his eye. From behind a dead tree that had fallen into the river, the croc attacked. Quickly he dodged, as the crocodile's lunge sent its dagger filled mouth in Mulumbe's direction. Like a loud clap, its jaws snapped shut just inches from his leg. Momentum carried the huge saurian body past him too rapidly to check its lunge.

Mulumbe dove for the shore as the massive tail of the croc splashed through the water sending a cloud of spray into the air. Momentarily unable to see, Mulumbe missed the back swing that put him in the tail's path. It swung out of the water striking Mulumbe just below the knee, snapping the bone cleanly. Mulumbe howled as he collapsed and disappeared beneath the surface.

Standing on the hood of the lorry, Ben Sheffield shot at the submerged reptile with the guide's rifle. Then he held his fire as both Mulumbe and the croc's location was lost to him. He and his wife anxiously searched the water for the missing man. Their search abruptly ended when the Wakamba surfaced near the far bank.

Mulumbe was in a bad way. Not only was his left leg broken, but the impact had severely twisted his spine causing him to cramp up. His only chance was to reach high ground before the croc returned and there was little time left to make it as Mulumbe could see the crocodile had surfaced and was turning around.

Desperately, Mulumbe pulled himself out of the water. His fingers dug into the mud, his eyes glued on the Acacia tree. Somehow, he still gripped the cable end. Mulumbe dragged it as he crawled up through the debris that littered the bank. Though he dared not look, Mulumbe knew the crocodile was closing the distance fast and he had to make it to the tree.

As Mulumbe reached the roots at the base of the Acacia, the sound of gunfire made him turn to look. The huge crocodile was already out of the water! It was coming at him slowly; ignoring the shots Sheffield fired that merely kicked dirt upon its snout, confide now that the Wakamba would be an easy meal. Mulumbe could see the many scars that ripped across the head of this eighteen foot monster. It was an old croc.

You are wise grandfather. You know you have me good.

A low hissing sound arose from the croc's gullet that sent a wave of fetid air into the hunter's nostrils. Too terrified even to gag, Mulumbe just stared back at the beast as he crawled frantically on his elbows towards the acacia. Mulumbe realized that he could not get to the tree in time. He could see the legs of the beast as they tensed to throw its titanic mass into an unstoppable kill strike. It opened its mouth ever so slightly, revealing the deadly triangles that framed his jaws.

Mulumbe knew that the crocodile would first grab him and then it would drag his body into the muddy water for a death roll. There would be no anger or passion in the act. He would just be another meal for this beast. His natural fatalism began to take hold. Mulumbe knew the end had come. It was calming to accept it. The naturalness of it seemed right. This was no ghost, no demon from a dream...just his life being sacrificed to maintain another's. As a hunter, he could accept that. Mulumbe stopped crawling and turned to stare fully into the tiny eyes of his death.

Suddenly a flash of light split the distance between Mulumbe and the croc. Then the beast was writhing as it struggled to get a long spear out of its mouth. With a high pitched yell on his lips, Kirakangano leaped past Mulumbe to land straddling the wounded monster's neck. Drawing his machete, the Masai chopped madly at the neck of the croc till he opened an area at the base of the skull. Turning the blade in his hand, Kirakangano drove it down in a savage stab deep into the exposed nerves. The croc shuddered as if electrified and then went limp.

The old Masai stood panting over his dead victim, his eyes wild with the madness of the kill. "Aiyeeah, my friend, this old Masai still owns the right to be Melombuki! This old devil was no match!"

Kirakangano stepped over to check his friend's injuries. "That old crocodile got you good Mulumbe. A broken leg for sure and maybe a few pulled ribs. You were lucky he missed on that first strike."

Mulumbe propped himself up and with a little help from the Masai, he arranged himself to a better position to view the dead reptile. Kirakangano left him momentarily retrieve his hat which had blown off his head when he leaped on the croc. Meanwhile, on the lorry, Ben and Angie were waving and calling franticly. Waving back at them, Kirakangano returned to the tree, set the cable and soon the lorry was headed for shore.

As Mulumbe waited, he studied the scarred old crocodile. Kirakangano reached over to pull the machete from its neck and when he pulled it clear, the other side of the beast face was exposed to Mulumbe's view. "Look at the empty socket, Kirakangano. What you make of that?" The old Masai followed his gaze.

"Something blinded this old boy, long before he tried to make you lunch." The Masai looked closer his fingers exploring a bulge near the dead eye. "Look here! This side of his face is swollen out. Maybe it's an old infection from a gunshot?"

Taking his knife he dug into the thickly scared flesh and pulled something out. "What do you make of this, then?"

Mulumbe recognized the object the old Masai was holding. His mind reeled with the knowledge of what that was...and what it meant. As he took the corroded fragment from Kirakangano's outstretched hand, he recognized the pitted shard as the broken edge of blade from a pair of scissors.

*

Perhaps there was truth to the Masai's claim of ghosts. Or perhaps, maybe a spirit spoke in Mulumbe's dreams. Was this the end the tall lady had come to? Why then had she come to him? In his mind, Mulumbe could see her stabbing desperately, in a futile attempt to free herself from the death that dragged her into the water. Mulumbe shook vision from his mind, but he knew it would always come back to haunt him.

Africa was a lady that never gave up all her secrets. Mulumbe knew that he would speak of this to his children and his grandchildren when they asked about his old scars and the odd piece of metal that would hang from his neck for the rest of his life. He would tell the tale many times in the coming years, but he would never completely understand it...or forget.

DIRE DEEDS AT GREYLIND MANOR

Within the hallowed halls of Greylind Manor, the chief of police of Wabash City stood surrounded by his detectives. Murder had occurred of a most foul nature. This was not an acceptable situation to the chief. He liked his town neat. Said opinion was his credo and what he had found was not at all fitting to that philosophy. He stood wrapped in his tan slicker pondering the events of the day.

It seemed the matriarch of the Greylind clan lay dead on the polished wood floors of the manor with her family bible clutched in each hand—the torn sections of said volume lay scattered over an estimated distance of twelve feet apart along with most of her anatomy.

On the table next to the couch sat a mint julep, undisturbed. Ethode Greylind would never sip the drink. The chief noted that the ice was still unmelted.

It was apparent that her attacker had left mere minutes ago.

"Chief—Look at this."

Officer Bradly pointed to the trashed litter box in the hall.

"We have one sick puppy here. Bradly, get a pooper scooper."

"Uh, sir?"

"Ok, a shovel and get us a sample of that, uh…stuff for analysis."

"Sir?"

"DNA, Bradly, the stuff will be loaded with it. Also check for bone fragments. Mrs. Greylind might be a part of that too." Ashen faced, Bradley left the house. The chief could here him calling outside, "Has anyone seen the gardener?"

184

Miles Simpson Greylind sat in the parlor twirling his moustaches caught between the shock of losing his mother and the joy of being heir to the family fortune. That his avarice had been rewarded without having to manifest any of the several plots he had envisioned to off the old crone was a stroke of luck that ranked celestial.

The debonair blue-blood dwelt upon this as he munched on the stale tasting snack the old woman had laid out earlier. Crunchy it was and smelled of dead meat and dog breath. Miles examined the bowl as he unthinkingly popped another nugget into his mouth. The bowl was labeled FARFY. To his horror, Miles realized he was nibbling on dog food.

Gasp...gag...cough.

Miles attempted to spit up the chunks, but they were already too far gone into his system. "Dog germs," he wondered, "Can I get rabies from eating this?" At least Farfy was AKC.

Quickly, Miles grabbed a bottle of New Rochelle 1968 and poured its contents down his throat, staining as he did, his apricot cravat with the red wine. In his mind's eye he pictured the combination and prayed it would not clash.

"Are you ok?"

A feminine figure stood at the door draped with lizard. It was Anne Highhedge, neighbor to the Graylinds. Miles looked upon her gossamer clad figure, which was svelter than svelte, and forgot his concerns about his discolored neckwear.

"I am as well as expected for one that has suffered such a loss," he lied. Sympathy could work well in his plan to gain the platinum blonde's affection.

"So sad, dear Miles," she said and clasped his head to her breast. Strangely, her wine colored wrap did not stain with the burgundy beverage that leaked from the heir's cravat.

The pet iguana she carried tucked into the crook of her arm licked at the liquor hungrily, whining as it struggled in her arms. Miles tried to ignore the scaly lizard as it slurped near his eye ball. Then it sank its teeth in his nose. Miles backed off with a yipe.

"Oooh...my little baby," Anne whispered in an annoying soprano, "Zookims, you just love Miles to death!"

The iguana flicked its tail in steady threatening motions and then dove into her purse. Anne withdrew its head from a box of mints it had found and released it onto a plastic hibiscus bush by the fireplace. The lizard chomped on the flowers happily.

Miles retreated to the piano—that being a Steinway grand, positioning himself in a seductive, yet mournful position.

"What are we to do, Darling? I feel so beside myself at this loss."

"Dear, Miles," she cooed, "I think you can do rightly well considering. Grams left you well seated, I should think. Try not to trouble yourself.

"I read in my Nancy Drew books that so many clues are just underfoot. Perhaps we should aid in this mystery."

"My darling, won't the constables suffice?"

"My Miles, I can see you are just being brave," Anne clasped his hand in her own.

"You mustn't feel the need to shelter me from the horror of this. I stand forthright to help you."

"Then if it be sleuth we play, then I must see to it properly."

Miles walked over to a cabinet and extracted a large reading glass. Thus armed, he pretended to examine the carpet—though in reality he used the glass to improve his view of Anne's long smooth legs. As he was thus engaged, Miles missed the entry of the chief into the room.

"So you noticed too, the chief said while chewing on the remnant of a stogie."

"Eh...what?" Miles looked up from Anne's ever so seductive gams. He cleared his throat and turned his glass to where the lawman pointed.

"What is it?"

The chief pointed to the large bloody footprints that stained the peach carpet. Midway the monstrous tracks changed to smaller more vile looking spatterings.

"We must determine which of these belonged to the beast that killed Mrs. Greylind," the chief said.

"If were a beast—or merely a man playing the beast badly."

The words came from a voice from the doorway. Their author spoke with singular authority.

"Do you think so, Detective Manhunk?"

Miles turned to see the man who entered and gasped. Anne fanned herself with her boa and almost panted. The iguana tugged on a plastic hibiscus— indifferent to the whole affair.

Detective Manhunk stepped into the room, his broad shoulders flecking off some paint from the doorframe as he passed.

"Good evening, all," he said and smiled handsomely.

Anne walked over to him, her cigarette holder tilted seductively. She purred at the sight of the stalwart.

"Do you have a surname...detective?"

"Yes I do, young lady. Manly."

Anne face flushed a deep pink. "Of course, Darling," she simmered.

"So…how fares your investigation," Miles sneered, unhappy that the handsome detective had caught the debutante's attention. The air was hot with testosterone, as the two men faced each other. Miles flinched from the twinkle in the detective's eye. It was cosmic.

"I feel this case might take a turn from what we find here. Note there—the window," Manhunk pointed.

All in the room looked to the sill where the blood trail seemed to end. There was a tell-tale drop of blood on the catch and what seemed the bloody hand print of a child sized hand.

"It is apparent," the detective said, "that our murderer is a midget, one that has remarkably large feet—"

A gunshot rang out, followed by a scream from the front door. The detective, followed by the others ran out to the living room.

There Officer Bradly lay, bespattered and tangled—wrapped around what was left of his shovel. Blood, guts and assorted entrails littered the floor with no sense or design. Not only was the officer dead, but the carpet was hopelessly spoilt.

"The poor fellow never stood a chance," Manhunk said, adjusting the fedora he wore. He picked up what was left of the shovel.

"Look here—its blade is dented."

"My good fellow, with all the blood, how can you tell?"

Miles looked at the shovel, his guts felt like they were going to explode.

"Look to the serrations on the edge," Manhunk said. "See those were made by teeth."

"Whose?"

"Uh...not mine sir."

Miles held up a denture," Just don't have the equipment."

"Nor I," Anne said extracting her own set. Miles looked at her in shock.

"Dearest, I was struck in the face by a polo mallet when I was young," Anne said (revealing to the detective the particularly cruel dangers that American blue bloods face—unbeknownst to the general populous).

Manhunk's eyebrow rose almost to the level of his slicked down hairline.

"We suffer so in silence," Miles said dispassionately, as he sipped on a gin and bitters.

"Those options being eliminated," Manhunk said, "There are just the chief and I to examine."

Manhunk flashed a smile filled with pearly whites.

"Dear boy," Miles said dryly, "weren't you in the parlor with us when it happened?"

"I should not presume to impede an ongoing investigation," the detective said scrutinizing his own reflection in the mirror above the liquor cabinet.

"We were both in the room, Detective," the chief said, "Can we move on?"

Manhunk shrugged his massive shoulders. The faint sound of tearing threads was heard by all as his gigantic biceps tore the threads his over filled jacket ever so slightly.

The air reeked of testosterone.

It was too much for the dainty sensibilities of the heiress to bear. Anne promptly swooned. Manhunk caught her as she fell, almost falling faint himself from the effects of the vibrant sexuality of the woman and the sweetly mint aroma of her breath.

Miles reached for some claret to give the girl, but when he did, the detective held a finger to his lips.

"We are not alone here," he said.

All looked to the bar. A slender shadow moved behind it, a dim reflection played teasingly across the mirror above it. Detective Manhunt raised his colt 45 taking deadly aim.

"Good lord sir," Miles gasped, "Hold fast, it's my cat!"

Miles groped behind the bar withdrawing a rather ticked off Siamese. It spat and displayed a large variety of harmonics.

"Are you certain Mr. Greylind that the thing you hold is indeed, your feline?"

"I presume, Detective, that the license on his collar would indicate that to be so." Anne staggered to her feet, her bola in total disarray. Her hair though remained picture perfect.

"Zookims?" she said weakly.

Detective Manhunk snickered, "Quite foppish, Mr. Greylind."

"That's not me she's referring to," Miles sneered.

"Where's my baby?" she gasped.

Manhunk took the cat from Miles, placing it into Anne's arms.

"That's not baby," she said gagging, "Where's my iguana?"

"Miles ducked back into the parlor. The lizard was gone. Only a few tell-tale chewed plastic hibiscus blossoms lay scattered on the floor.

"Darling," Miles called out, "Your baby is missing."

A thorough search of the manor ensued. Tables were looked under, lampshades were turned inside out, and even the dog dish was checked for signs of the missing unfortunate.

There were none.

At one point the chief thought he had found the undetected iguanid, but the green streak he spotted turned out to be just a moldy chunk of romaine lettuce that was rotting atop an old copy of BARTLETT'S QUOTATIONS, the remnant—apparently of one of the old lady's snacks.

"Oh dear," Anne said, "My baby is gone and a fiend on the loose as well." She sobbed into several handkerchiefs indiscriminately.

"Don't worry Miss," Manhunk said, "So far our attacker seems to favor humans for food. I feel I can assure you that your pet is quite safe."

From the dining room a howl sang out. One that was so wolf-like as to be almost feral. As the two policemen raced in they saw the maid's feet disappearing into the kitchen—leaving a trail of blood. Both men drew their weapons and stealthily approached the double doors.

Leaping in with a round ready in the chamber of his blue chrome 45, Manhunk followed the blood through the kitchen to where it disappeared in the dumbwaiter. Flinging open the door, he revealed the maid's head. Her glasses were on. The rest of her body however, remained missing.

"Check these for fingerprints," Manhunk said and removed the maid's spectacles, handing them to an officer. He examined the dumbwaiter and found several tiny bits of dark grey material. These he sniffed and then tasted with the tip of his tongue before they were placed in a plastic bag and secreted them in his vest pocket.

"What is it?"

"I am not certain, chief."

"It looks like it might be roach droppings—Shall I send it to the lab?"

"Not yet, Chief, I am beginning to have a theory. I am afraid we will have to go upstairs to learn what happened to the rest of the maid."

Several police officers ran upstairs on command of the chief. On the second floor the officers found a tray and what must have been warm milk in Mile's bedroom. On the third floor there were fragments what looked like soggy Sen-Sen leading from the dumb waiter to under the late matron of the house's bed.

Detective Manhunk fell to his hands and knees and sniffed the trail. Then he rose to his feet, the tip of his nose covered with gray particles.

"Miss Highhedge, do you carry candy with you?"

191

"I do, Detective, though Anne is much nicer to call me…don't you think?"

"Gad," Miles said, and reached for the bottle of claret by the bed.

The detective approached Anne and held her close to him. Anne raised her lips to him, but instead of receiving the kiss she expected, Manhunk sniffed her breath.

"Aha!" he said.

Anne squealed and jumped back as Manhunk drew his colt.

"As I suspected, Miss Highhedge, you are the murderer," he said authoritatively.

"That's ridiculous," Anne said. "I was with both you and Miles when the unfortunate officer was murdered."

"Oh," Manhunk said, crestfallen. "But your breath smells of Sen-Sen."

"And I do," said the displeased debutante, "carry some with me at all times."

Suddenly, yet another horrid howl happened.

"That came from the parlor!" the chief said. Everyone ran back downstairs. A furry tail tip disappeared into the room.

"After him," Manhunk shouted as he and the chief raced into the room in hot pursuit.

Within they beheld a sight to sear their sanity. A thing of deadly dimensions writhed before them. The creature was trying to shimmy up the fire place. It had fur, it had scales, it had claws, and it reeked of mint.

"Fire," the chief said, and let off several rounds from his 38. Manhunk unloaded his gun into the thing as it turned around. The beast's red rimmed eyes stared with pure bloodlust. Its furry ears flattened. A long red tongue flicked between massive canines.

"Miles, this isn't the family dog now is it?"

"I should say not detective, though that is Farfy's leash tangled in that thing's fur. This simply is not our pet. We would never be seen with anything less than an AKC," he sniffed, drinking down the claret he held.

"That Detective, I believe is a werewolf."

The beast raised its clawed hands and stalked towards the detective. As it did, the thing bumped into the trophy case, shattering it. A silver swimming medal flew through the air striking the creature on top of its skull. The creature let out an agonizing howl and fell to the floor.

"Good lord," said Miles.

"Good God," said the chief.

"Zookims?"

"What's that, Miss Highhedge?" The detective stared at Anne who just stood there, her face a mask of paleness as she pointed.

Manhunk turned back to the thing on the floor. Before him the creature shrank. As it did, the beast lost the fur and ears. The body became encased with scales as it shrank to a fraction of its size.

"Baby?" Anne lifted the lifeless lizard off the rug.

"This was your pet?" The chief poked at it gingerly with the barrel of his gun.

"Oh dear, poor Zookims was bitten by the neighbor's dog—or so I thought. The precious dear, how could he know what it would do to him?"

"You mean you knew?"

"Well…not really. It was just the neighborhood cats were disappearing every full moon. But I never thought Zookims would become—"

"A were-iguana?"

"Yes, detective," she said. "It's our family curse, ever since my great-great Aunt's pet gerbil came home from Hollywood infected after being an extra on the set of I WAS A TEENAGE WEREWOLF. But Zookims is supposed to be a vegetarian; I never thought it would pass to him."

"A tragedy indeed," Manhunk said.

"Then the case is finished," Miles said.

"It would seem," said the chief.

"Then I will thank you and bid you goodnight, gentlemen," Miles said as he directed the officers to the front door.

"Yes," the chief said, "I will return tomorrow with more officers to document the rest of the night's occurrences." He reached over and took the dead iguana from Anne's arms and dumped it into a plastic evidence bag.

Ann sniffled.

Detective Manhunk adjusted his fedora and flashed Ann a tooth-perfect grin as Miles shut the door on him.

Miles quaffed the last of the claret as the officers headlights faded into the night. His nose tingled still from the bite of the iguana. It had been a rough night.

Anne looked at him, her tears making a mess of her mascara. Miles held her close as she sobbed out her sorrow.

"Tis sad my love, the loss of your pet, but we will muddle through," Miles said.

The heir to Greylind Manor congratulated himself on his good fortune. The estate, the money, and now the girl were his at last. He openly salivated at the thought.

"Dearest, must you drool?" Anne stared in awe of his tongue which hung panting from his mouth to his chin.

Miles coughed. His throat felt hairy, his nose hairs grew. His neat tweed jacket began to feel tight.

194

"I dare say, Anne," Miles commented, as his form began to change into something massive and furry, "It's been a long night, Darling.

"Have you got a mint?

THE GORGON

DAY ONE: I see an ant crawling on my ceiling as I lie awake in the early morning hours. It is carefully picking its way across the popcorn terrain above my head, its little antennae wagging at the sky as if it's lost.

"Poor little thing," I sigh and the sound causes my wife to stir in her sleep. Ah my gentle Catherine, what does her innocent mind know of ceilings and ants and men?

I look over and caress the thick mass of her lovely hair, so wonderfully spilling out over the covers like tangled yellow strands of the finest gold wire.

I turn my attention back to the tiny insect above my head, as it struggles to achieve some goal that is lost to me. *What makes it stick to the ceiling?*

I ask such questions of myself, for I am bored and cannot sleep. Yet, though I am alert—I am so tired from lack of rest. What has it been? Three days now; three days and nights without batting as much as an eye.

I try to figure why this is so, but the reason escapes me. Three days without sleep. I wonder how many more till exhaustion wins and I sink into that pleasant oblivion?

I lay on the bed thinking about it, till the alarm rings and finally sets me free from the prison of my bed. *Did I just think that?* Then it must be so, as I find a certain sense of gratitude in the clocks harsh summons. I reach over and hesitate for a moment. I hear Catherine say, "Turn it off," in a voice that is still too flavored by sleep to be attractive.

I kill the alarm and then turn to find Catherine already half dressed, her back modestly turned hiding her beauty from my longing eyes. Wordlessly, she stumbles out to the kitchen and I am left unsatisfied without so much as a hug. *What of that?*

I eat my breakfast as she talks about neighbors and gossip that does not interest me. There is a story about a man in the paper, who was badly stung by hundreds of bees._*What would that feel like?* I wonder about things like that. I ask Catherine and she stares at me like I said something strange. I quickly finish my breakfast and leave.

At work, I am still wondering about the bees as I do my job on the line. The company I work for makes industrial filters. My task is to take the metal mesh that comes to my station on the belt stacked three sheets deep. I place the material into one end of an oven where it is baked and compressed. From the other end, I extract the finished filter, slide it out, and with a large cutter blade, I trim it to its proper size. Then I send it down the belt to the packagers. I look at the faces of my coworkers their expressions are blank *Like stone?*

The air stinks of hot aluminum, bitter to my nostrils. I wonder if I am breathing in too much of the gaseous metal and it might be crystallizing in my lungs. All day long I labor in the superheated factory. The only sounds are the steam hiss and the SLIDE—CHOMP, SLIDE—CHOMP… of the cutting blade.

I come home weary after the day's toil to find a note on the mantel. Catherine says that she has gone to play bridge with her friends and that there is dinner in the microwave. I heat it as instructed, but when I eat it, it still tastes like cold gruel.

Later on, I sit and watch an old Ray Harryhausen movie. In this one, Perseus has to get past the Gorgon Medusa without seeing her or he will turn to stone. Perseus uses the reflection of her in his shield to see where to swing and cuts off her head. Smart thinking, I conclude, but Medusa looks familiar.

After the movie I turn in early. Hours later Catherine comes in and slips into bed carefully, as not to disturb me. *Why is she so late?*

I lay there pretending to sleep, till her soft breathing indicates she is no longer awake…and watch the ceiling.

DAY TWO: I watch what is now a narrow line of ants above me and I can see the dust their tiny feet kick up. It falls from the ceiling like a fine powder, settling on my face and the coverlets. I can picture the fine dust settling in my nose and mouth choking me. If I lay here long enough—will it bury me? I can hear the loud thrumping of their feet as they march to off whatever destination their purpose takes them to. I look over at Catherine who appears to be sound asleep. Can't she hear the sound the ants make? She must…she must…yet still she lies motionless.

I look over the bed spread and it is covered with fine dust. Anxiously I await the alarm clock, as its slow ticking rattles my nerves. At the first ring I am up from the covers. Catherine looks up at me, surprised by my sudden departure from bed. I run into the bathroom to wash the dust from me.

Through the open door, I catch a glimpse of her dressing (reflected in the dresser's mirror). Her body is so perfect. Slender like a dancer, she stretches her arms up above her golden crown that settles like a waterfall to just above the small of her back.

At breakfast, I sit at the table and look in the paper for more on the 'Bee' story, but there is nothing there. Catherine has chosen to be quiet, so I let the silence fill our morning.

All day long work is the same. As I work, I picture my lungs turning gray as they slowly crystallize from the aluminum. Do crystals really form? I think they must. The thought terrifies me.

At lunchtime, I learn that one of my coworkers has been struck by a car and killed. All I can say is that no longer does she have to hear the sound of the factory. My coworkers are aghast at my statement, but one of them smiles sympathetically and offers her headphones. I try them out but it is no good. I can still hear it...SLIDE—CHOMP!

I get home and I hear Catherine speaking on the phone. She hangs it up fast as I come in and when I ask her, she says that the call was for her. I know she was talking about me because she hung up so suddenly. She looks pale. What is going on?

Catherine seems so different these last few days. Something has changed about her, but I am not certain what it is. We eat dinner as she tells me about her run in with an old friend. Someone she knew in college. I sit and try to be patient as I watch the line of ants preparing to go into the bedroom. She does not pay them any attention. I watch as the leader smiles up at me. We go to bed and Catherine falls asleep with her back to me.

DAY THREE: I have not yet figured the purpose of the ants. The line has grown to a column and they step in near perfect rhythm. THRUMP...THRUMP...THRUMP their united steps stamp out. The noise is deafening. I hide my head in my pillow to block the sound and almost miss the alarm clock. Catherine pokes me in the ribs and I turn it off.

There is nothing in the morning paper about the 'Bee' man. I check it twice before I go to work.

SLIDE...CHOMP!

That night I come home to find Catherine dressed seductively in her best red dress. She has done something to her hair as it now hangs in ringlets like coiled snakes about her shoulders. She offers me wine and then looks at me with sex in her eyes.

I am tired and go to bed alone right after dinner. After a while, I hear her storm into the room and undress. She gets into bed with me, but stays huddled up in her corner.

DAY FOUR: The column of ants has grown into an army. Their measured tread forbids any sleep. I watch as clouds of dust rain on the coverlets. I cannot move. I know that I am trapped and they will bury me! Then I hear the radio playing an old Bee Gee's tune. At least I thought it was the radio. Then as I listen closer it it is the ants. As they march they sing;

"Whether you're a brother, or whether you're a lover, your staying alive...staying alive..."

This can't be I groan, for a moment I think I really am going insane, but the ants smile at me and continue;
Ah, ah, ah, ah, staying alive—"

I scream in relief as the alarm goes off. Catherine jumps out of bed, runs naked into the bathroom and locks the door. Through it, I try to explain about the dust. She says I am crazy and that there is no dust. I look down and clearly see her footprints. *What of this?*

I go to fix breakfast and hurriedly I munch my cereal. Eventually Catherine emerges from the bathroom, but by then I am walking out the door to work.

SLIDE…CHOMP! The machine beats a rhythm that is draining what is left of me into the metal squares I cut. My co-worker has taken back her headset. She and the others have been sneaking sideways looks and whispering so I don't hear. I can see their ant lips move though… I know what they are saying.

I dare not sleep now; as if I do, the ant dust that is now liberally pouring on me will bury me as I lay. Catherine must know what the ants are doing, yet she still insists that I am over worked and possibly crazy. She has to be involved somehow and the thought of it depresses me. Catherine, my goddess…my love, has she betrayed me?

I shudder at the thought, but the possibility is there. Could she be planning my death, allied with these little vermin? Why else would they stare at me so gleefully as they shower their load on me? I can hear them marching loudly…Thrump…Thrump…THRUMP…

The alarm goes off and I run to the shower to remove the layers of ceiling dirt they have tried all night to choke me with. My skin, to my surprise looks gray (From the aluminum)? It can't be so, because I am here and the ceiling is as white as can be. I am confused.

I dress in the bathroom and leave my house without breakfast. I hear Catherine calling after me, but I know I cannot listen to her now. I drive away quickly. Then I hear on the car radio that the 'Bee' man has died.

SLIDE...CHOMP!!!

I come home to find Catherine talking with a man. At first I feel jealous and I start to say something, but then Catherine introduces him. She says he is Dr. Goldbloom, a psychiatrist. I ask him if she needed counseling and his eyebrow arches. By this I know that they are both lying, and I have possibly caught her with the mysterious man on the phone. I confront her about this, and Catherine tearfully admits that what I suspect is true. Then she says I need help.

Laughing triumphantly at the discovery of her thin plot, I withdraw to the den and slam the door. I hear her talking softly with the man and then he leaves. Catherine comes in a few minutes later and cries with her head resting on my knee as she apologizes, all the while still insisting that the man is just a psychiatrist. Looking down at her tear stained face I waver in my resolve, (she is so lovely) till one of her blonde locks falls near my hand and I catch a glimpse of its forked tongue. I carefully pull my hand away and hide my shock so Catherine will not suspect that I know. I clearly saw it though, the evil eye of the tiny malevolent beast as it stared its hate up at me. What am I to do? Catherine is changing...and I fear I know what to.

I pretend to act normally as the evening progresses, but my mind is working on a plan. I do not know how long I have till her transformation is complete and I will be doomed. I must think quickly.

We go to bed and she snuggles near to me. I can tell she is still crying and part of me is taken in by her sadness. But I see the ants on the ceiling are jumping up and down and I don't know how they can do that without falling on me. So I watch them and wait for them to fall.

I think I dozed off, for I awake and find I am covered with a thick layer of dust. Fortunately, the blanket over my face has protected me from suffocating.

I can hear the ants talking to Catherine. They say that tonight is the night and I should be dead before dawn. I smile at their presumption that I am asleep and do not hear them. Catherine's voice pierces the silence and I despair because she is agreeing with them, though how she has learned to speak the language of the ants is beyond me. But then I wonder, how do I understand them? Can it be that I am going mad? Can it be that I am so very wrong about my lovely Catherine?

The tears rise in my eyes as I start to roll over and apologize to Catherine, but that is when I catch sight of her shadow on the wall. I recoil as I realize her hair is all snakes now and I know that her transformation is complete! She is a Gorgon...and to look at her is Death.

I am not insane—I know it now. By morning, she will come to me and try to convince me of her love. I will look upon her face. That will be my doom. I squeeze my eyes shut as panic fills my heart. I dare not move now because she will know that I am awake, and she is waiting for that.

As she lies there beside me, I can hear her laughter and the horrible hissing of her loathsome locks. It is just a matter of time for her and she knows it. If I roll over, I will see her and the horror of her will turn me to stone.

In the bathroom there is a pair of scissors and a hand mirror. *That is how Perseus did it (isn't it?)*

One quick look at that horrid reflection and then stab-stab the vile thing till its loathsome face is no more! Then and only then, I will sleep and the ceiling will stay where it is and I will live.

I begin to slowly edge my way out from under the covers. "If I can just get out of bed and make it to the bathroom..."

RED

Red was the color,

So he had been told.

The color of passion

Of life,

Of ...death.

Only the reddest rose

Could hold the fire

Only the crimson of blood

Could hold the life.

Red from a fresh slain pigeon

Judged a ruby's worth.

Red flowing from a maiden

Called out her need to make life.

Red adorned the battlefield.

Testament to the slain.

Red second only in service

To the pure white vestments

Of the Pontiffs.

So very white,

Like teeth set in a red mouth,

Or nipple set in pale skin.

Red signals the way to fulfillment.

So sad to know that when such

Hues in shades of scarlet

Are gifted in the flow of night's feed,

Red is naught but black
Staining the moonlit ground.

THE DEAD PASSING

It took rare skill with a sword to cut the head off the undead in garbed in chain mail. When they charged you encased in heavy plate armor the task was impossible. As it was, Barin had neither skill, knowledge, nor the weapon to do so. He watched the troop of undead soldiers march through his village and tried to make sense of what the things were his eyes saw. The army was too solid to be ghosts and too immune to the effects of the crude weapons the villagers wielded to be men. The chain mail covered figures just walked through everything before them...and killed.

Unstoppable.

At first they had been hard to distinguish from the forest they emerged from. Their armor was so brown with rust that in the early twilight the soldiers looked as if they were moving tree trunks. What was left of the tunics and hose that hung from them was so rotted as to be almost indistinguishable from their mummified flesh. Here and there the stained remnants of red crosses stood out from the mud and decay on their chests. It was only when a goatherd went forth to examine the phenomenon and cried out as his guts were torn from his body that the villagers realized they were under attack. By then it was too late. An army of grim figures surrounded the village and moved in killing everything they could grab.

Barin saw near a dozen of the soldiers pull down an ox, slitting its throat and feasting even as the animal thrashed in its death throes. Tarinh the Weaver was torn from the saddle with his wife and child, his horse disemboweled by a cadaverous giant who wielded a two handed sword. What happened to Tarinh and his family was unspeakable.

206

Barin stood with his cross bow in hand as the giant in fine plate armor closed on him and his wife and boy who huddled behind him. Barin could see the eyes of the creature, so dead and dry that even maggots shunned contact with them. It raised its sword and came at him its dry mouth moving as if mouthing some obscene prayer.

The farmer aimed carefully and let fly a bolt that smashed through the thing's left eye jerking its head back and raising a large dent in the back of its helmet. The giant paused in its attack, dropping its sword and pulling with both hands to free the bolt from its brain case. Black liquid issued from the wound as the soldier dropped to his knees.

Behind him Barin heard his wife scream. He turned in time to see her brains jellied by the stroke of a mace. Another thing had his child in its grip. Already its teeth were sunk into the boy's belly.

Barin struggled to reload his crossbow and then as the horror of it overcame him he drew his knife and flung himself at the nearest soldier. Luck was not with him. Barin felt mailed hands grabbing him from behind. He found himself thrown to the ground with three of the creatures on top of him. The soldiers made no effort to kill him before they fed.

It was nearly ten minutes before the shredded thing that was Barin finally died.

It was in 1183 AD that Sir Guy de Birchen the 4th Earl of La Fontaine led twelve hundred knights and men-at-arms south from the Christian fortress of Acre south into the black lands in search of Solomon's treasure. Naught had been heard from them for nigh eighty years. All assumed the jungle ate their bones as not a soul returned from that green Hell. Then in recent years, rumors sprung up of men dressed in rusted iron, who

advanced on villages slaying the people; that and stories far more
gruesome.

Sir Bernard of Corey watched from the battlement of his cousin's keep in Rumania as the foul smelling army of the dead hammered at his gates. To his estimate, below there was near a thousand tattered warriors clad in mail or plate armor advancing in the cold grey dawn. There was little order to their attack, more of a mad scrambling to the gate which they struck at with weapons that were dented or broken. Some even clawed with what was left of their fingers.

"Pray, have the dead given up this day or must we suffer more of their assaults?"

The speaker was Bernard's cousin, Vangar. The Count looked below at the swarming mass of undead and sniffed.

"For years we heard tales from the east of villages that were wiped out mysteriously. Of course we thought it was plague that was doing the nasty, but then there were the survivors. When they told us their stories of horrific warriors long dead that fed upon the living we thought them mad or witches. We even burned a few to test the theory. Small satisfaction for them for them I suppose, as they apparently were right."

"Small indeed," Bernard said watching as some of Vangar's men poured boiling oil onto the group congregated at the drawbridge. The soaking had little effect except to make the wood beams slippery. Several of the creatures slipped and fell into the moat. Seconds later these emerged from the water and struggled to climb the muddy banks.

"Note there the tall one in plate armor. There is an emblem on his greaves and helmet. It looks to be a coat-of-arms. He must then be their leader."

"Gad Vangar, but I think your right there. Mayhaps we can slay him. If so might this attack cease? I mean no leader and all that."

"But how to get to him, I think it unwise to sally forth."

"That may not be a problem, Vangar. Look."

Several of the creatures that had been struggling on the banks had managed to reach the forty foot walls. Like giant ants they were climbing up the edifice their dried fingers clawing at the rough stone for purchase. They made painfully slow progress but it was obvious that eventually the creatures would succeed in scaling it. Below, others were detaching themselves from the party at the gates. They too began to climb.

"Archer," Vangar shouted to one of his men on the battlements, "Slay you and your comrades those who climb with fire arrows. All save the big fellow with the gold trim to his helm. Let him climb to the top and then seize him."

Vangar's men opened fire with a deadly hail of flaming shafts. Since none of the attackers were armed with bows the besieged men-at-arms could lean well over the walls sending arrow after arrow into the climbers. Some burst into flame immediately and were reduced to char even as they climbed. Others lost their purchase falling down into the moat. Those emerged from the water steaming and again began to climb. Unfortunately, being so soaked, further hits with fire arrows sizzled out when they struck. One mail clad figure made it to the top and was met with a javelin shot from an arbalete a tour. The force of the blow tore him from his perch and sent him flying nearly a hundred feet before pinning him to the ground. As Bernard watched, the soldier pulled himself up the shaft till he was free and then marched back to the wall.

"Cursed hard to kill," Bernard said.

"It would seem that only fire finishes them for certain," Vangar said. "Haste now, let us go to the wall to meet the prince that leads this vermin."

209

Bernard took a quick look out the window and saw that the armor plated warrior was near the top of the wall.

As they emerged at the base of the tower several men were engaged in trying to over-power the leader of the invaders. One man grabbed the arm of the giant and was rewarded for his efforts by having his arm grasped in a dead hand and removed at the elbow. Another had his head ripped off his shoulders as he fastened a noose around one leg of the thing.

"Look to his eye," Bernard said. Out of a dead eye socket the feathered end of a crossbow bolt stood out as testimony of an earlier combat.

"Chain it to the Baliste," Vangar said.

Four men carrying heavy chain charged at the giant placing the links before them to ward off its blows. As fast as they dared they tangled its limbs with the chain securing it to the war engine. One daring soul ducked under its flailing arm to retrieve the sword it carried in its rusting sheath.

Once secured, the two nobles approached the creature. It snarled at them with a breath as fetid as a week old battlefield.

"My God, I think I know this man," Bernard said catching his breath.

"It cannot be a man, look at the rotten leather that passes for skin. Even in the castle tombs I have not seen such a countenance."

"Yet it is…or should I say was. Look now at the coat-of-arms on its helm."

"La Fontaine, wasn't he of the Outremer lords, the one who went into the savage lands below Moorish Africa?"

"Aye, he was."

"The man's been dead near a hundred years!"

"Yet there is no mistaking the emblem he wears."

"Pagh, this reeks of Moorish sorcery," Vangar spat, "If we survive this I swear an oath to God that my neighbor, Mohammed Pasha will feel the edge of my blade on his scrawny-"

"I fear it may be too late. Did you notice some of these devils bear weapons of Moslem origin?"

A servant ran up and bowed to Vangar. "The enemy is breaching the walls!"

"Damn, but I didn't think these things had sense enough to employ sappers," Bernard said. Where do they enter?"

"Beneath the south wall, sire. The Devils must have dug whilst the others kept our attention. Now they emerge from the kitchen."

"You then," Vangar said, "Fetch a dozen men-at-arms and lead them to the breach. Mayhaps they can tarry with the things while we escape out the tunnel."

"What of the women and children?"

'Those we cannot save we'll have to slit their throats. Better that than to leave them to what succor these demons will supply."

Vangar gathered his wife and children assigning two strong knights to tend to them. Then he and Bernard went to the kitchen to survey the damage. The first thing they saw was the cook braining one of the undead repeatedly with a pan. With each stroke the things head crushed flatter and flatter. Black ichors streamed from its ears and mouth. Then its mailed hand reached out and tore off half of the cook's throat. This the thing stuffed into what was left of its mouth, the blood mixing with its black drool. It turned to Bernard and he shivered at the hunger in its eyes.

Behind it more than a dozen of the creatures poured through the hole in the wall. They had done their work well. The gap was over six feet across. There was no way to block access to the things. Several of the men-at-arms already had fallen in the tight battle. Men and Zombie were locked in a combat too close for the use of most weapons. One man rammed his dirk up into the throat of the creature he fought. The tip of the blade raising the mail drop on

211

the back of the thing's head as it emerged. The creature dropped moaning its death rattle eighty years too late. Two more took its place and the man went down with a pile of the undead on top of him.

Then Bernard heard a sound behind him. Six men carrying a battering ram and a door that had been removed from its hinges raced past him. As the other men fell back the soldiers shoved the door sideways into the teeth of the dancing creatures. Then they slammed the ram's carved head into the door. Another pair of soldiers carried pots full of oil which they poured over the door and then set alight.

"That won't hold them long," Vangar said, "we must make for the tunnel before they're through."

By the time they reached the escape tunnel there was a mob clawing to enter. Bernard and Vangar pushed pulled and tore their way past the refugees to the heavy door at the other end.

"Well, here goes nothing," Vangar said as he unlocked the wood door pushing it open. Then he, Bernard and a couple of knights emerged into the darkness. None of the dead army was nearby. Waving the refugees to silence Bernard led them out into the forest. Then Vangar ordered his men to grasp a hidden lever. When the first of the undead neared the tunnel exit, the men pulled the lever which released the support beams causing it to collapse.

"That's as near as any will receive in the way of Christian burial," Bernard said.

Three days later, Bernard and Vangar stood lined up on the banks of the Olt River which cut through the table lands south of Transylvania. An uneasy alliance had sprung up between the faithful men of Mohammed Pasha and the remnants of Vangar's guard. These were supported by two hundred pike men sent by Vlad Teppes. The combined forces stood ready at the river's steep banks and waited.

Pasha sat on his chair beneath a tent canopy. Bernard compared his calm with Vangar's constant pacing. ***How calm these men of the east. How would this translate in battle?***

"So, Mohammed you seem cool. Know you what manner of men we face?"

"Aye, they are the black scum of Africa, fashioned by the witch men of Kush, from Christian devils who died seeking the gold of the great Emir Suleiman. East they marched, past Jerusalem to the lands and around, then turning west sparing the holiest of holies in Mecca. They must have come that way, for the seas are too deep for even them to ford. They blaspheme Allah by their very existence, which is why I have ceased my quarrel and allied my servants with those of the unbeliever Vangar."

"We fought them in Vangar's keep but they were too strong to hold. Know you how to kill these things?"

"Flame and beheading are all that work with these. They are not true Jinn, which are evil drawn from fire. These are demons who occupy the souls of men, making walking cadavers…savage magic. It is an obscenity that must be stopped here."

Two hours later as the sun sent its final light to the Carpathian Mountains to the east a shambling noise issued from across the river. Oddly highlighted in the golden rays the army of the dead advanced towards the river.

Vangar ordered his archers to fire. The flaming shafts lit the pitch that had been poured liberally on the opposite bank. The foremost undead were immediately engulfed in oily smoke and fire. A loud huzzah rose from the defenders ranks.

For several minutes the fire burned on, blocking the view from the men. Then a flame coated figure emerged from the blaze like a walking coal. He was followed by a second and a third. Then dozens staggered forward walking to the steep river bank. As the reached it the dead slid or fell down the bank into the water. Smoke issued from the water like steam rising from an underwater volcano. Then as the last of the creatures slipped below the surface there was again silence.

"Are they dead?" a soldier whispered to his comrades. The flames began to die on the other bank. More of the creatures stepped across the burning pitch without effect. These too fell into the water. On Pasha's order, Greek fire was launched from Pierrier's, small portable catapults that operated by a single man pulling a rope that swung the arm upward throwing its load. These machines were capable of rapid firing. Soon the far bank was blazing again.

Then a man cried out as a blackened and scorched head emerged from the river. It gnashed its bizarre white teeth and howled. Following its lead more and more heads and then bodies rose from the water, some grimly waving swords and axes. Close to four hundred Bernard estimated. He stared in disbelief that the crumbling caricatures of humanity could still move. Chunks of soggy burnt material fell from their forms with each step. *Could it still be called flesh?* Bernard wondered.

Pasha raised his hand and from the back ranks men came forward with jars of asphaltum. The jars were emptied on the riverbank and the front ranks of the undead as they clawed for purchase on the muddy slopes. Then men with torches came forward and lit the mixture.

Then impossibly, some of the dead emerged from the second conflagration. Their bodies were too soaked to properly burn. In a steady crawl the remaining creatures climbed ever closer to the defenders. Vangar shouted an order. The pike men lined up at the top of the bank using their weapons to push the undead back into the flames. Here and there a creature succeeded in grabbing a pike pulling its wielder with it into the fire. Despite the pike men's efforts several dozen creatures succeeded in reaching the top of the bank. With a roar the Rumanians led by Vangar and Bernard charged to meet them.

With the first blow of his sword, Bernard realized the chain mail that had proved so difficult to chop thru no longer mattered. His overhand blow crushed the link armor pulverizing the body beneath. The creature—split in two, fell to the ground and thrashed. Bernard ground his heel into the thing's head and felt it squish into oblivion. A second one clawed for his sword and instead received the flat of it crushing its skull.

Then, in the midst of the press, Bernard saw the giant in armor plate swinging its huge broadsword. Men died with each stroke horribly, their death gurgles cut short by the demons that fed on them.

Bernard swung his sword for the thing that was Sir Guy's helmet. There was little effect save a new dent in the corroded iron of it. The thing in turn struck—shearing off the top of Bernard's shield and knocking him to the ground. As it reared back for a second blow, Vangar stepped in front of Bernard and locked its arm in his bull-like grip. Two more men seized the other arm and between them forced the giant cadaver to his knees.

Bernard tore the strap from the ruined shield off his arm. Then shaking the numbness from his bruised shoulder he stepped up to Sir Guy and lifted his helmet off his head. The crossbow bolt pulled through the braincase with little resistance. Bernard looked at the one eyed horror and spat. Then drawing his dirk, Bernard sawed off the creature's head.

Mohammed Pasha stepped past him and from a small pouch poured salt into the open wound of its neck. Sir Guy sizzled as if burnt, and then fell to the ground. With his destruction, the rest of the undead crumbled to dust before the defenders.

Bernard looked up the bank where the pike men were stomping out the flaming remains of the undead. Shaking his head he kicked at the soggy pile of armor and burnt bones. "How did you know to do that?"

Pasha threw the pouch atop the remains and grunted. "The black Africans call them Zombies. It is a foulness that Allah cannot tolerate. The salt purifies them breaking the spell that binds them to this world."

"May God finally have mercy on them," Bernard said.

"Let us hope, unbeliever that next time we fight, it will not be against so formidable a host."

"How do you mean?"

"Well," said Mohammed Pasha, "Next time you Christians seek gold in Black Africa, praise be to Allah that you go naked."

THE CORRUPTED VERSES

The priests howled as they slammed their bodies against the altar stone, its greenish hues stained a sullen red with the blood of dozens of sacrifices. Men, boys and even young girls had been flayed and skinned in search for the right material for the undertaking. Countless strips of flesh were compared and found wanting—till at last enough was gleaned from the hundreds of fresh corpses—to create the pages of the volume that chronicled the teachings of the dread god. Blood seared by lightening was used by blind scribes to place the whisperings of insane priests upon the pages. When it was done, their brains were smashed and the remnants smeared upon the bindings while the acolytes chanted obscene passages from memory. The leather of it—made from the tanned flesh of a virgin raped on the altar stone, took on its somber shades, the tattooed title and enchantments as starkly black—as they were when the foul letters were inscribed on the hopeless girl and skinned from her body while she was still alive. The book was bound and cursed, so the dark powers inscribed within those covers festered and grew.

Thus the worshipers of Kananzol blasphemed against the natural world and created their manifesto. Nigh a thousand years passed before them and their vile cult mercifully faded into obscurity.

"Quite the history this volume has," Idam Quizmat said as he displayed the large leather bound book to his guest, one Henry Bascombe, late of East Haddam, Connecticut. The hour was late and the cheeriness of his friend's White Chapel apartment did not ease the sense of foreboding the old book inspired in the American.

"In 1786, an English explorer Named Alfred Richmond found the tome when he infiltrated the keep of the Thuggee in Northern India. A linguistic expert, Richmond translated the verses and was appalled by the 'vileness of it'. He removed the text from its sanctuary and ordered one of his aides, Eland Foxright to destroy the volume."

"I take it Foxright failed to do so?"

"No, young Eland did indeed destroy the evil pages, but he took a fancy to the richly worked cover—so intricately marked with designs that made no sense to his European eyes. He saved it and years later sent the remnant to his friend, Lord Byron just weeks before dying in a knife fight in a tavern near Sebastopol."

"How unfortunate."

218

"Indeed, Henry. As one would expect, Lord Byron too was intrigued by the design of it and rebound the book, using it to pen darker verses and musings that came to him, none of which ever reached the public eye. He did share these passages with Shelly, Bram Stoker and others during a notorious gathering that birthed the horror classics Frankenstein and Dracula. Byron later died of a violent illness.

"From here the book's history becomes muddled, but it resurfaced, having arrived in England as part of a packet, part of the sum purchase of a lot of books bought at auction from the collection of the Greek bookseller, Adrian Scillious. You may recall, my dear boy that Scillious was the notorious Athens slasher; he who murdered seventeen people in six years of horror before dying—impaled upon the ironwork of Pathen's Gate after falling from the roof of the estate."

"I read about that, Idam, a nasty business."

"So it was. As a collector of the bizarre, I managed to wriggle this from the hands of the auctioneer at a pittance—mere shillings. But they did not know the history of the binding as I did."

"Quite the tale, Quizmat," Henry Bascombe said. "If such is its History, then this thing is accursed. It might be best to destroy the blasted thing, though I dare say, dark as it may be, this book is indeed handsome.'

"That would be a terrible loss," Idam said clutching the book to his breast defensively. "To destroy the pennings of great Byron, written in his own hand within—that would be monstrous."

"True enough Idam," Bascombe laughed. "Forgive me for subscribing to such a thought. Tis the Port I think. One too many draughts has fuddled my mind into taking this matter seriously." Henry shook his head.

"It is late and the hour demands that I retire to my chamber. We can resume this talk on the morrow?"

"But of course, Henry," Quizmat said, laying the book down on an end table. "Sleep well this eve, perhaps we can travel to Essex in the morning. My cousin Elaine would treasure the opportunity to see you again."

Henry Bascombe retired to his bed, but did not sleep well that night. His fitful dreams were filled with visions of black horrors and frightful obscene visions of thousands of young boys and tear stained virgin girls torn and stabbed by wild eyed priests in the worship of some dark and ageless god. The ground below the green alter was stained scarlet by impossibly thick rivers of human blood.

In the midst of the carnage a single figure stood, tall and darker than the rest. His eyes fixed on Bascombe's holding him in their hateful depths— trapping him, so the hand that held his knife fell unnoticed. Only the sound of his own scream as the priest's blade plunged into Henry's neck distracted the Englishman from the bonds of those horrid eyes. But then he found he was bound like the rest, flat on his back lashed to the green alter. Bound and slashed again and again...till Henry awoke with blood in his mouth from chewing on his own tongue.

"Henry, be a dear and fetch me my glass." Elaine Ducrea smiled with her cat green eyes. They had spent the better part of the morning together after Idam played the diversion on her ward. The two would not return till evening which left the better part of the day for the young mistress to work her wiles on her nervous subject.

"It is all too rare that you visit, Henry. I should think you less hateful though, if you openly scorned me, instead of this reticence in regards to voicing your feelings toward me."

"But I do not hate you, Elaine—"

"Then you love me?" The girl raised a lace clothed wrist from the back of the couch, resting her chin and cheek on a gloved palm.

Henry cleared his throat; the young redheaded woman had placed him in a precarious spot. He was fond, if not completely taken with the girl, but his bachelor ways still called softly to him. Henry was not ready for the altar emotionally, or financially. But still his passion was such that he was not willing to risk Elaine's displeasure or rejection. It was her insistence upon his immediate declaration of a mutual sense of amour that had him looking for any diversion that would free him from conversation that might inspire the folly of committing himself on the spot.

It was with no small sense of relief that the distraction of the telephone's ring allowed Henry to quit the couch. He crossed the room and picked up the receiver.

"How goes the battle?" It was Idam. From the sound of his voice, he had apparently taken Elaine's ward to the local pub.

"Blast man, she is all hooks and ties," Henry hissed, "At this rate she will have us married before you return."

"But don't you fancy the girl?"

"She is—Hold it, Idam, she is in the room. Let me duck to where I can achieve some privacy."

"Who is that, Darling?" Henry turned and smiled at Elaine, hoping his commentary had fallen on deaf ears.

"Just Idam; he and Wesley are over at Mogley's Tavern from the sound of it."

"Then I guess we will have to make due with just our own company," Elaine giggled.

"Ah, she's got your number old boy!" Idam burped loudly.

"You rascal, I should think you planed this ambush and now you've the gall to laugh in my face over a pint."

"Indeed my stalwart, you have caught me. The girl dotes on you and I would not break her heart by calling you false to her desires." Idam said.

"But she speaks of matrimony."

"Such might be the course for you to consider, after all Henry, she is endowed with more than just delectable feminine parts. Truth be told, she's quite wealthy."

"And listening too, Cad, you'd best to change the subject before her ears burn with the intrigue."

"That I can do," Idam said. "Now my dear friend and ally, I have a favor to ask."

"And what devices are you attempting that you seek to cajole me with such titles?"

"Nothing so bothersome but to ask that when you leave, please see that my satchel goes with you. I plan to finish the week here and I would not be burdened by it. Take it to your place and I will collect it upon my return.

"I shall see to it."

"Mind that you do, my friend. I would not want to suffer the absence of it because of your carnal endeavors."

"You are a beast," Henry snorted, but the line was already dead. He looked over at Elaine and bit his lip. The girl was making lamb eyes at him—the kind that would break even a priest's resolve. Keeping single was not going to be an easy task.

Back at his apartments, Henry laid aside his belongings clearing a place on his dining room table for the black leather satchel he had carried home for Idam. Even before he opened it, a sense of what was within, overcame him chilling his blood. Then the book was in his hands, its dark stained leather cover cool against his skin…like the dead thing he knew it was. Odd that it should affect him now more profoundly then when he had first seen it in Quizmat's apartments. Revolted by it, Henry sought to toss it away, but something stopped him. Oddly, it was a feeling of curiosity, strangely contrasting with his first impression. Though consciously Henry could feel the malevolence that issued from the book, a desire to open and read the verses within compelled him like a drug. Perhaps, he thought, there might be secrets within the volume that would make his loathing seem foolish. After all, weren't the pennings of one of histories greatest poets bound within the rich leather of it?

Henry sat at the table, his hands trembling as he placed the tome before him and opened it. Within, he read in letters still sharp and legible, the introduction by Byron to his work within;

MUSINGS IN TONES OF DARKNESS~A collection of thoughts unusual and extreme—placed here on these pages for providence to decipher or destroy, for I, alas cannot explain the reasoning's within—or their source. May God grant me the answers to the questions I have copied here, in the hope that in understanding what I have written may yet know it for a lie—a fiction, rather than the vile truths I feel I have stumbled upon. And may he— in his wisdom—grant me forgiveness for committing to paper this blasphemy.

I turn now from this detestable enterprise. My mind no longer can stand the abominations that come forth unbeckoned. I lay down my pen forever, in the hopes that in seeking action in some noble enterprise I might redeem my poor soul from the fire that it certainly deserves.

~ George Byron, October, 1823

The hour was late when Henry tore his eyes from the volume. Part of him was disgusted by the obscene rituals and narratives described within it. The book was the history of some ancient and incredibly evil cult. Its bloody perversions staggered the American's soul. Henry knew such writings deserved to be destroyed for the corruption their mere existence hinted at.

Yet, as offended as he was by the narrative, Henry felt strangely elated by the passion expressed within the pages. Something shocking and liberating, something that spoke to him of pleasures denied the sane and sober civilized man he had been raised to be. It was as if the chains of his Victorian existence had been flung aside, in an orgy of sensual enlightenment. Henry laughed a deep and guttural laugh. The world made sense to him now in a way that hours before he would have shunned as madness.

He rose from the table, suddenly thirsty. Grabbing a bottle of Claret, he bit into the cork, tearing it from the bottle and downed its contents. Unable to satisfy his thirst, he tore open another and another. Minutes later, all was lost to darkness.

"Wake up old boy," Idam said as he shook the senseless American out of his stupor. "Bad news, Henry, the kind you need to be sober to hear."

Henry felt the hard wood of the table beneath his cheek. The sour smell of his wine soaked cravat reminded him of his binge. He raised his head and fought back the pounding in his brain.

"What happened, Idam?"

"Just blocks away from here, another harlot was stabbed to death. A bloody mess it is too."

"That's terrible. Any thought as to who may have done it?"

"There is talk that some well dressed fellow might have been seen leaving the scene. God man, he opened her up like a melon." Idam shook himself.

"Anyhow, there is a mob afoot seeking out anyone strange to the area, which made me think of you alone here. It might get a bit dicey, so I figured you might want to consider moving in with me, at least till the police solve this thing and the locals settle down."

"Do you really think it could come to violence?"

"I fear the rouges might be more interested in revenge than pedigree. Best pack a few things and get going before they think of you."

As Henry and Edam stepped from the building they heard the shouts of the mob. At the sight of the two gentlemen several of the company made to intercept them before they boarded Idam's carriage. Snatching a small pistol from his vest, Henry raised it above his head and fired off a round. The leaders of the pack dove for cover.

"Best be gone before they summon some courage," Henry said. Idam dove into the vehicle with the American close behind.

"You know of course, the Bobbies don't like us using guns," Idam said.

"That's for the best, my friend. For on my oath my aim is terrible." Idam tapped on the carriage side with his cane.

"Driver."

The carriage sped through the cobbled streets without incident. Quizmat, who had fortified his resolve in Henry's rescue with a flask of good Scotch, offered his friend a dram.

"Its guaranteed to shake the night chills off you,"

"No thanks, I prefer to breakfast with a more sober mouth, Henry said, "Besides, I think you are correct in that we should keep our wits about us."

"How pedestrian," Quizmat said, "Guess there is more here for me." Idam up-ended the flask, draining its contents. Henry marveled that he managed the feat without coughing or other ill effects.

"You are a medical mystery, my friend."

"Years of dedicated assaults on my liver, dear boy. I am a devout believer in the wages of gin.

"However, we must address what to do with you till this nastiness in White Chapel quiets down. You are of course welcome to stay with me or you may fancy going back up to Miss Ducrea's, I'm certain she would not mind."

"Like a shark minding bait I should say." Henry said. "Perhaps it is better the good fellowship of bachelors at this time."

228

"She will be so disappointed." Quizmat said.

#

As they stepped into Quizmat's apartments Henry noticed a surgeon's bag tucked into a corner of the cloakroom.

"I say, Quizmat, I did not think you followed the medical arts."

"It's nothing, just a leftover from an inebriated houseguest. I have been meaning to send it along, but the bloke's name escapes me."

"Curious, that."

"But enough of this prattle. I have some exciting news about that book," Quizmat said producing it from under his coat. "You look funny sir...a bit pale." Henry felt clamminess about his throat as if dead hands sought to constrict his breath. Forcing a laugh he shook the feeling off.

"Just in need of some bangers and mash, it's been a lean morning and I'm afraid the lack of food has gotten to me."

"My poor boy," Quizmat said pulling a nearby silken bell cord. "I will see that Mrs. Maupin fixes you up directly. Now as I was saying about—"

The door to the dining room opened, but instead of Mrs. Maupin young Elaine entered carrying a tray of teas and biscuits. Harry shot an evil look at Idam who just shrugged and tried to hide his laughter.

"I dare say sir, How did this happen?"

"Henry darling, you look starved," Elaine said, "Won't you sit here by the fire. I would despair if you caught a chill."

"Note she isn't inviting me over," Quizmat whispered.

"So Idam, what news have you on that wretched volume?" Henry said plucking a biscuit from the tray and spreading some Marmite and butter on it. "I should think we can manage well in the parlor, Elaine." Elaine nodded and smiled, but Henry noted it didn't hide her disappointment. *Curse the girl for having such a one track mind.* He seated himself in a comfortable chair under a small portrait of one of Idam's ancestors.

Quizmat reached into his vest pocket and withdrew a letter that looked to have—by its tattered appearance—to have traversed the distance from its source via a camel route.

'This is a letter from a Doctor Hampshire who resides in Rampur State;

Dear Mr. Quizmat,

In regards to your inquiry about the 'Bryon volume' I can understand why you took the measure of sending the sample of the cover material to me for analysis rather than having the tests preformed there in London. As you suspected the book is indeed bound in human skin. No doubt such a revelation would have prompted Scotland Yard to investigate.

I took the measure of conferring with Raji Hammeran who was a great local historian. I dare say—when he was approached on the subject he recoiled as if snake bit. All he could tell me of it was that the book was—according to local legends the cover for the religious text of some vile an ancient cult of devil worshipers. He implored me to destroy the cover fragment I held and to beseech you to do the same with the rest of the volume. I thought naught of it—just some local heathen mumbo-jumbo superstition—till this morning, when I was informed Dr. Hammeran was found dead in his bed. His throat had been slashed and his body desecrated. Oddly, the police said his apartment was locked and the windows sealed from within.

I know not what plans you might have for that thing, but I suspect there is something dreadfully wrong with that book. I think you might consider entertaining the late Hammeran's suggestion and consign that tome to the fires that should have been its fate centuries ago.

Your servant,

~Ambrose Hampshire MD.

"Oh dear, that sounds horrid," Elaine said. "And you have this book in your house, Idam?"

"Yes I do, Cousin," Quizmat said.

"Good heavens—why?"

"Because Elaine…"

Henry listened to the conversation, but found himself distracted. India as a place to visit had oft intrigued him. The thought of visiting Delhi, or going on a man-eating tiger hunt in the Kumaon Division to the northwest of Nepal; as he thought about the journey he drifted off…

It was near dusk when the hunter found the spoor of the beast, its front left paw missing a pad. It had left the soft leafy trail and disappeared down a ravine—leaving the one pug mark to betray its passing. The depth of the mark suggested that the tiger was still carrying his prey—a poor unfortunate village girl that had wandered too far from safety to do her washing. Bad, but good news as it would slow the beast down so possibly he could get a shot off. Carefully he climbed down. To his left was a grove of trees, to the right a faint trail led further down into the ravine. As the hunter climbed down he was suddenly aware of the sound of wheezing. Bringing his gun to bear on the trees he saw—not fifty feet away—the tiger. It stood up and the hunter could see its left leg looked crooked. The cat it self looked mal-nourished. Apparently at some time a villager had let fly at the beast with a shotgun. The pellets had not killed the tiger but had crippled the leg and punctured the left lung—hence the wheezing. Reason enough he figured, for it to go man-eater.

Beneath the beast lay the girl. The hunter could not tell if she were alive or dead. The tiger watched him as he licked the dried blood from her throat. That was when Henry realized—he no longer the hunter, but instead was the tiger. And the green eyed victim whose blood tasted so delicious, was Elaine.

"Henry. Dear God man…are you alright?" it was Idam's face that met his opened eyes.

'What…why do you stare?" Henry sat up in his chair. Elaine rubbed his hands looking very worried.

"Because dearest, you passed out here before us. You look ashen, Idam, have you been starving the poor dear?"

"I'm fine blast it," Henry said. Looking up he could see the whiteness of Elaine's throat and sense the pulsing of the carotid artery. Just inches it was from his…*what am I imagining?* Henry shrank from the horror his mind had envisioned. Turning his back on his two friends, he feigned dizziness to hide his expression.

"Easy old boy," Idam said. "Elaine, please, some tea for Henry."

"Should we fetch a physician?"

"That's it! Dr. Burgess," Quizmat said jubilantly, "That's who the bag belongs to. Elaine, have Mrs. Maupin give him a ring and we can have him see to Henry and return his surgery to him."

233

"Yes, Idam." Casting another worried look at Henry she caressed his forehead and then walked to the kitchen to locate the housekeeper.

"I'm telling you Henry, That girl is good for you. Pledging your troth to her will give you a lifetime of pampering."

"At the cost of my freedom," Henry said. "Really now, I am feeling much better."

"Sorry lad, there's nothing to do but wait for the sawbones. Elaine will hear nothing to the contrary till you're examined."

For near a week, Henry stayed as guest at Idam's house in relative peace. His nights were restful—without the reoccurrence of the bizarre dreams that had troubled him. Instead he spent the days fending off the amorous attentions of Elaine who now considered him not just her beau—but also her patient. Then one evening Idam announced that he was going to his club.

"I say, I have been too saintly these past few days. Henry, I need to go out and commit a suitable amount of depravity on my wretched self. Elaine will endeavor to stop this unless I give her the slip. Can I trust in your aid?"

"Certainly, Quizmat, I am in your debt. I will be your agent in this."

"That was too easy," Quizmat laughed, "I think my cousin may well have snared your affections!"

"Balls, it's just that I have nothing better to do on a wet London night."

234

"Paugh, maybe I'd best stay here to keep you two from mischief," Idam said as he collected his coat and hat. "Shush…here she comes! I 'd best be away."

"Get out of here," Henry said as he pushed Idam out the door. The short Londoner waved and tipped his hat as he got into his coach and sped down the damp street. Henry chuckled to himself at the thought of Quizmat's foibles. It was his friend's imperfections that added to his charm. Henry closed the door.

As he was walking past Idam's study, he heard a noise. A mouse raced across the top of Quizmat's desk. Henry watched its path skitter over Byron's book.

"This will not do," he muttered and picked the volume up to check for damage. As he did the volume fell open and Henry read…

"What was that Henry?" Elaine walked to the door looking past the American. "Idam's sneaking off to the pub?"

"No my dear," Henry said—noting the smile the use of the affectionate brought. He set the volume back on top of the desk and turned to her.

"Idam is off to business. I heard him say he had a client to meet at his club."

"You lie delightfully, darling," Elaine said, "his business is with Port or Sherry this night. He will be gone till late and…well, I suppose it must fall on me to save you from boredom. Do you think I can manage?" Elaine moved close to Henry who took her into his arms. She felt warm and his nostrils drank in her perfume. Unable to resist, he kissed her. Surprised, she struggled briefly and then relaxed into his embrace.

"Henry," she sighed. Henry kissed her again and then pressed his lips to her neck—just above the white lace neckline of her dress. Again he became aware of the warm blood smell of her throat—so soft, so delicious.

"My dearest, why do you withdraw?" Henry felt his passion build as suddenly he held her at arms length. In the back of his mind he heard chanting. He could smell strange scents that spoke of rituals to the god—his God of the book. Part of him wanted to force her from him—to save her. More powerful was the urge to bend her, crush her body over something…a chair maybe? Henry looked around the room and seeing nothing suitable dragged her into the parlor. There he saw a couch that looked perfect. Flinging her onto it he tore at her petticoats.

"Henry, what are you doing?" For the first time a questioning look—a twinge of fear was in her eyes. Elaine tried to sit up, Henry pushed her back down into the cushions. She looked afraid, but also aroused. This was as it should be, he knew. Henry relished the look, the smell of fear. In his mind strange verses chanted that he knew would make her understand. He sang them to her as he ripped at her clothing.

"My God," Elaine moaned. "Must you take me like this?" Henry slapped her face and she went limp, tears welling from her eyes.

"If you must, my love," she said between sobs. Elaine tried to unbutton her blouse. Henry saw this and instead, tore it open to the waist. Elaine fainted.

A glint caught Henry's eyes. On the table next to them was a letter opener. Henry pictured the long blade passing just an inch under her skin. But no—it was too dull. Seeing her sprawled limp on the couch Henry left her and went into the kitchen. There in a drawer he found a filleting knife. Satisfied, he walked back into the parlor where Elaine lay conscious and apparently resigned to her fate as she held her arms out to him. Held them till she saw the knife.

"What is that, Henry?" Somehow Henry felt sad. He knew she was probably thinking of the murderer in White Chapel. *Poor child, no wonder she is afraid. I must explain to her that she is not a victim of that low fiend. Why she is too afraid to even scream.*

"Darling, it is not what you fear," he said with tenderness in his voice, "I am not that madman of the east side. Your flesh is a gift. The knife is love, my dear. Can you not understand that our blending of blood is the truest seal of our passion?" Henry opened his shirt and drew the blade across his chest.

"You are mad, Sir," Elaine said. He could see the disgust mixed with the fear in her eyes. Slowly he began to chant louder as he drew near to her.

Elaine was confused by the words—born of an ancient and obscene tongue. She shrank back as far from him as she could, her hands reaching out for anything she could use to defend herself. Finding nothing, she balled her fists in a futile attempt to punch her way free. Henry laughed ignoring her blows. Terrified, Elaine tried to close her eyes. Through her tears Elaine saw Henry reach for her then grasp her hair—and finally the knife rose…and he handed it to her

Idam Quizmat arrived just as the Bobbies were securing his house. Casting about he caught sight of a large man who appeared to be a sergeant. The burly policeman started to push past him when Quizmat gripped his sleeve.

"Sir, Sir…can you hold for a minute?"

"Watch how you grip there, I'll have no hands on me," The sergeant growled.

"It's my house you have come from—what happened?"

"It's your home?" the bobby turned and stared at Idam as if the impress his features into a mental photograph. "Have you been here this evening?"

"No, I was over to Mogley's Pub as the owner can assure you. He is a good friend of mine."

"Well be glad you weren't here, tis murder within…and not the kind for the squeamish. Can you tell us who was there while you were out?"

"Dear God, My housekeeper, Mrs. Maupin, and my cousin Elaine Ducrea…are they all right?"

"And no one else?"

"Oh, yes…my friend Henry Bascombe. He has been staying with us for a week."

"Well, he won't be any longer, the sergeant said, "He and the young lady are both dead. Your housekeeper found them and called us."

"How can that be, was there an intruder?"

"Naw, the old lady said the front door was locked from within," the sergeant said as he flipped through his notes. "Nasty business there…looks like they took turns cutting each other with a knife. Then there was the book."

"A book…what of it, Sergeant?" Quizmat shuddered as he guessed what was coming next.

"They were holding the blasted thing in their hands like they were reading it. Looks like it might have contained some heathen drivel, but I'm not certain."

"Why?"

"Because what ever was written in it is ruined—by God's good justice I reckon, the pages are soaked and spoiled with the two of them's blood."

The bobby went back to examining his notes. Quizmat watched him as he went to the kitchen. *How horrible, so much blood—so much lost.* Idam stared for a moment, with his head bowed, at the bloody sheet that covered his two friends. Then he stepped into his library. When Idam was certain no one was looking, he opened a hidden panel. Within was a plain cloth-bound volume. Quizmat smiled as he wrapped his hand written copy of Byron's tome in brown paper. He didn't need it as his memory of its contents was perfect. Mrs. Maupin would take the parcel later to be posted to his pen pal in Massachusetts. Quickly, he jotted down a note to enclose;

My Dearest Miss Borden.,

Lizzie you are going to love this…

THE MOGLOTH

Beneath the bowels of Karnatoran,
Down where the sewers deposit their flow;
Lays the home of the rats and the worms.
A place where only the foolish go.

The ancient city casts out its filth,
To places where sunlight has never shown.
There in the dark, the Mogloth rules-
And sharpens its teeth on dead men's bone.

There are those who seek to venture there.
Tales abound of hidden wealth.
Riches to have and glory to find,
If one can tread the slime with stealth.

Many have gone into the pit
And died with screams shared underground,
With snarls that chills the listener's blood.
A horrid-rasping-mewing-sound.

So why do they go to meet an end,
That shatters their senses and burns them so?
How did the story of treasure begin?
They wonder, but no one can know.

Yet some and more have ventured there.
None return and none are sought.
All who wait above the mire,
Wonder what their quest has bought.

Beneath the walls of Karnatoran,
A foulness laughs amongst the dead;
And whispers things to those above,
In obscene verbs…or so it's said.

I ask of this thing that dwells below.
The answers are refused to me.
What is this Mogloth, which scares them so?
I guess I'll have to go and see.

Also available from Trashed Cat Publications…

THE BARD BUSINESS

Heroes and monsters travel through different worlds in search of glory and fried chicken.

SIDEWAYS THRU TIME

Twin assassins; one trying to escape her life of death dealing – the other trying to decipher the deadly secret of her existence as she faces the worst murder of her time and the secret behind SIDEWAYS THRU TIME.

TALES OF THE GUANO BANDIT

A young man is forced to turn to robbery after the Guano mine he works at is destroyed. An adventure in the old west—and the story of a writer who searches for the truth behind the legend.

More titles coming soon from TRASHED CAT PUBLICATIONS